Advanced Acclaim for

"*Hidden Blessings* is a beautifully written, deeply moving story about a woman going through breast cancer. It reaffirms God's lifting us up through our darkest times. I highly recommend this book and this author."

—CARRIE STUART PARKS, BREAST CANCER SURVIVOR
AND AUTHOR OF *A CRY FROM THE DUST*

The Color of Hope

"The author has a gift for bringing God's love and light into even the darkest situation."

—*ROMANTIC TIMES*, 4-STAR REVIEW

"In *The Color of Hope*, Kim Cash Tate weaves a powerful story that will shake you to the core. You will laugh, your heart will break, and, ultimately, you'll be uplifted by the many colors of hope."

—STEPHANIE PERRY MOORE, AUTHOR AND
COEXECUTIVE EDITOR OF *SISTERS IN FAITH*

"Tate's engaging storytelling and eloquent prose journeys us through the challenge of breaking through prejudice and hurt for the sake of love and faith. Tate is definitely a voice of influence in today's Christian fiction."

—RACHEL HAUCK, AWARD-WINNING, BEST-SELLING AUTHOR
OF *THE WEDDING DRESS* AND *ONCE UPON A PRINCE*

Hope Springs

"Tate expertly crafts an intriguing narrative that explores unrequited love, true faith, and the complicated politics of change in the Christian church."

—*PUBLISHERS WEEKLY*

"Tate has penned another meaningful novel about the lives of three distinct women. Themes of faith and trusting God for direction in life and family resonate throughout this novel. The author has a gift for writing characters that are so realistic readers will be able to see all parts of themselves—good and bad—mirrored in them."

—ROMANTIC TIMES, 4-STAR REVIEW

Cherished

"Tate's amazing ability to connect with the reader on both personal and spiritual levels elevates this novel far above the rest. Those looking for hope and encouragement will find it on the pages of this superb book."

—ROMANTIC TIMES, 4 1/2-STAR REVIEW, TOP PICK!

Faithful

"Tate has an amazing ability to put difficult but realistic emotions on paper and show the reader the redeeming love of God in the process."

—ROMANTIC TIMES, 4 1/2-STAR REVIEW

"Kim Cash Tate's enjoyable novel is true to both the realities of life and the hope found through faith in Jesus. Romance meets real life with a godly heart. Hooray!"

—STASI ELDREDGE, BEST-SELLING AUTHOR OF *CAPTIVATING*

"The author skillfully ties the concept of sexual purity, whether married or single, to the idea of faithfulness on a spiritual level . . . Tate avoids the unrealistic "happily ever after" ending while still offering a message of faith, hope, and love. Readers will not be disappointed . . ."

—CROSSWALK.COM

hidden blessings

ALSO BY KIM CASH TATE

Faithful

Cherished

Hope Springs

The Color of Hope

hidden blessings

KIM CASH TATE

THOMAS NELSON
Since 1798

NASHVILLE   MEXICO CITY   RIO DE JANEIRO

Published in Nashville, Tennessee, by Thomas Nelson. Thomas Nelson is a registered trademark of HarperCollins Christian Publishing, Inc.

Author is represented by the literary agency of The B&B Media Group, Inc., 109 S. Main, Corsicana, Texas 75110. www.tbbmedia.com.

Thomas Nelson, Inc., titles may be purchased in bulk for educational, business, fund-raising, or sales promotional use. For information, please e-mail SpecialMarkets@ ThomasNelson.com.

Scripture quotations are taken from the NEW AMERICAN STANDARD BIBLE®. © The Lockman Foudnation 1960, 1962, 1963, 1968, 1971, 1972, 1973, 1975, 1977, 1995. Used by permission.

Publisher's Note: This novel is a work of fiction. Names, characters, places, and incidents are either products of the author's imagination or used fictitiously. All characters are fictional, and any similarity to people living or dead is purely coincidental.

Library of Congress Cataloging-in-Publication Data

Tate, Kimberly Cash.
  Hidden Blessings / Kim Cash Tate.
    pages cm
  ISBN 978-1-59554-999-0 (paperback)
  1. African American women--Fiction. 2. Cancer--Patients--Fiction. 3. Christian fiction.
I. Title.
  PS3620.A885H53 2014
  813'.6--dc23

                              2014011025

Printed in the United States of America

14 15 16 17 18 19 RRD 6 5 4 3 2 1

To those who are experiencing affliction . . .

CHAPTER ONE

June

KENDRA WOODS HIGHTAILED IT DOWN THE SPIRAL STAIRCASE of Fleming & Stein to the K Street conference room as fast as her heels and the burden of a hefty legal file would allow. It wasn't like Grace to go into a client meeting unprepared, or for her legal assistant to let her. And Kendra had no idea why *she'd* been called upon to rectify the matter, since she wasn't an attorney on this case. But Buddy from the mailroom had poked his head into her office, said Grace needed the file ASAP, and asked if she could find it. And Grace was head of litigation and her boss of eight years, not to mention a trusted mentor. Whatever she needed, Kendra was happy to oblige.

She strode past offices and cubicles, the sound of printers and copiers still buzzing late on a Friday afternoon. Fleming & Stein was seldom quiet. One of the largest law firms in the world, the Washington, DC, office was its flagship, and business churned evenings and weekends as frantically as it did during "business hours." Kendra had been told in her first year of law school that she would never work here, to set her sights lower. At the time there was only a handful of black attorneys at the firm, and Grace was the sole black female partner. But the challenge had motivated Kendra all the more. And these halls were now like home.

Rounding a bend, she saw the shades drawn on the internal floor-to-ceiling windows of the conference room. She knocked on the door.

"Come in," Grace called.

Kendra opened the door.

"Surprise!"

Attorneys and staff filled a room teeming with colorful balloons, gifts, and the delicious aroma of hot appetizers.

"What is this?" Kendra said, taking it all in.

"What does it look like, silly? It's a wedding shower." Beaming, Grace relieved her of the file. "Thanks, I'll take that." She parked it on the floor.

A knock sounded behind her, and Kendra realized the door had been closed again.

Roger, head of government contracts, stepped forward with a Cheshire-cat grin. "Come in," he said.

Kendra's fiancé, Derek, entered with a file, too, and the room dissolved into self-congratulatory whoops and applause because they'd pulled the whole thing off.

Kendra joined him, giddy. "Can you believe they put together a shower for us?"

"Men get showers now?" Derek had a cute, confused look. He took Kendra's hand and leaned in. "Not with games and stuff, right? Because I'm buried with work."

Grace chuckled. "Yes, it's the twenty-first century, and men get showers at Fleming & Stein," she said. "That is, when they're marrying another attorney in the firm, thus making it a big celebration. They get champagne too." She put a half-filled glass in his hand, and one in Kendra's, and quieted the crowd.

"Many of you enterprising souls like Derek need to get back to work shortly," Grace said, "so Roger and I want to give a quick toast at the start. Maybe a glass of bubbly will give you the kick you need to get that work done."

"Hear, hear," one of the attorneys called, lifting his glass.

"Kendra," Grace said, "I've had the unique honor of recruiting you as a summer associate, bringing you on board after you graduated law school, helping you hone your legal skills—and watching you get swept off your feet by this fellow here." She smiled at Derek. "I have to confess that I always regarded the government contracts group as, well, unexciting."

"I take offense to that." Roger frowned in his humorous way.

"*But . . .*" Grace smiled at Roger and turned back to Derek. "The just-because floral arrangements, the carryout dinners on long work evenings, the elaborate proposal . . . Watching your courtship took my breath away. I can't wait until the wedding because I'm sure you'll have something wonderful up your sleeve." She raised her glass. "To Kendra and Derek, who've filled these offices with the beauty of romance and the promise of happy-ever-after and a gaggle of kids. Cheers!"

Derek's glass went up only partially. "Wait, we promised a gaggle?"

Laughter and a chorus of "Cheers!" filled the room as everyone raised a glass and took a sip.

"I admit," Derek said, "this is pretty nice." His arm slid around Kendra's waist. "And you *look* nice. I can't believe I haven't seen you yet today."

She felt flutters from his touch. "Your fault," she said, eyeing his dark and handsome face. "I tried to steal you away for lunch."

"And I almost went, despite my deadline." He squeezed a little tighter. "You know my day's not the same without you. We should share an office after the wedding."

Kendra laughed in her champagne glass. "I can see it now—totally distracted, no focus, fired by year's end . . ."

He laughed with her. "True, true."

Roger stepped forward next. "I'll be brief since everyone knows I hail from the unexciting government contracts wing." He winked at Grace. "I knew when I stole"—he cleared his throat—"*plucked* Derek from one of our rivals a year and a half ago that he had special talent. But oh, the things I learned through that elaborate proposal. Who thinks to get a judge and jury involved? Who's *able* to get a judge and jury involved?" He eyed Derek even now, as if questioning. "This man knows what he wants, and he's got the skills to go after it. In Kendra, I think we'd all agree he got quite a prize." He raised his glass. "To the soon-to-be husband and wife, Derek and Kendra."

Loud cheers and champagne sips were followed by cries of "Speech! Speech!"

Kendra and Derek looked at each other, smiling. She nudged him. "You go."

Derek shrugged as everyone quieted. "I don't know what to say." He looked at Kendra. "I just love this woman."

"Aww," a few of the women chorused.

"Oh, stop it," one of the government contracts attorneys said. "You've set the bar too high already for the single guys."

Derek held up his hands in defense. "But how's that possible in a room full of overachievers?" When the laughter died down, he continued, "Seriously, thank you, everyone. I'm blown away by this show of love and kindness. Coming to Fleming & Stein was one of the best decisions of my life."

Kendra squeezed his hand, looking around the room. "I'm not an emotional person, but you all know I lost my mother last year to cancer, and my father's on a sabbatical overseas. I would've never thought a big firm could be like family, but in the years I've been here, that's what you've become." She scanned their faces. "I can't tell you what it means that you would do this for us." She swiped an eye. "Okay, really? I will not cry," she declared as another tear came. "Let me stop while I'm ahead, and just say thank you."

Grace hugged her, then turned to the crowd. "We'll open gifts soon, but for now, enjoy the food. Or get back to work!"

"Thank you, Grace, really." Kendra spoke above the rising chatter. "You're always there for me. I'm sure this whole thing was your idea."

"No way," Grace said. "I can't count the number of people in litigation who came to me about giving you a shower. We all wanted to celebrate with you. You're getting married, girl!"

"And it's starting to feel really real," Kendra said. "I've got my final fitting tomorrow."

"I'm going with you," Derek said. "Since it's the twenty-first century, the dress doesn't have to be a surprise."

"Uh-huh," Kendra said. "You're the one who didn't want to schedule pictures before the ceremony."

He conceded with a nod. "Who knew I was a traditional type of guy? I never thought so until we started planning this wedding." He linked fingers with her, pulling her close. "I can't wait for you to become Kendra Richards."

His whisper drew butterflies. "I can't wait to *be* Kendra Richards."

Kendra stood atop the podium in the dressing room, loving every angle of her gown in the mirror. She'd tried it on at least three times before, but now, so close to the date, it woke something new in her.

Her maid of honor, Charlene, circled her. "Classic. Elegant. Exquisite." She nodded, arms folded. "Killer. That dress was made for you, Ken."

The strapless silk sheath with a Swarovski-beaded bodice fit her five-foot-six frame like a glove. Kendra felt tingly looking at it. She'd never dreamed about marriage. Even back when she thought her parents had the perfect marriage, marriage itself wasn't uppermost in her mind. Her dreams had always been career driven. But what *did* she expect from marriage? What did she long for?

The bridal consultant had been checking every aspect of the fit. "It's just perfect," she said, "but it's formfitting"—she shook a warning finger—"so no fried foods between now and the wedding."

"Or rich desserts," Kendra said. "That's my weakness."

"Whatever." Charlene rolled her eyes. "You never gain a pound."

"Let me see if those adjustments were made to the veil," the consultant said, "and I'll also grab the undergarment you need." She looked at Charlene. "And I'll show you how to help Kendra with the dress on her wedding day, as well as how to bustle it."

"Awesome," Charlene said. "I'm so excited to be part of this."

Kendra smiled at her. "It wouldn't be the same without you."

She and Charlene had met the first week of the first year of law school at George Washington University and quickly became best buddies. The grind of working at a large firm kept them from seeing each other as much as they'd like, especially since Charlene worked in Baltimore, so wedding moments like this were a treat.

Kendra smoothed her fingers over the hand-sewn beading. "You think Derek will like it?"

"For him to like it, all that's required is that you be in it. That man is head over heels." Charlene sighed. "Why can't I find a man like that?"

"I told you I think you'll like his best man," Kendra said.

"He lives in Philly—several-point deduction," Charlene said, "but definite points for hotness, from the picture you showed. What does he do?"

"He's in banking."

Charlene looked impressed. "Kids?"

"Nope."

"Married?"

Kendra gave her a look.

"Then what's wrong with him?"

"I think he's been focused on his career, like all of us. Now everybody's feeling the itch to settle down." Kendra got an idea. "He'll be in town next week. The four of us can go to dinner."

"I'm not going on another blind date," Charlene said.

"How is it a blind date? This is prewedding . . . stuff." Kendra laughed. "But that other blind date was hilarious."

"You mean Jared? God's gift to mankind? I should've stopped speaking to you after that." Charlene laughed with her. "And how is it you always get the nice, fine guys making big money, and I get the sidekicks, who always have a major defect?"

"Obviously the ones I dated had defects, too, because they didn't last."

"Um, no, hon," Charlene said. "They didn't last because you were working 24–7, trying to make partner. You and Derek must've been meant to be, because he landed right in your world at Fleming & Stein."

Kendra pondered that. From the beginning, it did seem meant to be, a whirlwind romance culminating in a memorable wedding. But the whirlwind and the wedding would pass. What kind of husband would he be? What kind of wife would *she* be? And why the anxious feeling all of a sudden?

Kendra shook it off. Prewedding jitters . . . bound to surface.

Her phone chimed with a text message.

"Can you get that for me, Charlene?"

Charlene reached in Kendra's purse and handed it to her. Kendra smiled at Derek's text as the jitters evaporated.

THINKING OF U. LOVE U. 21 DAYS.

CHAPTER TWO

"I'D BE GETTING KICKED OUT OF THE NEST—PREMATURELY." Lance Alexander's elbows rested on a tabletop in the St. Louis Bread Company, coffee cup in hand. "You said to give you my straight thoughts, right?"

"I did." Pastor Lyles gave a slow nod, the nod that meant he was considering every word. "You've done that from the beginning."

Lance nodded with him. That was certainly true. He'd told the pastor exactly what he thought when he met him as an inmate—that the gospel he was peddling was garbage.

Pastor Lyles added, "And I wouldn't want you to stop now. Tell me what you mean."

"Okay," Lance said. He tried a different metaphor. "It would feel like somebody stole my training wheels in the dark of night. I mean, I'd rather you took the whole bike." He got more worked up thinking about it. "To take the training wheels only? And expect me to ride, with no support?"

"On the contrary, Lance," the pastor said, "you'd have the full support of Living Word. You know that. That's the whole point of this church-planting endeavor—to send and support qualified leaders."

"And that's *my* point," Lance said. "I'm not qualified to lead a church plant. It took awhile to wrap my mind around leading the youth ministry at Living Word. But at least with that, I'm under the overall leadership of you and others at the church."

Pastor Lyles was nodding again. He sipped his coffee. "I'm sure you want me to be straight as well?"

"Hey, Lance." A Bread Company worker stopped at the table. "What are you doing back in this corner? Your office is over there." He gestured at a table near the main door.

Lance laughed. "This was the only way I could get a little privacy."

The guy nodded, smiling. "If anybody comes looking, I'll tell 'em you're not in the office right now." He pointed at their cups. "Can I get you some more coffee?"

"No thanks, man." Lance was touched by the gesture. This guy's job was to clear tables, not get refills. "I appreciate it, though."

"Anything for you, man."

Lance watched him walk off and turned back to Pastor Lyles, remembering his question. "Absolutely," he said. "You know I want you to be straight."

"Lance," the pastor said, "I think this is fear talking."

"Fear?" Lance looked at him crosswise. He couldn't recall ever being accused of fear. He was the one who'd taken a bullet for a friend. "I'm just being real. Why would I agree to do something— something as serious as this—if I'm not ready?"

Pastor Lyles leaned in, engaging Lance in his fatherly way. "I don't think I've ever felt ready for anything God called me to do."

"Pastor, come on. You had a PhD from seminary when you started Living Word. The only letters after my name are GED."

"I had some book knowledge. That's true," Pastor Lyles said, "but I didn't have near the experience you've got. I can't count the number of young men you've discipled, many of them right here in your 'office,' over coffee and a cinnamon roll." He continued, "Your high school students bring so many friends that we had to put you all in a bigger space. And that's aside from the fact that you've submitted yourself to discipleship over the course of several years, and you're a confirmed elder." He sat up, spreading his hands. "Son, how much 'ready' do you need?"

Lance sipped his coffee, mulling over the pastor's words. "I don't know how to explain it. Living Word has been my home. I've been able to do everything you mentioned because of you." He added, "Come to think of it, I wouldn't even be a photographer if it weren't for you."

Pastor Lyles chuckled. "Oh, I get credit for that too? The man who couldn't take a decent picture if he tried?"

Lance smiled. "You know what I mean. If you hadn't vouched for me, I wouldn't have gotten a job at the camera shop, which is where I discovered my passion for photography."

"Listen . . ." Pastor Lyles leaned in. "You've been able to do everything you've done because of God," he said. "I'm just happy I've had a front-row seat to watch Him work. But as you consider the church plant—assuming you're considering it—I do have an update since we talked last."

"What's that?"

"We'd been talking about a plant on the north side of St. Louis."

Lance nodded. That was the one positive. It would be near the neighborhood in which he grew up.

"But we were approached by Church of the Redeemer. They're targeting the same area for a plant and are much further ahead. They want us to partner with them in terms of financial resources, and I think they'll serve that community very well."

Lance looked confused, but Pastor Lyles wasn't finished.

"And wouldn't you know, God put another location on my heart."

"What location?"

"Clayton."

Lance frowned slightly. "That's the last place I expected you to say."

"Exactly," the pastor said. "My first thought was, 'No, the inner city needs us, not the people who are well off.' As if they're not sick and in need of a Physician too."

"Pastor, I hear you, but I *know* I'm not called to lead a church plant in Clayton."

"Why do you say that?"

"I can't believe you forgot," Lance said. "That's where I went to high school for a short while, got in big trouble, and got expelled."

Pastor Lyles shrugged. "I didn't forget."

"How would it look to go back there and start a church? People have long memories. And considering the other things in my past . . . it just wouldn't work. If I was called to do something like that, I believe God would make it real clear."

"I would absolutely want you to hear from God about something like this. So I won't say another word. If it's His will, I trust He'll establish it in His timing."

Lance gave him a look. "You used that tactic when you raised your kids, didn't you?"

"All the time," the pastor said, smiling. "And you should know you're like a son to me."

It took a moment for Lance to respond. "That means a lot."

"On another note," the pastor said, "are you still looking for a place to stay?"

"I am. My roomie's getting married next weekend. He said

there's no rush, but it's his house, and three would definitely be a crowd. You know of a spot?"

"Marlon Woods called me."

Lance's eyes widened a little. "Really? Isn't he still overseas?"

"University of Ghana."

"How's his family doing?"

"His daughter is doing well," the pastor said. "Getting married this month out east. But his son dropped all his classes last semester and has been majoring in partying."

"Trey? No way. That's not the guy I had in youth group."

"Marlon's tried to get Trey to return to church, but the last person he'll listen to is his dad. Anyway, as he's telling me this, he also mentions that he's thinking about renting out the lower level of his home because he needs someone to help look after the place. I told him that you were in need of a place to stay, and he said it sounded like an answer to prayer. He also said you could stay for free."

"What?" Lance said. "Why?"

"He holds you in high regard, and I think he wants to be a blessing. But I also think he's hoping you'll do what you do and kind of help Trey through this." Pastor Lyles stood. "I've got to run to another meeting, but I'll text you his info."

Lance was about to ask where Mr. Woods lived, when he suddenly remembered—Clayton.

CHAPTER THREE

MEET ME DOWNSTAIRS AT 11:00 AM. CASUAL/COMFORTABLE. LOVE U. 20 DAYS.

Kendra read the text while in bed, loving the feeling it gave. What outing had Derek planned now? How did he come up with this stuff?

She rose and headed to the bathroom. It was the first Sunday in weeks neither of them had felt compelled to go into the office. They'd probably pull out their laptops later and do some work, but right now she wanted to soak up the leisure in the morning. And the second she walked into her bathroom, she knew how to do it—a bubble bath. One of her favorite things, but one she never had time for.

In no time, she lit scented candles around the perimeter of her bathtub and found the bubble bath in the back of the cabinet. She ponytailed her hair, safeguarded it in a shower cap, and turned on the bathwater, liberally pouring in the lavender liquid. It felt like a minor luxury to step into the semi-hot water and sink down into the bubbles. She closed her eyes, determined to erase thoughts of due dates and court deadlines.

Twenty days. In twenty days she'd be Kendra Richards. Her heart smiled at the sound of it. Shortly after their engagement, Derek had asked what she thought about taking his name. She could tell it meant a lot to him, though he assured her he'd be fine either way. She hadn't thought much about it until that moment, but knew at once—to her own surprise—that she wouldn't have it any other way. She'd happily ordered new business cards and asked her secretary to order the new nameplate that would go outside her office door. She was ready to make the switch.

For thirty-two years she'd been Kendra Woods, and in the small suburban St. Louis enclave where she'd grown up, the Woods name meant something. Her dad had been a prominent sociology professor at Washington University in St. Louis, and her mom had been active on the school board of the Clayton School District. Kendra felt the weight of their expectations early in life, and it drove her to succeed. She'd attended college and law school in DC, then started her career there. Now, DC would play host to her wedding and married life. She didn't see herself ever returning to St. Louis to live.

Kendra raised her left hand above the bubbles and gazed at her engagement ring. She'd asked herself a thousand times how she could be so blessed. Making partner at a prestigious firm. Marrying the man of her dreams—though maybe not a man of strong faith. She'd had to admit that to herself. But she wasn't where she needed to be either. Once they were married, they'd find a church home and grow together as husband and wife.

Shifting in the melting bubbles, she turned on the water, re-steaming her sanctuary, and turned her attention to the checklist that would consume her between now and the wedding day. The RSVPs would be the biggest headache—contacting those who hadn't responded, and even some who had, to tell them they couldn't just add a guest. Space for the wedding and reception was limited at the Textile Museum, not to mention expensive. Once she had the final number, she had to confirm with the caterer and plan the seating chart for dinner. Oh, and make sure out-of-town guests had booked their rooms. It would be nice if she could get a little gift basket to leave in those rooms, but she wasn't sure if—

Her eye caught something on the inside of her left breast. Swishing away a few microbubbles, she looked more closely. Where did that come from? It looked like she'd bruised herself somehow, a weird reddish-orange color, about the size of a quarter. Her fingers examined the area, then the entirety of both breasts, relieved she didn't feel any lumps. Still, a slight tremor passed through her.

Her mom had found her illness in a similar way, not in the bathtub but casually, while reclining on the sofa. Her hand had run across a mass in her abdomen the size of a small apricot, and weeks later, after ignoring it for a time, she discovered she had Stage IV liver cancer. She was dead in less than a year.

Kendra didn't want to overreact, but she took seriously anything that half looked like a symptom. She bathed quickly, stepped out, and slipped into a terry robe as she walked, water droplets trailing. How long had the bruise been there? Why hadn't she seen it before? And what about Derek? He wasn't a stranger to her body, but their time together was usually at night, when it'd be too dark to notice.

She got her laptop from the nightstand and, sitting lotus style on her bed, powered it up and opened her browser. On her Google home page she typed "bruise" and "breast" into the search box, then surveyed the results. "Common causes" seemed a good place to start. She clicked the link and skimmed the first paragraph, landing on a sentence that might as well have blinked in neon: "One of the most feared causes of breast bruise is inflammatory breast cancer."

Her heart pounded. She'd read a fair amount about breast cancer over the years, but why wasn't she familiar with this kind?

Only a brief description was given, which thankfully branded it "very rare." Still, her hand twitched as she scrolled down for other possible causes. Injury or trauma to the breast . . . ill-fitting bras . . . anticoagulant medications . . .

She clicked the next link, then the next, swinging from relief to alarm at the possibilities. Then she stared at the laptop, exhaled, and typed "inflammatory breast cancer." Her breath caught at images of breasts with similar bruises and coloring. But most were also swollen, with a pitted orange look to them. She examined hers closely again. Was it slightly pitted? Or was she imagining?

An image led to a story, which led to several stories and profiles and blogs of women who'd been diagnosed with inflammatory breast cancer—including one who'd discovered it in the bathtub, with a casual glance. Kendra began reading this woman's daily accounts as she walked through the reality and fear of the diagnosis to the first stages of treatment. She was so engrossed that the phone startled her when it rang.

"Hey, I'm downstairs."

Kendra looked at the clock. 11:05.

"Sorry, I lost track of time. I'll . . . be right down."

She jumped up, threw on a pair of jeans and a top, finger-combed her hair, swished on light makeup, and tried to catch her breath on the ride down the elevator of her building, which housed renovated condos.

Derek's sports car was parked at the curb. He got out and opened the passenger door as she approached. "I almost came up to check on you," he said. "You're never late. Everything okay?"

Kendra had debated whether to tell him. But tell him what? That she'd found a bruise and let her imagination run wild? Besides, she didn't want to put a damper on the day he'd planned.

"I got caught up doing some research," she said. "Everything's great."

⁂

Derek's arms enveloped her waist from behind as they stared out into the vast landscape of downtown Washington.

A perfect summer breeze lifted her hair from her shoulders. "I didn't think you could outdo yourself . . . but you outdid yourself. Rooftop picnic, spinach quiche, this view—incredible." She turned, embracing him. "What did I do to deserve you?"

He kissed her softly. "I ask myself the same question. I don't know what I'd do without you." He twisted a lock of her hair. "I didn't know my father, and my mother wasn't much interested in being home." He stared away, remembering. "I basically raised myself, and I had a vision of what my life would be like one day—wife, two or three kids, dog, house, sports car . . ."

Kendra smiled into his chest. "You've already got the sports car."

"And twenty days from now I'll have the wife. And nine months later, our first baby."

"Umm . . ." She leaned back. "Did you say nine months? Can we get a little more honeymoon than that?"

"Okay, twelve." He laughed. "Speaking of honeymoon, as promised I've been doing my due diligence on Paris, taking notes on all the must-see places. And, of course, the out-of-the-way romantic spots."

"We've been counting down to the wedding," she said, "but we need to count down to Paris too. I can't believe we'll be there the day after."

"I like the sound of that . . . 'the day after.'" Derek kissed her cheek. "The first day of the rest of our lives."

Kendra turned back around, facing the view once more. "You mentioned having a vision for your life." She stared at the Washington Monument. "Graduating from law school, landing a position at Fleming & Stein, making partner. *That* was my vision. I could control those things." She was thinking it through even now. "Then you came along and gave my life a dimension it had never had. I've never felt this way about anyone. And it's all . . . unexpected and out of my control. It's like I've *stumbled* into a new vision—a longing—for true love and relationship." She looked at him once more. "And it's scary."

"And beautiful." He kissed her. "I've never felt this way about anyone either, Ken." His voice was a whisper. "You're everything I've always wanted."

He kissed her again, deeply, and led her to their private picnic area. As they lay together, Kendra feared he might see her bruise, given the daylight, but he didn't seem to. Still, she couldn't get it off of her mind. One question circulated—*What if?* With all she had to do to prepare for the wedding, honeymoon, and life afterward, one thing had suddenly leapfrogged them all. She needed to see her doctor. Tomorrow.

CHAPTER FOUR

GOD HAD A SENSE OF HUMOR; LANCE WAS SURE OF IT. IN THE last ten years, he'd spoken of Clayton as part of his testimony. It was the place that had represented promise, then failure, the last stop before his life took a turn for the worst. He'd always felt like an outsider here, but for a time he'd been welcomed into houses like this.

Lance gazed at the Woodses' home as he came up the tree-lined walkway, remembering the first time he'd seen the inside of such a house. His schoolmate had laughed when Lance called it a mansion. "This is small compared to a few streets over," his friend had said.

Lance had wondered what he'd say if his friend saw where *he* lived. Only once did he invite friends over—and only because they insisted—and he took them to a great-uncle's condo, where he sometimes stayed. No one saw his real environment. Even he wanted to forget it at times.

Lance noticed that the grass at the Woodses' home was under-watered and overgrown, and weeds choked the flower beds. If he didn't know better, he'd think the owner had taken an extended vacation and left the house unoccupied. He rang the doorbell, then rang it again. Seconds later he looked at his watch. Hadn't he said Wednesday evening at six? He'd had a late-afternoon photo shoot and had come directly after.

The door was opened finally, partially, by a young Caucasian woman with multicolored short hair. She wore shredded denim shorts and a crop top with a great deal of midriff showing. She blew a bubble beyond her dark red lips. "Yeah?"

"I'm looking for Trey Woods." Lance stepped back and checked the number by the door. "Is this the right house?"

Another bubble stretched big and wide, then popped to reveal an amused smile. "So you're the babysitter?"

Lance was confused about everything in this picture. "Excuse me?"

She stepped back inside, leaving the door slightly ajar. "Trey, get the door," she called. "Trey!"

Lance shook his head. He'd been intrigued by Mr. Woodses' offer and told him he'd take a look. But based on the first thirty seconds . . .

The door opened again. A guy with a white T-shirt, low-riding jeans, a lopsided Afro, and scraggly facial hair stood before him, holding a bag of Doritos.

Lance blinked. "Trey?" He hugged him. "Hey, it's good to see you."

"I look a little different from that youth group kid, huh?"

Lance smiled. "Only a little."

Trey had always been the best-dressed kid in youth group. Clean-cut, nice jeans or khakis, collared shirt. But he'd filled out, too, more muscle on his over-six-foot frame.

"Come in, I guess," Trey said.

Lance could hear music from the lower level when he stepped inside. He glanced at the young woman as she looped her arm through Trey's. Next to him, she was short, but the hair, the combat boots, and the gum she hadn't stopped popping made her a spunky short.

"I'm sorry," Lance said, extending his hand. "I didn't get your name. I'm Lance Alexander."

She shook with a firm grip. "Molly."

"Good to meet you." Lance shifted his gaze. "How are you, Trey? I've been praying for you."

"Look, I don't really want to hear about your prayers. I'm not gonna pretend I'm up for this." Trey dug out a chip and popped it into his mouth. "I know what my dad is up to," he said, speaking through the crunch. "He's bringing in an overseer, and if I don't shape up, he'll kick me out. But it's his house, so do what you feel."

"Trey, I'm not planning to be anybody's overseer." Even as he said it, it was clear to Lance that the *house* needed overseeing, if not the residents. He could see stains on the living room carpet, *a hole?*— he did a double take to be sure—in the hall off the entryway, and junk in various forms everywhere. "I'm just here to check out the place because I need somewhere to stay."

Trey shrugged. "Knock yourself out." He motioned to Molly, who followed him down the hall.

Lance stared after him. Trey's attitude and conversation were more foreign than the new look. "So . . . I should just show myself around?"

Trey turned, walking backward. "Yeah, pretend it's an open house."

Trey opened a door. The music got louder, and Lance heard another voice before they disappeared, closing it.

He blew out a sigh. Mr. Woods had practically begged him to move in. Said he trusted Lance—with his house and his son—and believed his presence would make a difference. But Trey probably had people in and out of the house—at all hours, no doubt—and that wasn't how Lance wanted to live. He'd grown up like that and had come to appreciate home as a place of peace and quiet. He could continue praying for Trey, get together with him from time to time if he was willing, but he couldn't see himself living here.

The front door opened behind him and two guys walked in, strolling past Lance and heading directly downstairs. They proved his point.

Lance didn't need to see more. He headed for the door, but the sound of angry voices rose suddenly, making him pause. If a fight was breaking out, especially with a woman present, he couldn't walk away. He walked toward the lower level as the voices grew louder. The new arrivals had left the door open.

"You're paying up," one guy said. "Today."

"Timmy, why are you tripping?" The voice was Trey's. "Just pay them their money."

"Do you not understand the nature of this rip-off?" another voice said. "They charge half the price on the street for the same product. Why do students get the overinflated prices? And I buy in bulk! Squeeze somebody else."

"I warned you yesterday," the first guy said. "Remember what I told you, Timmy?"

Lance heard a sound like a punch as Molly shouted, "Dillon, stop!"

Lance hustled downstairs, where the smell of weed hit him. In the dim light he saw a guy on the floor, arms raised to block the next blow. Trey was mediating still—"Timmy, just give them the money"—while the other two stood over him.

Lance entered the fray, stepping between them and raising his phone. "My finger's on emergency, and I'm calling the police if you don't get out now."

"Man, you can't call the police," Trey said. "That's so lame."

Lance would've said so, too, back in the day. If Trey only knew . . . His first instinct was to knock these dudes out.

"I'm not going anywhere until I get my money." The main aggressor stepped toward Lance. He was a big guy, but Lance was taller and more muscular. "It would take a few minutes for the police to get here anyway," the guy said. "If I were you, I'd head back upstairs."

Old wiring kicked in. Lance closed the gap even more between them. "Or what?"

Timmy broke just then, scrambling to his feet and running out the back door. The other guys took off after him.

"Trey!" Lance called.

Trey stopped, turning slightly, poised to keep going.

"Why are you caught up in all this?" Lance asked. "This isn't who you are."

"That's where you're wrong," Trey said. "You never knew the real me."

CHAPTER FIVE

THE SOFT NOTES OF A CELLO SET OFF A TIDAL WAVE THROUGH Kendra's body. She took a deep breath, staring at a court opinion on her desk that blurred before her. She'd assigned a special ring-tone to her doctor so that her expectations wouldn't rise and fall with each call. But the call she was waiting for was a roller coaster unto itself. She picked up the phone, closed her office door, and braced for the ride.

"Kendra Woods."

"Miss Woods, this is Dr. Matthews's office," the woman said. "Are you available to speak with her?"

"Yes." Her mouth was cottony. "I'm available."

"One moment, please."

Kendra walked to the window and looked down at the hustle and bustle of sidewalk travel, people moving inside of normal. She hoped to join them once again. Maybe she'd been wrong, paranoid even. She'd read so much online that when her gynecologist prescribed antibiotics to rule out infection as a cause of her bruise, Kendra pushed back.

"But what if it's inflammatory breast cancer?" Kendra had said.

Dr. Matthews had touched her shoulder. "I don't want to jump to the worst case. There's no swelling or tenderness or pitted orange appearance, which often present with IBC. Let's rule out the infection first, then do additional tests if needed."

"I'm getting married in less than three weeks, Dr. Matthews. Please. I'd rather start the additional testing now."

Kendra had had a mammogram, ultrasound, and biopsy two days later, and kept it all to herself as she waited for this call.

"Kendra?"

She sat in one of the guest chairs on the other side of her desk. "Hi, Dr. Matthews. You have my results?"

"My first thought was to have you come in, but I knew you'd want to know right away."

She stared at the pattern in the carpet.

"Kendra, I'm so sorry. It's inflammatory breast cancer."

She continued staring.

"We need to schedule a CT scan and a bone scan to see if it's spread. I've already checked with radiology, and they can see you this afternoon at three o'clock. From there, we'll have a better sense of your treatment options. This is an aggressive disease that requires an aggressive plan . . ."

❧

Kendra knocked on Derek's office door and entered when he gave a shout. He faced the computer, typing furiously.

"Oh hey, babe," he said over his shoulder.

"I forgot you have an administrative court deadline today," she said. "We can talk later."

He switched screens to check an online court opinion, then

switched back to his document to finish a sentence. He glanced up briefly. "What's the latest fire?"

Lately they'd been putting out several a day. "No fire this time." Her stomach clenched. "Well. Not wedding related."

He swiveled his chair toward her. "What's going on? You don't sound like yourself. Sit down."

She did, closing the door first, trying to figure out how to have a conversation that didn't seem real. *Just say it.*

"Sunday morning, before you picked me up, I saw this spot on my breast, like a bruise." She clutched a notepad in her hands, not sure why she'd brought it. "I didn't want to say anything because you know I can be a hypochondriac."

"True. You and Google are dangerous. You'll convert a single symptom into a rare disease within a few clicks of the—babe, what's wrong?"

Kendra doubled over as the news hit, as if the doctor had just repeated it. Derek was at her side, rubbing her back. "What's wrong?" he asked again.

"That's what I have, a rare disease." Hearing herself say it made her nauseated. She swallowed and focused on breathing.

"What are you talking about? What rare disease?"

"Inflammatory breast cancer."

"I've never heard of that."

"I hadn't either." She gathered herself. "I had some testing done, including a biopsy, and the doctor just called with the results."

"What? When did you have tests? Why didn't you tell me before now," Derek said, "so I could be with you?"

"I wanted to hear that it was nothing, just an infection, and move on."

"So what does this mean?" he asked. "What happens now?"

"I go for more tests this afternoon," she said, "to see if it's spread."

"To see if it's spread?" He stood and leaned against the desk. "I'm not understanding. Why would that be the next thought? Wouldn't it have to be an advanced stage for that to happen? You're not even sick."

Her body twitched. "That's the thing. I . . . I *am* sick. The nature of inflammatory breast cancer is that once it's diagnosed, it's already advanced. That's why they scheduled further tests right away."

Derek's gaze moved into the distance, for an eternity it seemed. "What time is your appointment?" he said finally. "I'm going with you."

"You've got a deadline today." She never would have expected him to go, or even asked.

"I'll work it out." He took her hand and pulled her up. "I know it's scary, but we'll get through this. Together. I love you, babe."

Derek pulled her closer, embracing her, and Kendra felt herself trembling. Over the last few days she'd researched every facet of this disease, imagined endless scenarios, and gone to bed with a million what-ifs. Until this moment she hadn't realized how afraid she was, afraid of enduring this alone . . . the way she had moved through all the hard things of life alone.

But she needed to get used to a new way of thinking, a new way of operating. She had a man—a soon-to-be husband—who loved her. His words were like a balm—*We'll get through this. Together.*

As scary as this was, knowing Derek would be with her today and every day ahead made all the difference.

Chapter Six

Lance had been at the Woodses' home off and on since Wednesday evening. Once Timmy and the others ran, he'd debated for a moment what to do, fearing what might happen if they caught him. He'd never forgive himself if he simply left and Timmy ended up hurt. But just as he'd resolved to call the police, Molly emerged from the lower-level bedroom. She'd slipped inside during the ruckus and made the call herself.

As it turned out, a neighbor called as well, after the guys caught Timmy and beat him down in the neighbor's yard. Between then and now, Timmy had pressed charges; Trey had gotten hauled down to the station; Timmy's parents had come from Nebraska, shocked that drugs were involved; campus police stepped up an ongoing investigation; and somewhere in the midst, Lance felt the divine nudge that he really needed to move in.

And today was moving day. Sort of. Lance had stopped by yesterday to get a house key and clean up the lower level. He planned to drop off a few things this morning before a photo shoot and return later with a team of friends to help with bigger items.

He entered through the door to the lower level, arms filled with clothing, appreciating the living quarters he would have. He had a bedroom, his own bathroom, and a living area with a sectional sofa, a large-screen television, and a desk to set up his computer. He spent a great deal of time at the computer, editing photos and—

Lance stopped on his way to the bedroom. What were Trey and Molly doing down here, sprawled on the sofa asleep? Empty beer bottles, fast food trash, and Doritos chips were on the floor. And was that weed he smelled?

Lance gaped at them. "Are you serious? After everything that happened this week? And I just cleaned down here yesterday."

Neither moved. Lance dumped his clothes in the bedroom, walked back out, rolled the vacuum near the sofa, and turned it on.

Their heads popped up, Molly's freshly dyed red.

"What are you *doing?*" Trey rubbed his eyes. "What time is it?"

"Now that I've got your attention"—Lance shut it off—"why are you getting high down here?"

Trey let his head fall on the arm of the sofa. "I live here, in case you forgot."

"Actually," Lance said, "as of today, the lower level is my own personal space, according to your dad."

Lance had talked to Mr. Woods after the Timmy ordeal, and he not only was pleased that Lance was moving in, but hoped the extra-curricular activity in the home would be curbed, at least somewhat.

"I'm sorry. I thought he told you," Lance added.

"My dad says a lot of things, mostly lies."

Lance let that one sail. "Anyway, I asked why you were getting high down here after what went down this week."

"What about it?" Trey asked.

Molly stared back and forth between them, mascara smudge marks around her eyes.

"I thought you might see it as a wake-up call," Lance said.

"And what was I supposed to awaken to?"

Lance sighed. "To understand that marijuana isn't the harmless recreational drug you think it is. There's a whole world associated with it."

Trey looked at him. "Who said I thought it was harmless? You're the one who needs a wake-up call."

Lance glanced at Molly and back to Trey. "Can we talk privately somewhere?"

"Why? I don't care if Molly hears."

"I know you're in pain, Trey. I hate that you lost your mom and got hit with all the stuff about your dad." Lance sat down on the sofa. "But you don't have to make these kinds of choices. There are people who can help you through."

Trey half laughed. "What, you picked up some pop psychology from somewhere? Nobody can 'help me through.' You don't know the half of my pain."

"You're right. I don't know everything you're dealing with." Lance felt he was talking to a wall. "But God knows. He sees you. And I know that you know because you were the one who always carried your Bible around, always memorizing passages of Scripture. Whatever it is, Trey, please give it to God. He cares about you."

Trey stared downward, and Molly moved closer to him, taking his hand.

"You okay, Trey?" Lance asked.

Trey just stared at a single spot on the carpet, and when he looked up, Lance was surprised to see tears in his eyes.

"I wish it were true, that God cares about me." He looked at Lance, his eyes hardening. "I used to think it was. But what do you do when you realize it's not?" He stood, his hand grasping Molly's.

"Huh? What do you do when part of your pain is the realization that God *doesn't* care about you?"

He led Molly upstairs, and Lance remained where he stood, replaying Trey's words.

CHAPTER SEVEN

IT WAS THE SHAKING THAT UNNERVED HER. SHE COULDN'T STOP the shaking.

"I'm sorry." Kendra held herself, trying to focus on the oncologist. "I can't . . . stop."

Derek moved closer and draped an arm around her. Their chairs, upholstered with fabric in a pattern of brightly colored leaves, were positioned across from a doctor Kendra had met minutes before . . . who'd pronounced her fate quickly.

"It's metastatic." Dr. Watson's voice was even, his hands folded on his desk. "The cancer has spread to your neck."

"This means it's . . . it's Stage IV?"

"It's Stage IV, yes."

She should've brought a sweater. Was the AC on blast?

"I advise aggressive chemotherapy," he was saying, "followed by a mastectomy, radiation, and likely more chemotherapy."

Kendra was reeling. "And if I do . . . do all of that, is there a chance it'll be cured?" She had to ask, though her research had already supplied the answer.

"This is not treatment with a curative intent. This is terminal."

His expression was empty. "But if you respond well to treatment, you might live a little longer—although I can't give you any guarantees."

Derek came forward in his chair. "What do you mean 'a little longer'? How long are you giving her?"

"The five-year survival rate for inflammatory breast cancer is about 30 percent."

"Only 30 percent live five years?" Derek asked. "And given Kendra's particular diagnosis, what's your best guess for her?"

The doctor looked at Kendra, as if questioning whether he should say.

"I'd like to know," Kendra said.

"I've seen dozens of IBC patients, and my best guess is that two to two and a half years would be optimistic, if she responds well to treatment."

Kendra had read story after story. She knew the life expectancy, even of a metastatic IBC diagnosis. But hearing it about *her* life . . .

She scrambled for air, scanning family pictures on the doctor's desk, one of his wife and him as bride and groom. They probably had a perfect wedding, both in perfect health.

Dr. Watson was jotting notes. He looked up briefly. "I'm also advising that you start the chemo next week."

Kendra's eyes went wide. "Doctor, I'm getting married next week. We've been planning this for months. I can't take the chance that I'll be sick on my wedding day because of chemo."

The doctor paused his pen. "Miss Woods, you're sick *now*. I don't think a dream wedding is your goal at this point."

Kendra stared at him, dumbfounded. Did she no longer have input in her own life? Had she relinquished it to a man she'd known all of ten minutes?

"With all due respect, Dr. Watson," she said, "you just told me this is not a cure, and there's no guarantee it'll even extend my life. So I'm not understanding why I can't put it off for one week, to enjoy the wedding we've planned."

He removed his glasses and looked pointedly at her. "My job is to effectively treat the cancer, Miss Woods. I can't do that when patients get in the way. I need you to put all the 'life' things you want to do behind you and focus on the matter at hand."

Kendra stood. "Thank you for your time, Dr. Watson."

Kendra left the doctor's office, almost more upset about his attitude than her diagnosis. Put the wedding behind her? Is that what he was saying? Chuck all the planning and money invested—not to mention how much her heart was invested—and do what? A quick vow exchange outside the chemo room?

She needed another oncologist. But she also needed a second opinion, just in case. She needed to know that her desire to proceed with her wedding as planned wasn't insane.

Kendra remembered Dr. Myra Contee, a former neighbor back home and an oncologist who specialized in breast cancer. On staff at the Siteman Cancer Center at Wash U, Dr. Contee had made herself available for questions and support during Kendra's mom's illness.

Kendra called, and Dr. Contee said to fax her medical records ASAP so she could take a look. And while she waited to hear back, Kendra was determined to stay in the swing of wedding planning. She was inside the federal courthouse, making her way to the chambers of the Honorable Jayne Cardwell to discuss the final order of the ceremony. Derek had planned to come, too, but got called back to the office to handle a client crisis. They would connect a little later this evening, when they'd have dinner with his best man and Charlene.

It was after five, and the judge's assistant and current law clerks were gone. The judge buzzed Kendra through the door herself.

Kendra smiled big when she saw her, sans black robe, impeccably dressed in a summer suit and top. They hugged like old friends. "Judge Cardwell, it's so good to see you."

The judge, nearing retirement age, smiled from her eyes. "Always a joy to see my favorite clerk."

"You say that to all your former clerks."

The judge laughed, neither confirming nor denying. Kendra had learned much from her about diplomacy in the year she'd spent there.

"How are you?" The judge always asked in a way that questioned the soul.

Kendra's gaze faltered. "Fine, thanks."

The judge's eyes sparkled at her. "Can you believe the wedding is almost here? This is the most exciting thing on my docket."

"Well," Kendra said, "I guess I'm flattered that our wedding beats the trials of hardened criminals on the excitement meter."

The judge chuckled. "And don't forget those month-long patent infringement suits on the intricacies of computer hardware wiring. They're a rousing good time."

"Ah, yes, I remember well."

"Let's have a seat and get comfortable."

Kendra followed Judge Cardwell from the outer chambers to her office, where she took the sofa and the judge took a chair.

"First, I want to say again that I am humbled that you've asked me to officiate your wedding. I consider it a great honor."

"The honor is ours," Kendra said. "We didn't want anyone else to marry us."

When they'd first gotten engaged, Kendra considered getting married back home, since her mother was sick and doing little travel. But the only pastor she knew was Pastor Lyles of Living Word Church, and she hadn't been there in over a decade. Then her mother died, mooting the question.

Judge Cardwell grabbed a notepad from the side table. "So, the service starts at five o'clock in the evening," she said. "What time should I arrive?"

"There's another wedding before ours," Kendra said. "Our party will be allowed in as early as three o'clock. Maybe since you won't be able to attend the rehearsal you could arrive at four, for any last-minute instructions."

"That's a good plan," the judge said. "In terms of the ceremony, when the string quartet signals the start of service, I walk out with Derek and the best man. Correct?"

"That's right," Kendra said. "Then our attendants will partner up and walk down the aisle—we have four bridesmaids and four grooms-men—then the maid of honor, flower girl, ring bearer, then yours truly."

Kendra got butterflies picturing it. How often had she dreamed of that moment, when Derek would see her in her gown for the first time?

"And you'll be walking down the aisle alone?"

"Yes. My father won't be there, and it doesn't make sense for anyone else to give me away."

"Okay," the judge said. She looked at her notes. "I have the Scripture verses that will be read, two songs, and"—she glanced up—"I believe I have the final copy of the vows?"

Kendra nodded. They'd cut and pasted different versions of traditional vows they'd found.

"Okay, and one more question—"

Kendra's phone sounded. She'd given Dr. Contee a special ringtone too. "I'm sorry," she said, "but I need to get this."

A million beats per second. That was her heart's rhythm as she walked into the outer office. "Dr. Contee, hi."

"Hi, Kendra, sorry to make you wait all day."

"Not at all," Kendra said. "Thank you for taking the time."

"Even now, I only have a second before I see a patient," Dr. Contee said. "But I wanted to give you my thoughts on this."

Kendra closed her eyes. "Okay."

"You're not insane, is the short answer." Dr. Contee had a soothing tone. "I see no problem with your moving forward with the wedding as planned. But you need to postpone the honeymoon and begin chemo right after the wedding."

"Dr. Contee, I can't thank you enough. This is the best news I've heard in days."

"Kendra, again, I'm so sorry," she said. "I'm still stunned. If you need anything, don't hesitate to call my private number. I'll also compile a list of recommended oncologists in the DC area, as you asked."

"I appreciate everything, Dr. Contee. Thank you."

Kendra held the phone after she'd hung up, turning over her words.

I see no problem with your moving forward . . .

She couldn't wait to share the news with Derek.

CHAPTER EIGHT

KENDRA SAT ACROSS FROM DEREK AT ONE OF THEIR FAVORITE restaurants on Capitol Hill, staring at a curious text message from Charlene.

U 2 LOVEBIRDS WANNA BE ALONE, HUH? I GUESS I'M NOT MAD AT YA, EVEN THOUGH I DON'T GET TO MEET THE SIDEKICK YET ;-) CALL ME LATER.

"Charlene's not coming now?" Kendra flipped the phone around to show Derek. "I don't know what she's talking about. Let me call her."

Derek covered her hand. "No need to call."

"Why not?"

"I texted Charlene and Phil and asked them not to come. We need some time, just the two of us." He paused. "It's been a lot today, Ken."

She stared at him a moment, then tucked her phone inside her purse, slightly irritated that he hadn't discussed the change with her. It *had* been a lot today, but for that reason she'd been looking forward to escaping, just for a night, in laughter and wedding talk. Maybe he wanted to process it aloud. She had to remember that he was in this too.

"Good to see you two this evening." Franklin, their preferred server, appeared with their favorite bottle of wine. He glanced at the place settings. "We're waiting for two more?"

"Actually, no," Derek said. "It'll be just us."

"Very good then." He lifted the bottle toward Kendra. "Shall I pour you a glass?"

She almost nodded. Would alcohol be harmful? There was so much she had to learn about her life now. "Not tonight," she said. "Water will be fine, thanks."

Franklin tipped it Derek's way. "Sir?"

"Yes, thank you."

Kendra settled in as he poured, inhaling her surroundings . . . the soft lighting, light jazz, tables spaced with intimacy in mind. Maybe Derek had the right idea. They needed this time.

"Shall I start you with the pan-fried calamari?" Franklin asked.

Kendra's mouth watered. She remembered the warning to stay away from fried delicacies so she could fit into her dress perfectly. But with the day she'd had, she might order the chocolate hazelnut cake for dessert as well. "I'd love that," she said. "Derek?"

His thoughts were with his wine. He finished a sip and looked up, his brow questioning.

"Calamari?" Kendra said.

"Oh. Yes, sure."

"Excellent," Franklin said. "I'll return shortly for your order."

Kendra sipped her water. "You didn't say much on the ride over here." She stared into his eyes. "Were you upset that Dr. Contee advised postponing the honeymoon? I know how excited we were about Paris." She added quickly, "Now that I think about it, it was just a recommendation. We could still go and—"

"Kendra . . ." Both hands cupping the glass, Derek stared into the red wine for long seconds, then looked at her. "I don't think you're operating in reality."

"Why would you say that?"

"You received a terminal diagnosis of cancer this morning, and by evening you're ready to hang out with friends and talk honeymoon in Paris?"

"Derek, my world was rocked this morning," Kendra said. "You saw me. I could barely breathe, couldn't stop shaking until we left that office." She felt a shiver now thinking about it. "Is it wrong to try to find a little joy in other aspects of my reality? This is supposed to be the happiest time of my life."

"I guess that's what I'm saying." He was staring at the glass again. "Nothing is as it was supposed to be. It's all changed." He looked at her, and his face wore an expression she'd never seen.

A different kind of shiver went through her. "What do you mean?"

"Kendra, it was a *terminal* diagnosis. Have you played that out in your mind?" His words were slow, pained. "We had so many plans for the future, for our careers, our kids, where we'd live, other trips we'd enjoy. That's all . . . lost."

His words pummeled her gut. She hadn't *wanted* to play all that out in her mind. She wanted to focus on next week. The wedding. Then she'd deal with the rest of her new reality.

"But it's not all lost." Kendra needed him to see. *She* needed to see. "I've read a lot of stories of women who beat the odds, lived longer than expected, accomplished more than anticipated. It wasn't easy, but they didn't give up. They adjusted their plans."

Derek nodded slowly. "I love you, Kendra, so much. And that's one of the things I love about you, that you don't give up. You go hard after everything in life. Even . . ."

The emotion in his voice tugged at her. She leaned in, to hear, to understand.

"Even . . ." he said again, "with this wedding. You wanted to do what you could to make it happen."

"I'm just glad I thought to ask Dr. Contee," Kendra said.

"But, Ken, you didn't ask me."

His words, almost a whisper, lunged at her. Her insides staggering, she couldn't find her own words. Didn't know if she wanted to.

"Hot and delicious pan-fried calamari." Franklin set it down between them with two appetizer plates. "Are we ready to order?"

"We need a few minutes, please," Derek said.

"No problem at all," Franklin said. "Enjoy."

She was shaking again. "I don't . . . know what you mean."

"You didn't ask what I wanted to do about the wedding, what I wanted to do about *us*."

She only stared at him.

"I love you, Kendra, but I've thought about it and thought about it." He sighed. "I can't do this."

"Can't do"—her breath stuttered—"what?"

"I can't go through with this wedding next week."

Her mind struggled to find nuance, to overthrow the obvious and claim the unlikely. He said next week—maybe he needed more time?

"I can't go through with it at all," he added. "I'm sorry. I really am. I feel awful, but I have to be honest with you and with myself. This is not what I envisioned."

"And I did?"

"I know, babe." He reached for her hand, and she pulled it back. "I just . . . What do you want me to do?"

"How about thinking about it for more than a few hours? How about *that*? You don't think you owe us that? You don't think I'm worth that?"

"I considered that," he said. "But the only thing that'll change by tomorrow or the next day is we'll be that much closer to the wedding. How would that be fair, to let you get your hopes up that much more?"

"Oh, now we're talking 'fairness.' Is it 'fair' to keep one's word? Because what happened to 'we're in this together'?" She heard her voice rising and pulled it down. "I believed you. I thought you would be there for me."

"None of this means I won't be there for you," Derek said. "I still love you, Ken. Whatever you need, I'll walk with you through this."

"I have to go." She got up, covering her mouth, afraid she might vomit.

"Go where?" he said. "We took my car." He stood. "I'll drive you home."

She pointed back at him. "Stay away from me."

Kendra passed Franklin on the way out of the restaurant. Outside, she doubled over suddenly. The valet rushed to her. "Miss Woods, are you okay?"

"Yes." Her forehead beaded with sweat. She fanned herself with muggy air. "Can you hail me a taxi, please?"

He looked confused, especially as Derek walked outside. "Of course," he said.

"Kendra, please." Derek held her up. "Let me take you home. I can't let you leave like this."

A taxi swerved over to the curb, answering the valet's signal.

She jerked away, wobbly, wanting the strength of his arms but needing to embrace the truth. She was alone. And she'd be alone the rest of her life, the little life she had left.

Kendra's eyes hit her engagement ring. She pulled it off and dropped it in Derek's hand. Then she made her way into the taxi and crouched into a ball in the backseat.

CHAPTER NINE

LANCE QUIETLY SCOOTED BACK HIS CHAIR, POISED TO SNEAK OUT of a meeting of various church leaders. They'd been at it more than two hours, and no one in the room seemed aware of the hugely urgent matter begging his attention—the VBS carnival kicking off outside.

Vacation Bible School wasn't Lance's ministry area—a dedicated children's ministry staff and tons of volunteers pulled it off beautifully every summer. But for years he had spread the word in his old neighborhood and arranged transportation for as many as wanted to come. And this year, their new sister church was bringing a busload of those same kids.

Lance became a kid himself at the carnival, hyping the fun with his popular photo booth. He'd set it up earlier, with all kinds of silliness for the backdrop and props for the kids to dress themselves in. Many came straight from the face-painting booth. Others planted their faces in a mound of cotton candy. But it was all about capturing the moment and taking home pictures as souvenirs. Hearing the first squeals of laughter outdoors made him anxious to get out there.

"Anything else?" Pastor Lyles was asking.

Lance inched forward, hopeful.

"I just thought of something."

Lance slumped in the chair, foiled by his friend Darrin, the worship pastor, sitting next to him.

"We've talked sort of informally about our next church plant," Darrin said, "and a possible Clayton location. I'm wondering if and when we'll take the next steps to flesh it out." He nudged Lance. "I do know there's a growing consensus that my man here would be a great choice to head it up."

"Growing consensus?" Lance gave him the eye. "You got jokes?"

"It would be funny if *my* name were mentioned," Darrin said. "I don't know why you can't see it. You're made to be a pastor."

"That's what I am. A youth pastor."

"You know what I mean," Darrin said.

"If I may address the question," Pastor Lyles began.

Lance waited. No way could he sneak out now.

"You're right, Darrin," Pastor Lyles said, "our discussions about the church plant have been informal, but there's been a lot of prayer and deeper discussion among the elders." He cleared his throat. "I don't mind sharing that I did approach Lance to get his thoughts on heading it up. He says he's not ready, so we continue to pray. We want to have a lead pastor in mind before we take the next steps."

"Wow." Patricia, head of women's ministry, was looking directly at him.

Lance returned her gaze. "I guess I don't need to ask why you said that."

"Lance, I remember when you first came to Living Word," Patricia said. "You were like a kid in a candy store, reading everything you could get your hands on, making sure you had a ride to church for every Bible study." She spoke like a big sister. "I saw God's hand on you, young man, and years later when the youth pastor position opened, there was no question who should fill it." She gave him a look. "But what did you say?"

Lance looked a little sheepish. "That I wasn't ready."

"And what did I tell you?"

"To stop looking at myself."

"And what am I about to tell you now?"

Lance smiled. "But, as I shared with Pastor Lyles, Clayton wouldn't be a fit for me anyway."

"Well, here's what brought all this to mind," Darrin said. "I'm sure you all heard about the frat guys beating down another student over a drug transaction."

Lance couldn't believe it had gotten news coverage.

Darrin continued, "That's just the latest in a string of stories. A few months ago, a different fraternity got kicked off of Wash U's campus for drug use. People tend to put Wash U on a pedestal, but it's like any other college campus—students are lost and need Christ. I think it would be so cool to target the area that surrounds the campus." Darrin nudged him again. "Man, you'd be perfect for that."

"Something's wrong with you, Darrin." Lance shook his head, chuckling. "I can read the headline now: 'High School Dropout Leads Church Plant Targeting Some of the Best and Brightest College Students in the Country.' Right."

"Wow," Patricia said again.

Lance looked at her. "What?"

Patricia only shook her head.

"Can we all commit to praying on this?" Pastor Lyles asked.

"Yes" rang out in the room, with all eyes on Lance.

He laughed. "Why do I feel like there's some conspiracy here?" He raised a hand. "Can I be excused to go outside and play now?"

Pastor Lyles had that fatherly twinkle in his eye. "I'll walk with you after we pray to dismiss."

A few moments later Lance stood near the door, wondering if the pastor had more to say about the plant. But Darrin approached him first.

"Hey, did Adrienne contact you?" Darrin asked.

"About what?"

"She said she needed some photos, and I gave her your number," Darrin said. He grinned. "Can you believe that? Providence."

Darrin had been talking up Adrienne, saying Lance should get to know her. A newer member of Living Word, she shared an apartment with Darrin's girlfriend.

"If it's Providence, it's only because it's meant to give me more business." Lance touched his shoulder. "Stop playing Cupid."

"What? I'm just—"

Pastor Lyles walked up, interrupting them. Lance walked with the pastor, shaking his head at Darrin.

"How's it going?" Pastor Lyles asked.

"Sir?"

"At the Woodses' home. I understand you moved in."

"Yes, this past weekend," Lance said. "It's been . . . interesting. Please pray for Trey. His life is totally spinning out of control."

"I'm definitely praying for him," the pastor said. "When it rains it pours with that family."

"What do you mean?"

"I got word today that Kendra canceled her wedding."

"Really, why?" Lance hadn't heard Trey mention the wedding at all, but he'd seen the invitation on the refrigerator.

"No reason given. Her maid of honor said it was due to unforeseen circumstances."

"Was Mr. Woods planning to return to the States for the wedding?"

Pastor Lyles hesitated at the bottom of the stairs. "From what I understand, he wasn't invited."

***

Lance got home past one in the morning, after holding open his booth until every kid got a turn, then breaking it down and packing it up. But that wasn't what prolonged the night. Cleanup time among the volunteers had become battle time as popcorn began flying. The challenge: to pop someone directly on the nose. Having been accused of starting it—though Lance maintained it was Darrin—he stayed, industrial broom in hand, until the lot was kernel-free.

Lance entered through the back door and walked to his room, impressed by the quiet. He hadn't seen much of Trey this week and wondered what he might be up to. But he had to remind himself that he wasn't here to keep tabs on him. Trey was a grown man. The only way Lance could help him was if he wanted the help.

Lance dropped his camera bag and other backpack full of equipment in the room and headed upstairs. He'd eat some of the spaghetti he'd made last night and hit the bed. He had a photo shoot first thing in the morning.

Lance walked into the kitchen and stopped short, startled to see Trey and Molly—at the table, eating his spaghetti. "Good evening," he said.

Trey nodded at him, sucking up a noodle. "What's up?"

"Hiya," Molly said from under a black fedora hat, her fork twirling pasta.

Lance spied the spaghetti container on the counter, empty. "Is it good?" he asked.

"Real good." Trey looked back at him. "Wait, you made this?"

Molly looked at him. "Who else could've made it?"

Lance was thinking the same.

"My bad," Trey said. "You were saving it?"

"It's cool." Lance's stomach growled. "Did you get some French bread?"

Trey stood, looking. "There's French bread too?"

Lance got it from the bread basket and turned on the broiler. "I can toast it a little, with butter, if you want."

Trey eyed him, as if trying to figure out the catch. "Cool. Thanks."

Lance brought it to them minutes later. Spaghetti gone, they now tore into the toasted bread. He joined them at the table, taking a piece himself.

"So what'd you two do tonight?" Lance asked.

"Why?" Trey licked his fingers. "So you can report to my dad, and he can kick me out sooner rather than later?"

"Just making conversation."

"Okay then," Trey said, "what did we do tonight? Let's see . . ." He let his head rest on the back of the chair, staring upward. "Partied with friends. Drank. Got high. No arrests. And no sex, yet." He looked at Molly. "That about sums it up, right?"

"You can be such a jerk sometimes," she said.

Trey popped a piece of bread into his mouth. "You're always crabby when you're coming down from a high. I love you anyway, though." He deftly snatched her hat from her head.

"Stop playing." Molly stood, reaching to get it back, her little dress hiked high.

Lance diverted his eyes.

She got it, hitting Trey over the head with it before putting it back on.

Still amused, Trey looked at Lance. "So, what'd you do this evening, Pastor?"

Lance went with the question, though Trey's tone was insincere. "We had the VBS carnival at church."

Trey toyed with his bread. "So you worked the photo booth?"

"You know it." Lance pulled out his phone, scrolled to a picture, and handed it to him. "Check out the backdrop I made this year."

"Oh, that's dope," Trey said, and seemed to mean it.

"Let me see," Molly said.

Trey passed her the phone and got up seconds later, leaving the kitchen.

Molly scrolled through pictures he'd taken of the kids. "Whenever I saw a photo booth as a girl, I wanted to stop and take a picture. But we barely had money for essentials, so anything 'extra' was out of the question."

Lance was tuned in. He'd wondered what her story was.

"Same with school pictures," she was saying. "Not in the budget. And then my dad would say . . ." She hesitated. "He'd say, 'You don't need to be in front of the camera anyway. It's not like you're pretty.'"

Trey breezed back into the kitchen. "I can't believe I found these." He held them up. "Carnival photo-booth pictures I took when I volunteered to help in high school."

"You saved them?" Lance said. "Let's see." Lance couldn't remember taking the photos, but he remembered this Trey, fun and playful.

Molly came to see. "I see you were into hats yourself."

Trey laughed. "The kids picked that Dr. Seuss hat out of the prop basket and dressed me."

"Aww, you looked so cute," Molly said, pinching his cheek.

"I'm not cute now?"

She folded her arms, studying him. "I guess you still got it."

He put an arm around her. "Good. We can look cute together at my sister's wedding."

"I didn't say I was going." Molly rolled her eyes. "I'm tired of trying to fit in where I'm not wanted."

"Whatever. My sister's tripping, telling me I can't bring a guest."

"Um," Lance said, "you haven't heard the wedding's canceled?"

"Kendra's wedding?" Trey said. "How do you know?"

"Pastor Lyles told me today. Said the maid of honor called."

Trey took out his phone. "I got a call from a number I didn't recognize and let it go to voice mail." He listened. "This is the message. But why am I not getting the news directly from my sister?"

"Why was it canceled?" Molly asked.

"Didn't say," Trey said. "Derek probably made her mad, and she cut him off." He put his phone in his pocket. "One thing I know. Kendra's gonna do Kendra. Always has, always will."

CHAPTER TEN

FOR TWO DAYS KENDRA LAY ACROSS THE WIDTH OF HER BED, head angled near the side with a bucket below to catch the vomit, in case she couldn't make it to the bathroom. Or didn't care to. But the vomit never came—just dry, horrible heaves that stalked her while awake.

So she slept. And when she was tired of sleeping, she made herself sleep some more, to dodge the nightmares that haunted her every waking moment. Nightmares like having to notify every single guest that you've canceled your wedding.

"Let me contact everybody for you," Charlene offered after the first day. She had called umpteen times and finally came banging on the door. What a joke that Derek had broken the news—only part of the news—and asked her to check on Kendra. "What should I say, just that the wedding is canceled?"

"Tell them life is canceled."

"Oh, there'll be life without Derek," Charlene said. "He did you a favor, showed you what he was really about."

Ready to heave, Kendra had only half listened. Charlene didn't know her diagnosis, and Kendra wasn't ready to tell her.

"What about the Textile Museum—you contacted them, right?" Charlene was saying. "And the photographer, videographer, florist . . . ?"

"Ugh. No." The fog of her new existence . . . doing nothing that needed to be done and not caring.

"I'm sure you've got all the information detailed in some computer file. I'll make those calls too."

Kendra thanked her and slipped back into the arms of slumber, unaware that another night had passed until she heard incessant banging at the door again.

Deep down she hoped it was Derek. Maybe he'd been calling. He'd realized his love—*their* love—outweighed anything that might come against them. They'd endure together. And they didn't need a big wedding anyway. They could get married today, a week earlier. The man full of romantic surprises had probably called and arranged it with Judge Cardwell.

It was the fog talking.

Instead of finding Derek at the door, Kendra found her litigation supervisor, Grace. For an hour she wept in Grace's arms on the sofa, unloading everything from the past two weeks. And Grace listened, weeping with her at the news of the diagnosis, sharing the hurt of the breakup, even rolling her eyes at the realization that Derek had gone to work the next day as if nothing had happened. When Grace couldn't reach Kendra for two days, she had gone to him, and he'd told her the same thing he'd said to Charlene . . . "You should go check on her."

Grace looked Kendra in the eye. "I hope I can speak plainly to you, not as a boss or colleague, but as your friend."

Kendra nodded.

"You've grieved the relationship for three days," Grace said. "I'm not saying it will be easy, but it's time to put Derek and the wedding behind you and focus on your health."

Kendra looked down. "I know."

Grace continued, "And this is even tougher for me to say . . ."

Kendra focused on her.

"I think you need to go home," Grace said.

"What do you mean, go home?"

"A new environment would do you well right now," Grace said. "You said you need a new oncologist. Dr. Contee would be the perfect choice. You could receive your chemo treatments in St. Louis."

Kendra struggled to understand. "Why would I do that? I've got responsibilities on some pretty big cases, with deadlines approaching. Many people work through their chemo treatments."

"If they're able," Grace said. "Josh tried it for a while . . ."

Kendra remembered. Early in her time with the firm, an attorney named Josh had been diagnosed with lung cancer and eventually succumbed to it.

"I'm not concerned about your caseload, Kendra." Grace was earnest. "We were making accommodations anyway for your time away for the wedding and honeymoon, and we can extend that. I'm concerned about you." She looked at her dead-on. "You've had not one, but two major life shifts. Give yourself time. You have so much to think through and process." She paused. "And would you really want to be coming to work every day, where you could run into Derek at any time?"

Kendra hated him even more at that moment. Fleming & Stein was her firm. She'd been there eight years, even longer if she counted her time as a law student. He'd been there less than two. Now she had to avoid the place—and the people and the work she loved—because of him?

But Grace was right. She didn't want to see Derek. Ever.

"Kendra, honestly," Grace continued, "this is a time to be with family."

Whatever family she had left. Kendra sighed. She hadn't considered going home, but maybe that was what she needed. Maybe Trey could even help get her to chemo appointments, since she didn't think he was working or taking classes this summer. Then she could re-evaluate things toward the end of the summer.

The more she thought about it, especially the prospect of getting away from Derek and the entire wedding fiasco, the more she liked it.

The taxi pulled up to the Woodses' home late Sunday night. Kendra paid the driver and stood with her bags on the sidewalk, remembering the last time she was home, for her mother's funeral. She hadn't lived here since she left for college fourteen years ago. And with all that had transpired in the last year, the soul of the place seemed to be gone. In another year her brother would graduate college and head who-knows-where for grad school or a job. She wondered if her father would sell the house then. What would it be like when there *really* wasn't a place to call home?

Kendra grabbed her luggage as a car came down the street and parked a few houses down. As she glanced around she noticed lots of cars in the immediate area. Somebody must be having a get-together.

She headed up the walkway as footsteps and voices came nearer, then joined her on the walkway. Two girls and three guys moved past her, up the front porch and into the house.

Kendra stopped, frowning. *What is this about?* As she approached the door she felt the throbbing beat of a bass. And when she opened it, she couldn't believe the scene.

Music pulsating. Bodies gyrating—in the hallway in front of her, on the stairs, in the dining room to the right, all over the living room to her left. In almost every hand was a beer bottle or plastic cup.

A party—*a wild party*—in the Woodses' home? Only once, near the end of senior year, did she dream of it, when her parents had planned a short overnight trip and left her in charge. But she was too afraid of neighbors telling, or more likely, her Goody Two-shoes little brother. She couldn't get away with anything around Trey.

Now it dawned on her that he must be the one hosting this. Leaving her bags near the door, she began scanning faces for Trey. She moved through the living room, thinking she must be getting old because she was almost embarrassed by the way the young women were dancing with the young men. More people were in the sunroom off of the living room, and when she opened the French doors, she couldn't believe she smelled smoke, *marijuana* smoke.

She doubled back, making her way to the kitchen. Standing over a big pot on the counter, stirring some sort of red punch, was her brother.

"Trey, what is going on?"

Trey turned. "Hey, what's up, sis?" He dropped the wooden spoon in the pot and hugged her tight. "I didn't know you were coming, but you're right on time for the party."

He took her by the hand, bouncing to the music, and twirled her around.

Kendra took a step back. "Are you *drunk?*"

"Molly!" He waved an arm to someone down the hall. "Kendra's here!" He pointed downward, above her head.

A young woman with bright-red, faux-hawked hair breezed into the kitchen. Even with the new hair, Kendra recognized her from the funeral, where she'd worn a short plaid grunge dress. Now she sported black skinny jeans and a corset top.

"Trey's sister!" Molly grinned, hugging her, holding a plastic cup aloft. "Oh hey, I'm so sorry about the wedding." Arm draped around Kendra, she lowered her voice to almost a whisper. "I was looking forward to it." A giggle escaped. "Trey was making me crash."

Kendra eyed her brother. The last time they'd talked, he'd been upset because his invitation didn't include a guest. He'd accused her of excluding Molly because she didn't fit Kendra's "uppity DC crowd."

"What happened anyway, Ken?" Trey was back at the pot, now with a ladle in hand, scooping punch into a cup. "You investigated the dude? Found out he was cheating?" He tasted his concoction. "Didn't want to be the last to know like Mom, huh?"

"I can't believe you'd bring Mom into it like that," Kendra said.

"Trey, where's the punch?" someone yelled.

"I'm coming!" Trey poured the contents of the big pot into another container and walked it out, with Molly behind him.

Kendra leaned against a chair, feeling nauseated, head hurting. *I just need to lie down.*

She moved back down the hallway, dodging bodies. "Excuse me . . . Excuse me . . . Hey!" A woman, dancing, jerked around and bumped into Kendra, spilling her drink. Kendra brushed the liquid off her shirt, feeling increasingly hot, almost suffocated.

She grabbed her two bags from the entryway and headed upstairs, past pockets of people.

Kendra walked into her room, clicking on the lights and dropping her bags. It was mostly unchanged from high school days, but she was too spent to reminisce. She collapsed on her queen bed as music vibrated beneath her. She peeked at the clock—12:20.

How long will this thing last?

Her head pounded with every pulsating beat. And the malt liquor, or whatever it was, that had spilled on her shirt was making her feel even more nauseated. She rose up a little, yanked off the shirt, and threw it on the floor, entertaining thoughts of calling the police. She was surprised none of the neighbors had. The only thing that stopped her was the possibility of Trey getting arrested. But it was tempting.

Kendra closed her eyes, chasing sleep in a den of hoots and hollers and chants of "Chug! Chug! Chug!" Was this supposed to be her respite? A frat house?

She hadn't made any commitments yet. She could easily return to DC.

But then she'd be back near Derek.

Kendra felt her world closing in on her. She had nowhere to go.

CHAPTER ELEVEN

LANCE LEANED AGAINST THE SIDE OF HIS CAR, WAITING FOR THE tank to fill at a rest stop near Montgomery, Alabama. He'd left Tallahassee at four a.m. and planned to make it back to St. Louis by early evening.

Seeing his mother behind bars was always painful, though she tried her best to make it easy on her son. Smiling in prison khakis, Pamela embraced him and asked how he was doing, as if he'd come through the front door after a long day rather than through barbed wire and metal detectors. Every time he wanted to cry. She'd made a lot of mistakes, but this was his mom. Locked up. She'd served six years and wasn't even halfway done.

He walked across two islands to the convenience store for gum and more snacks. He'd made this trip dozens of times, and each time he filled the tank and restocked here. Each time he grieved. For her. For them. For bad choices they'd both made, always wishing they could turn back the hands of time.

But he was grateful too. Over the past year he could tell his mom wasn't pretending to be okay for his sake. She *was* okay. In her words, "everything clicked" that he—and others in prison—had been telling her. And now she was telling others.

Lance paid for his goods, enjoying the memory of their conversation the day before.

"I don't see how she couldn't see it." Her mother spoke of a fellow inmate. "How could you not see your life is messed up when you're in a prison cell? How can you not see you need Jesus?"

Lance got a kick out of that. "Momma, you were in a prison cell for five years and didn't see it." He smiled at her. "Cut her some slack."

"But she could die tomorrow." Her voice was animated. "She needs Jesus *today*."

She told Lance she was talking to more of the women, hearing their stories. Of the women in the visiting room alone, she seemed to know something of how each had gotten there. Alice's boyfriend had asked her to pick up a package from a cousin in Florida, which turned out to be drugs. Convicted of conspiracy and intent to distribute drugs and given twenty-six years, she'd see her two young kids grow up from the visiting room.

The woman across the room had a story that seemed unreal. Teresa had three kids, the youngest a cute four-year-old who was styling her mother's hair. She'd never used or dealt drugs, but had agreed to hide her boyfriend's stash. For that she'd gotten life in prison, because she'd been unwilling to turn others in.

His mother's story was similar: caught up with a boyfriend, letting him deal from her house. They'd both gotten arrested. But though he was the dealer, he got a fraction of her time because he rolled over on someone else. She had no one to roll over on. She got twenty years.

Unlike Teresa, though, his mom had been a user . . . and it had impacted much of his life.

Lance returned the nozzle, screwed the gas cap on, and jumped into the car, ready for more highway. He ramped up his speed, set the cruise control, and sank back into his thoughts. Maybe the stories made him sad more than anything. And not just those stories, but stories he heard almost daily in ministry about hardship, pain, and deep struggles. Who was exempt? He was starting to think that if he could see into people's lives—their real lives, not the ones they wanted to show—he'd find everyone going through something, something that hurt.

He stared at the stretch of highway, eyes welling with tears. *Lord, there's so much pain in the world. Sometimes I just wonder . . . where are You?*

Chapter Twelve

KENDRA STOOD BEFORE HER CHILDHOOD DRESSER, GAZING INTO a mirror that had seen so many of her faces: hope, joy, anticipation, sadness—or what she thought was sadness—boyfriend problems, girlfriends gossiping behind her back, a less-than-perfect ACT score.

But never had it seen despair. Or fear.

Overnight, it seemed, her breast had changed. She examined it all the time now. It was her first thought in the morning and her last thought at night. And this morning when she looked, she gasped. Her left breast had swollen and grown more tender to the touch and gotten that pitted orange look she'd seen so often online.

She'd known it was coming, but seeing it made it tangibly more real, more serious—more frightening. How much worse would it get? Would it stay so . . . deformed? Would she really need a mastectomy?

She felt her arms begin to twitch, anxiety rising like goose bumps. There was so much to consider. So much she needed to know . . . and do. And she couldn't even nail down whether her next few weeks would be spent in the Midwest or on the East Coast.

Kendra sighed, moving away from the mirror. It was eight

forty-five, and she wanted to be gone by nine. The facility at Wash U was only minutes away, but she needed extra time to find parking and fill out paperwork.

She dressed quickly, threw her hair into a ponytail, and went out, glancing at Trey's room as she walked past. It was empty. Descending the stairs, she spotted him and Molly camped in a messy living room. With everything on her mind, she couldn't begin to figure out what was going on with him. But she couldn't wait to talk to him—sober—to see where his head was.

Kendra walked through the kitchen to the garage, thankful they'd kept her mom's Toyota Camry. Originally it was meant for Trey, but when their father went overseas and left his BMW, Trey naturally preferred to drive that. The old Camry with a zillion miles was perfect for her right now though. Comforting. It was almost like she could feel her mom with her as she made her way to this appointment.

But only almost. As she walked through the doors of the cancer center minutes later, the scene was striking, for a lot of reasons. Patients young and old in wheelchairs, with shaved heads, walking alongside IV drips, smiling, sullen, looking hopeful, falling asleep. But no one else was alone.

***

Dr. Contee was everything Kendra thought she would be. Knowledgeable. Attentive. Soothing. Unhurried. After an examination, Kendra pulled out a pad of questions she'd written, and Dr. Contee took her time answering each as best she could. It was a no-brainer. Kendra needed to be under this physician's care.

"Kendra, over the weekend you seemed fairly certain about wanting to pursue treatment here in St. Louis." Dr. Contee, in her early fifties, wore stylish glasses and her hair pulled back. Even her white lab coat looked chic on her. "But today I'm sensing a hesitancy. May I ask why?"

"I thought my brother might be able to help get me to treatments," Kendra said, "but now I'm not sure he can commit to that." She thought about it. "But the situation is really no different in DC. Being single . . ." She paused, swallowed the tears. "It's just hard."

"Your mom had friends from church who occasionally took her to appointments. Would that be an option for you?"

"No. I've been gone a long time and haven't really kept in touch with anybody."

Dr. Contee typed something into her laptop. "Let's work on this, because I'd like to get started with your chemo this Thursday."

"In three days?"

"There's no reason to wait, if this is where you'll be."

Maybe she could drive herself, though it wasn't recommended. Or take a taxi. Better to figure it out here in St. Louis, with Dr. Contee, than in DC.

The doctor wasn't done. Before she sent Kendra on her way, she walked her through next steps, ordered pre-chemo tests, and gave her a packet of material regarding local support groups and resources for cancer patients.

Cancer patient.

That's who she was now.

Kendra left with a cloud of thoughts. It was a lot to process, her time with Dr. Contee. She needed to drive somewhere and think. She navigated her way to Forest Park, less than a mile away, and in a flurry of twists and turns wound up near the zoo. Somehow it seemed just about right. She parked and walked in, starting as always on a path to the left. She hadn't been here in years, but she remembered. That's the way her mom would lead them. This was one of their favorite things to do when she was a girl.

Thankfully, the midday St. Louis heat wasn't oppressive. There was even a slight breeze once she entered the forest-like environs of the River's Edge. She took her time, idling to watch the hippos romp through the pool and nose the viewing glass, staring at the slow gait of the Asian elephant. It was peaceful, communing with nature and animals. Almost too peaceful, as it coaxed a myriad of thoughts to the fore.

Kendra had been many things. Daughter. Sister. Friend. Student. Attorney. Almost-bride. But cancer patient seemed to engulf them all. It was demanding. Exacting. It had stormed into her life and taken over. It had displaced her from her job and her condo, at least for now.

It had taken Derek.

Kendra moved on, amid running toddlers and strollers. And moms. She stopped, her breath sucked away. Would she never have that identity—*mom?*

She found a bench and sat, a new grief washing over her. This was bigger than Derek, the wedding, the condo, or a job. This was everything. Her life had been swallowed up. Hopes, dreams, everything she'd envisioned—gone. And what did she have to look forward to instead? Two and a half years of treatment. Oh, and if it was "successful," maybe three or four.

The sights and sounds all around were almost haunting now. Even the bees and the flitting birds. All flaunting their joie de vivre. "Vivre," for her, in any meaningful way, was over.

CHAPTER THIRTEEN

LANCE PULLED UP TO THE HOUSE AT FIVE THIRTY, SPENT BUT surprisingly refreshed. The last half of the trip he'd cranked the music, washing the sadness and even the tears in a sea of praise. That was probably the weirdest thing Jesus had done in his life— made a tough guy emotional. He felt things he didn't feel before, which meant he hurt in ways he hadn't hurt before. But praise music always brought him up. He had to laugh when, dancing with a single arm swaying as he drove, he got double takes from the occupants of other cars.

He parked and got out, ready to walk around back to his entrance, when he spied trash in the front yard. Beer cans? He collected what he could carry and entered through the front door to find Trey and tell him to pick up the rest.

A bigger mess greeted him inside. Maybe he shouldn't have told Trey he was leaving. But he probably would've partied either way.

Lance shut the door with his foot and headed toward the kitchen to the recycling can. Hearing footsteps, he looked up. "Trey, I'm glad you're—" He could barely see in the shadows, but it was a woman, and not Molly.

"Whoever you are, please turn around and go," she said. "There's no party tonight."

He walked closer. "Kendra?"

She came down a few stairs, studying him. "Do I know you?"

"It's Lance. Lance Alexander. I don't know if you remember me"—he wasn't sure he wanted her to—"but we were in the same class at Clayton for a little while."

Kendra hesitated. "I do remember you." She stayed the distance between them, arms folded around her. "You're here for one of my brother's get-togethers?"

"Oh. No." The cans clinked as he put them down. "These are empty. I picked them up in the yard. I just got home."

"Just got . . . home?"

Lance cleared his throat. "I'm guessing you don't know I moved in about a week ago, into the lower level."

Kendra descended a few more stairs, where he could see her better. She looked tired, as if she'd just awakened, her hair half ponytailed, half out, with stray pieces all around. But she was still as pretty as he remembered.

"I'm sorry. I'm confused." She took hold of the rail, as if to steady herself. "You moved in? How did that happen?"

"I needed a place to stay, and your dad was looking for a tenant . . ." He shrugged, feeling awkward. He'd always felt awkward around her.

She slumped suddenly, leaning on the rail.

"Kendra, are you all right?" He went to her and helped her sit on the stair.

"I just . . . have a headache . . . kind of dizzy." She heaved like she was about to vomit. "I'm sorry . . ." Tears appeared, seemingly from nowhere. "It's just been a lot. I'm so tired . . ."

"I'll be right back." Lance went to the refrigerator and got a bottle of water. "Here," he said. "Drink some of this."

Kendra shifted and lifted her head a little. "Thank you."

Lance watched her struggle with the cap. "I'll get that." He unscrewed it and gave it back. "When was the last time you ate?"

"I had a granola bar this morning and a hot dog at the zoo."

"Let me help you to the kitchen," he said.

"You don't have to do that. I'll just go back and lie down."

"Let's just see what's in there."

He lifted her by her hand and supported her as they walked down the stairs and into the kitchen, where he placed her at the table. "Can I warm you up some chicken noodle soup?"

"You don't have to," she said again, her voice barely above a murmur.

Lance couldn't *not* do it. He'd grown up making sure his mother ate. It was in his blood. "How about this," he said. "I'll warm it up, and if you don't like it or don't eat it, my feelings won't be hurt."

Hungry himself after the trip, he prepared two bowls and brought them to the table. "Try a little," he said. "I think it'll help."

Kendra sat up and spooned only a tad, blowing the steam. She tasted it, followed by another spoonful. "It's really good, thank you." She looked at him. "This is homemade."

He nodded.

"You made it?"

He nodded again.

They ate in silence a few minutes, then Lance asked, "So when did you get here?"

"Last night, at the height of the party."

"I bet that was fun."

"Exactly."

Seconds more passed. Then he said, "Look, Kendra, I feel bad being here. I don't know how long you'll be in town, but I won't be in your way. I pretty much stay in the lower level, unless I'm grabbing something to eat."

She stared into her bowl. "It doesn't matter. Don't worry about me. Please, just . . . live your life."

He quirked a brow, taking a breath to speak, then thinking better of it.

"What?" she said. "Go on and say it."

"It's just . . . I heard about the wedding cancellation," he said. "I wondered if you were okay, that's all."

The spoon on its way to her mouth began to quiver. She set it down, stared vaguely ahead, then looked directly at him. "I guess I have to get used to saying it, so I might as well start now. I'm not okay. I'm dying. Of cancer."

"What?" Lance stared at her, waiting for the punch line.

She went back to eating her soup.

"So your family knows?"

"No one knows yet," Kendra said, "except the head of my department at work. And my ex-fiancé. That's why he canceled the wedding."

Trey and Molly came through the garage door.

"Hey, cool," Trey said. "I was hoping dinner would be ready." He tossed his keys on the table and looked closer. "Oh, y'all are eating that? I don't like soup. That's why it was still in there."

"And hello to you, too, Trey." Kendra sat back, looking at him. "How are you? How was your day? Nice to see you."

"What's that about?"

"It's called trying to have a conversation to see how you're doing, since I haven't seen my brother in months, and the one I saw last night I didn't recognize."

"Oh, so you decide to come home when it suits you—because heaven forbid you should come home and help your mother when she's sick—and you expect everything to be like you remember."

"You're going to stand there and accuse me of not helping Mom?" Soup had refueled Kendra. "For your information, I offered to come home and stay for a while, but she said not to, that she had plenty of help."

"Which was mostly me, since Dad was caught up in damage control on campus."

"And you're throwing it up in my face?"

"I'm just saying you hardly came home at all. Always so busy. Kendra, the high-powered DC attorney." Trey got a bottled water. "You're only here now to lay low because you're embarrassed about the wedding. I heard you got dumped."

Kendra looked undone. "Who told you that?"

"Your maid of honor called to see how you were because you wouldn't answer your phone. She thought I knew." Trey paused. "And do you know *why* she thought I knew, Kendra? Because in normal families, they share things. In normal families, people don't keep secrets for years. But we all know this family is far from normal, don't we?"

Trey snatched up his keys, and he and Molly were gone again.

Kendra took the soup bowls to the sink and rinsed them, then got a trash bag and walked to the living room. Lance followed and picked up empty bottles and cans while she picked up cups and other trash. While he took his collection to the bigger recycling bin outside, Kendra got out the vacuum and plugged it in.

"I can get that," he said.

"I'm not helpless."

"I know."

She vacuumed the downstairs rooms as he cleaned the kitchen counters, washed a pile of dishes, and spot-mopped the floor. He joined her back in the living room as she walked around the room dusting and looking at photographs.

He sat on the piano bench. "So what kind of cancer?"

She didn't turn from the shelf. "It's called inflammatory breast cancer."

"What stage?"

"Four."

Lance felt a pang inside. "When does chemo start?"

"Thursday morning." She put a picture of her mom back on the shelf. "But I don't want to talk about it right now." She turned. "You know what? This is weird . . . Lance Alexander living in my house. I used to be afraid of you."

"Ah, much nicer topic," he said.

Kendra smiled for the first time, a little.

"Why were you afraid of me?"

"You're a nice-size guy," she said. "Probably what, six two?"

He shrugged. "Between six two and six three."

"And muscular," Kendra said. "And you walked around looking so mean and hard . . . and that *fight*. When I saw all that blood . . ."

"You saw it?"

"I was on my way to chem lab. I was there when you threw the punch that broke Mr. Magnetti's nose."

The punch that got him expelled. "I'm sorry you had to see that. The whole thing still grieves me."

She seemed a little surprised. "Where did you go after you left Clayton?"

"To my neighborhood school, for a little while. Ended up dropping out."

Kendra's brow furrowed. "Then what?"

"A lot of stuff that's not pretty."

She stared at him, and he stared downward.

"What are you doing now?" she asked.

"I'm a photographer. Also on staff part-time at Living Word."

"So that's the connection," Kendra said. "You knew my parents from there?"

"Mainly Trey, from youth group," Lance said. "But I got to know your parents somewhat too." He paused. "I was at your mom's funeral."

Kendra fell quiet. "So you know about my dad?"

"I knew enough to pray for your family."

Kendra grabbed another picture and resumed dusting. "And you just got an earful as to how dysfunctional we are."

"Whose family isn't?"

Kendra stared into the picture, one of herself as a toddler with her mom and dad. "You know what I want to do more than anything right now?"

"What's that?"

"Watch a silly, animated movie and forget everything else happening in life." She pointed at him. "The problem is, the big-screen television is in your part of the house. That's no fair."

"Funny you should say that," Lance said. "I sell movie tickets."

Chapter Fourteen

On Thursday morning Kendra tiptoed quietly through the kitchen, hoping to slip out unnoticed. She drank some water and packed another bottle, some baggies of snacks, a book and some magazines she'd bought—Oh! She scurried back upstairs and got her iPod from the nightstand, passing Trey's closed door. They'd barely spoken since Monday. She'd barely seen him, and when she did, Molly was joined to his hip. They needed to talk, though, just the two of them. Everything about their interactions this week bothered her.

She scurried back down and found Lance in the kitchen.

"You're about to go?"

She nodded.

"Can I help you with anything? What do you need?"

"I'm good," she said, picking up her satchel.

"What did you eat for breakfast?"

Kendra gave him a look. She'd learned in three short days that he was something of a health nut. "Granola bar." She lifted it from the satchel.

He didn't look impressed.

A light honk sounded outside.

"I've got to go," she said. *Don't follow, don't follow . . .* She walked to the door, and he followed and looked out the window.

"I thought you said you had a ride."

"I do have a ride."

"Kendra, you know what I meant. I could've taken you."

She opened the door. "I appreciate that," she said. "But I decided I'm actually worse off when I begin to need anybody for anything."

She made her way to the taxi and, after a short ride, arrived again at the cancer center. She'd been here every day this week for one thing or another, including blood work and a tour of the chemo room. But this morning there were more patients in the chairs, along the right side of the unit especially, presumably because it was near the window. She was clearly the new kid on the block, with all her hair. She'd grown it to well below her shoulders so she could wear a pretty updo for the wedding. Now she wondered how quickly it would all fall out.

"Kendra, let's get you settled and started on some paperwork," said the nurse, who'd introduced herself as Lori. "Is anyone with you today?"

"No," Kendra said, attempting a smile. "No one's with me."

"Well, you've got all of us," Lori said. "So if you need anything, don't hesitate to ask. That's what we're here for."

Kendra chose a spot and glanced around again. An older woman was there, accompanied by a younger woman, maybe her daughter. Kendra's heart was moved by a boy, maybe twelve, with a bald head, there with his dad. A woman about her own age held her husband's hand as she prepared to start her chemo. Kendra moved her gaze around the width of the room, finding only one other patient who was there alone—but several minutes later, another woman arrived to join her.

Kendra soon finished the paperwork and waited a good while with her magazines, a wait that convinced her how afraid she was. Of how it would feel, and how she would feel afterward, particularly how sick she'd get. The last thing she wanted was to be rendered incapacitated and needy.

"Miss Woods, how are you?" A new nurse appeared. "I get to spend the morning with you. Are you ready to get started with the first IV?"

Kendra remembered something close to this feeling only once, when she was a teen and her family visited Vancouver. She'd wanted to go whale watching, but seasickness forced her belowdecks to lie down, the nausea touching every inch of her being. She felt like that now as she lay in the taxi—as though if she moved one inch, she would vomit for days.

The taxi's sequence of turns let her know she was near home. She dug her money out, tip included, and shouldered her satchel so she'd be ready as soon as the driver stopped. She stepped out quickly, her aim to get to her bed. Or the bathroom. At this moment nothing on earth was more pressing.

Thankfully, the front door was unlocked, saving her a step. She took the stairs as fast as she could, which wasn't fast at all. But the fact that she could keep moving was a win. Down the hall and alll . . . mossst . . . there. She kicked her door closed behind her and collapsed, tucking herself into a ball on her bed. At some point she'd have strength to get up and take some meds for this splitting headache, but no way was it happening right now.

Why is the light so bright?

Kendra buried herself beneath her arms, blocking sunlight from her window. Things had to be better on the other side of sleep.

But her head hurt too much to doze off.

A knock on the door sounded. If she opened her mouth to answer, she'd vomit.

"Kendra?" It was Lance. "I heard you come in." He poked his head in. "Are you okay? What do you need?"

Water and headache medicine. Part of her wanted to say it, part of her didn't. She'd get it herself eventually.

"Kendra?"

She shook her head and turned farther from him, but the movement must've been too much. Everything inside of her was out in a matter of seconds. On the floor.

She'd never been more mortified.

And worse, she only had strength to lie back down, flat on her back this time, forehead beading with sweat.

She only realized Lance had left when he returned with who-knows-what kind of cleaning supplies. She couldn't look, and if she could, she'd be too embarrassed to do so.

He took two or three trips to the bathroom across the hall, then left. But minutes later he was back with a tray, setting it on her nightstand.

"I brought you some water," he said. "You probably don't feel like eating, but here's some apple slices just in case, and grapes. You need protein, so I put peanut butter on here, too, and some crackers. Oh, and there's ibuprofen." He placed a cool washcloth on her forehead. "And tonight I'm making grilled chicken, brown rice, and steamed broccoli. You might not want to eat, but if you do, it'll be good for you." He lifted a piece of paper from the tray. "Here's my number if you need anything. I'm right downstairs."

And he was gone.

Chapter Fifteen

Lance settled at his computer to upload photos from an early-morning shoot. He'd met a couple from church, with their newborn in tow, at Forest Park. They'd wanted to take as many shots as they could while the baby and the weather cooperated, since rain was forecast. He felt they'd gotten some good ones, but seeing them in thumbnails on the screen now got him excited.

He loved this, capturing precious memories, and capturing them in creative ways. That's what he'd become known for—innovative shots. He much preferred the creativity of camera angles and natural lighting to the creativity of Photoshop.

Once every photo was uploaded into Lightroom, he scanned them for the perfect shot. There could be dozens of pictures his clients loved, but he had to find the one or two that stood head and shoulders above the rest. And he always knew when he'd found it.

He smiled at the various shots, all of them adorable. But this one . . . He sat forward in his chair and magnified it. Father holding son tenderly in his arms, kissing his forehead, with a beautiful backdrop of trees and a slight burst of sunlight through the branches. Bingo. He five-starred it.

He went back to the beginning, whittling out the least favored ones, then paused when he heard footsteps coming downstairs. He waited for Trey to show with some sort of request. His dad kept him financed, but taking time to buy what he needed wasn't Trey's thing. Now that Lance was here, he'd taken to asking, "Hey, man, are you going by the store?"

But it wasn't Trey who appeared; it was Kendra, in yoga pants and a GW Law T-shirt, hair brushed into a neat ponytail, eyes telling the tale . . . She was drained.

She walked closer. "Lance, I had to come tell you . . . You can't do this."

"Do what?"

"Help me."

He turned toward her in his swivel chair. "Why not?"

"Because . . ." Kendra lifted her hands as if it were obvious. "It's ridiculous. You don't even know me, not really, and you're cleaning up my vomit and bringing food on a tray? No."

"Was it helpful?"

"That's not the point." Her eyes narrowed. "And how'd you know to bring headache medicine anyway?"

He shrugged. "I Googled to learn a little about chemo effects. It said headaches were common."

She stabbed the air. "Right there, that's what I'm saying. Why would you do that? Why do you even want to help me?"

Lance was incredulous. "I live here."

She spread her hands. "And?"

"You think I could live here, watch you go through this, and do nothing? What kind of human would I be?" He crossed a leg over the other. "You know what I think? I think you're stubborn. Why else would you refuse help when you know you need it?"

"You can call it what you want," Kendra said, "but I'll do what I need to do myself. And when I can no longer do it—what'll happen? I'll die?" She threw up her hands. "I'm dying anyway. I mean seriously, who cares if I choose fried chicken over grilled or ice cream over apple slices? What does it really matter if my health fails in 1.8 years instead of 2.5? I'm dying, Lance." A hand went to her face, covering the tears. "I'm dying."

Lance didn't know what to do, so he did the only thing he could do. Tentatively, he got up and brought her head to his chest. And she sobbed, the pain of it bringing him nearly to tears.

"I'm sorry," she said, chest heaving. "This is not . . . what I wanted to . . ."

"Stop." He spoke gently. "It's okay."

"It's not . . . okay . . . to be crying on you like this . . ."

"Yes, Kendra, actually it is."

She allowed herself a few seconds more, mostly because the pain seemed determined to express itself whether she liked it or not.

"I need to sit down," she said. She took the closest spot, his desk chair, wiping her tears into submission.

"What can I get you?" he said.

She gave him a look.

"I can't help it. Shoot me."

She glanced at the computer screen. "When did you take these?"

"Earlier this morning."

"May I look?"

"Sure."

She clicked thumbnail after thumbnail, gazing at the photos of mom, dad, and baby. "This is where I thought Derek and I would be in about a year, happy with a newborn." She kept going. "You're a good photographer," she said, her voice barely present. "I bought a nice camera once and never learned how to use it. I like your style."

He watched, pained by her pain. "Thank you."

She got lost in the images again, clicking through more than a dozen. "I was supposed to be taking pictures today too. Our photographer was planning to capture photos at the rehearsal and dinner."

Lance winced inwardly. He hadn't realized this was the big weekend.

Kendra stopped and swiveled in her chair. "Do you think God is punishing me?"

He stared at her. "Why would you say that?"

"I went to Living Word when I was younger, Sunday school and all that. But I haven't really been to church since I left for college." She paused. "And haven't exactly abided by the things I learned."

Lance got a folding chair from the corner—*Lord, You know I need wisdom for this one*—and sat near her.

"The short answer is no," he said. "God is not punishing you. He loves you."

"He loves me." She nodded. "And He shows His love by giving me cancer and taking my fiancé." She continued, "Because God can do anything, right? He could've made it so I *not* get cancer, or so that Derek would stay with me regardless."

Lance took his time to respond. "I wish the answers were that easy, but nothing is easy with fallen people in the mix, and fallen bodies that suffer horrible diseases like yours." He looked her in the eye. "But, Kendra, I do believe with all my heart that God is in control always and has a purpose in it all."

Her eyes cut away.

"Can I ask you a question?" he said. When she didn't refuse, he continued. "Why did you say it wouldn't matter if your health failed in 1.8 years instead of 2.5?"

"Because it wouldn't."

"I don't understand that."

"What's not to understand?" Kendra shrugged. "I have terminal cancer. The life I've known is gone, and the life I've dreamed of will never happen. If I'm only living from one treatment to the next and feeling like crap in between—who wants that?"

"Okay, I get it," he said. "I wouldn't want that either."

She looked at him.

"It's a choice, Kendra."

"What's a choice?"

"Whether you're going to live from one treatment to the next, or *live*."

Kendra frowned. "Now I'm the one who doesn't understand."

"All I'm saying is, maybe it's not the life you've known, and maybe you won't have the life you dreamed of. But it's life, and it can be a rich one if you let it."

CHAPTER SIXTEEN

KENDRA PLAYED WITH HER MORNING OATMEAL, HER MIND CYCLING through the day—the day she'd planned for months. Right now, ten in the morning Eastern time, she'd be finishing breakfast with her bridal party, a limo waiting to whisk them to a day spa for massages, manicures, and pedicures. Afterward they'd return to the hotel suite to dress, and a hairstylist and makeup artist would make them gorgeous.

She tried another spoonful, and the oatmeal mushroomed in her mouth, making her gag. She didn't know if it was a chemo effect or the nausea that came with any conscious thought of Derek. She swallowed anyway. Gaining strength was the most important thing, or something like that. Lance had given her a pep talk yesterday on food and nutrition during a forced trip to the grocery store. She'd promised to eat well during those times she could eat. And this morning she'd awakened feeling decent, unfortunately. She'd half hoped to feel cruddy as an excuse to sleep through the day.

One more spoonful.

The door to the lower level opened as she put it to her mouth.

"There you go!" Lance was grinning. "Go 'head and eat that oatmeal with your bad self."

Kendra scowled. "I hate this stuff."

"That's okay," Lance said. "You don't have to love it—"

"—for it to work for you." Kendra fake-smiled at him.

"Hey, I'm just glad you're listening."

She watched Lance pull out his camera equipment on the kitchen table. "You've got a shoot this morning?"

"Later today." He glanced at her. "How are you feeling?"

"Okay, actually. Why?"

"I thought it'd be fun if we had a photography tutorial."

"We who?"

"You and me."

"Why?"

Lance was attaching a different lens to his camera. "You said you wanted to know."

"I said I never learned how to use that one camera."

"Which means you wanted to know." He wiped the lens with a cloth. "Plus you clearly like taking pictures. The shelves in your room are full of them."

"I was definitely the one always taking pictures with my little point-and-shoot," she said, "going way back to elementary."

"The point-and-shoot is cool," he said. "Extremely basic, but cool." He smiled and shrugged. "If you don't want a tutorial, that's fine. Thought it'd be something nice to do today."

She eyed him. "You're not slick. You're trying to help again."

"Help with what?"

"To get my mind off the would-be wedding."

His mouth dropped. "Today was the day?"

A laugh bubbled inside her. "Okay, Mr. Alexander, I admit I've always wanted to go deeper with photography. I just never had time." She pushed the last of her oatmeal aside and stood, surveying the gadgets. "The question is, what kind of teacher are you?"

"You'll get to the point where the first thing you'll notice in any setting is the lighting," Lance was saying.

An hour into the tutorial, Kendra had found a notepad to jot things down, surprised at how much she was learning.

"Look at the light in here," Lance said. "Describe it."

Kendra lifted her eyes, looking around the living room. "Let's see . . . all the light is coming from the big picture window, diffused by the sheer white window covering."

He nodded. "The bright sun outdoors is filtered through those sheers, which makes for perfect pictures. No harsh shadows." He grabbed her hand. "Come stand over here by the piano." He began focusing the camera.

"You're not taking my picture, are you? I'm not camera ready."

He kept fiddling with his settings. "Do you want to focus on learning or on looking cute?"

She made a face at him and heard a click. "You didn't!"

He brought the camera to her and showed her. "Look at the way the light falls on that face you gave me. Perfect."

"So wait, though." Kendra looked closely at it. "It's not just the lighting. How'd you get it to look like that?"

"Remember the triangle I drew for you with exposure, aperture, and speed?"

Kendra looked back at her notes, nodding.

"You'll get to where you have a feel for what the aperture should be in certain lighting, or what the speed should be, to get the look you want."

He backed up, adjusted the settings, and took another, then showed her. "See how there're more shadows in this one? You'll learn as you play with the settings. The key is to stay away from automatic mode."

"But automatic mode is my friend." Kendra pouted. "I don't have to fuss with any settings in automatic."

"Nope, it'll do all your thinking for you." He smiled. "And you won't learn a thing."

Kendra felt herself losing energy and moved to the piano bench. "How did you learn all this, Lance?"

"Well, after I got out of prison—"

"Prison?"

"I told you it wasn't pretty." He sat across from her on the sofa. "After I got out I couldn't find a job, but I was going to this weekly men's discipleship gathering at Living Word." His thoughts seemed to go back there. "Turned out one of the men was manager of a camera shop. They needed somebody to do odd jobs, run the print-ing machines, things like that. I ended up working there five years. They let me learn as much as I could soak up."

"When did you know you had a passion for photography?"

"My first outdoor shoot. I know it sounds weird, but being in nature, capturing its beauty that way . . . It was like worship to me. God came alive."

Kendra looked at him. Such a walking paradox. "So, can I ask . . . ?"

He focused on the camera. "Why I went to prison?"

She nodded.

"Short answer . . . drugs."

"I know you like those short answers. How about the slightly longer answer?"

Lance took his time, absentmindedly moving the settings dial. "I didn't grow up like this, Kendra." His eyes took in the surround-ings. "I grew up in the city, poor, with a mother who was hooked on drugs, so I had to take care of her and myself. When I got bused to Clayton for high school, a whole new world opened up. It was my ticket out. Saw myself going to college. I was gonna get a basketball scholarship." He smiled faintly. "A few guys from my neighborhood went to Clayton, too, which means some of the neighborhood stuff came along as well. The day of that fight . . ."

Kendra waited, moved by this vulnerable side of Lance.

"It started because I found out Dewey, who was my boy, had sold my mother drugs. And he knew I was trying to help her get off them. So I approached him about it at school, and he said . . ." Lance's voice faltered. He stared downward, then put his camera aside and stood at the window. "He said my mom begged him and offered to sleep with him for payment. And he *slept* with her. He slept with my *mom*. I just . . . I snapped."

Kendra's heart reacted at the emotion in his voice.

"I never talk about this." Lance faced away from her still. "It's too hard . . . you know? I'd rather people think I was a thug who got in a gang fight than know the real reason." He paused several seconds. "I threw the first punch, the other guys jumped in, and Dewey kept at it, talking about my mom in front of everybody. With everything in me, I wanted to knock him out, but I didn't see Mr. Magnetti jump in. When he fell to the ground . . ."

Lance blew out a sigh. "So . . . I got expelled. I was distraught, all hope of doing anything in life was gone . . . After a few months at the neighborhood school, I just said forget it. I became the person I said I'd never be—a drug dealer. Didn't take long for trouble to escalate. Got shot—"

"*Shot?*"

Lance nodded. "Drug deal went bad. The bullet was actually

meant for a friend of mine, but I jumped in the way because he'd just had a little baby and—"

Kendra couldn't keep up. "What? You took a bullet for a friend? You were willing to die?"

"I wouldn't go that far," Lance said. "My mind was so warped. I probably thought I was invincible. It wasn't long before I had run-ins with the law." He turned. "God was gracious. I could've gotten locked up for a long time, but I only did two and a half years, and that was mostly local jail time. That's where I met Pastor Lyles."

Kendra had so many questions. "What about your mom, Lance? How is she?"

He returned to the sofa with a sigh. "Mom's in federal prison in Tallahassee."

"Are you serious? Oh, Lance . . ."

"I just saw her last weekend," he said. "It's hard. But the crazy thing is she's seeing God's purpose in it. She's off the drugs. And she's living for the Lord. It's amazing really."

Kendra cocked her head, staring at him.

"What?" Lance said.

"I'm seeing why you're so good at cooking and cleaning . . . and *helping*. You grew up doing it for your mom."

"That's true."

Kendra watched his gaze fall again, the way it did whenever he spoke of his mother or his past. "Thank you," she said.

"For?"

"For sharing all of that with me. I know it wasn't easy."

His gaze met hers. "Actually, for some reason, it was easier than I would've thought."

Chapter Seventeen

Trey could feel the battle raging for his soul. The constant barrage of thoughts. Relentless accusations. Unending pressure. It was getting harder to escape, harder to fight.

"What are you doing?" Molly blew a bubble, glancing around. "I thought we were headed to my apartment."

He'd pulled into a small park near home, cut the engine, and dropped his head on the steering wheel. "I need to think through some things."

Fight through was more accurate, except the fight had dwindled. He was tired.

"Let's walk," he said.

Trey slipped his key from the ignition. They walked past a toddler playground along a short trail to an area of benches. He chose one closest to the waterfall. Over the years, it had become his thinking spot.

Molly pulled her feet up in front of her on the bench and hugged her knees, staring with him at the waterfall. She knew that in times like this, he didn't feel much like talking.

Trey kept his gaze fixed, focused on the crossroads before him.

He knew clearly the path of each—and which he should take. But he couldn't do it in his own strength. Wasn't God supposed to help him? Why wouldn't He help him?

Stop waiting on God, Trey. Don't you think you've waited long enough?

He definitely had, and he'd told God that.

I'm tired of waiting, Lord. I'm tired of trying to do everything right, and seeing nothing from You in return.

He'd cried out to God as he walked across campus this past spring, having just dropped all his classes.

How many prayers do I have to pray? How much pain do I have to endure? Huh? How is this fair? If You won't help me, forget it. That's where I'm at, Lord. I can't take this anymore.

He'd made up his mind. He would take the path of least resistance. Smoking and drinking made it easier. Numb the pain. Silence the voices. Stoke his inner rebel until he no longer cared what God thought.

Why should I care anyway? You don't care about me.

Exactly. Trey's eyes welled. Part of him had hoped that dropping his classes would get God's attention. Maybe He'd finally show up, do something. So he still waited, in a sense. He'd put boundaries on his current path, to go only so far. So he could easily turn when God tapped him on the shoulder.

But God was still nowhere to be found.

This is the path that makes sense. Stop constraining yourself and live.

Trey turned to Molly. "I'm moving to Atlanta in two weeks."

"You're what?" Her feet dropped to the ground. "How did that come about?"

"I told you about my high school classmates who are at Emory," he said. "I might transfer. Meanwhile, they said I could come stay with them and see how I like it down there."

Molly shook her head. "You said if you ever look to move away, I should make sure you talk to somebody."

"I am talking to somebody."

"You know what you said, Trey. One of your Christian friends."

Trey waved her away. "That was a year ago. I don't even hang with them anymore."

"Your sister's here now," Molly said. "Why don't you talk to her?"

"Kendra's the last person I would talk to."

"Why?"

"She's never had a real problem," Trey said. "Everything has always come easy for her: A's in her sleep, cheerleading captain, gazillion friends—and boyfriends. She wanted to work for one of the biggest law firms in the world. Bam, she got it." He looked away. "She'd never understand my struggles."

"You can't say she's never had a real problem. You were supposed to be in DC right now, dancing at her wedding."

"Perfect example," Trey said. "Kendra's fiancé breaks up with her, and it's like the world ended—because she's never been through anything. She comes home, all depressed, even has Lance tending to her." He shook his head. "In a few months, she'll be seeing some-body else, saying Derek was never worth anything anyway."

"Okay then." Molly folded her arms. "Talk to Lance."

"Why are you on me like this? It's not a big deal if I move to Atlanta."

"We made a pact, Trey Woods." Molly's green eyes bored into him. "We said we'd be there for each other. You've been there for me when I've gotten weak and wanted to start sleeping around again. This is my chance to be here for you. You're my *best friend*."

Emotion choked her last words.

"You just had to go there." Trey moved closer to her on the bench, put his arm around her. "You really care about me, huh?"

"I love you, you jerk." She blew a big bubble. "Promise me you'll talk to Lance. If you end up moving anyway, fine." She elbowed him. "Promise me."

"What am I promising to tell him exactly?"

"Everything."

"What?" Trey rose up, frowning at her. "No way. Come on, Moll."

"What's the point otherwise?" Molly said. "You have to. That was the deal."

"Are you sure I wasn't high when I made that deal?" Trey blew out a sigh. "All right, whatever." He sighed again. "I promise."

CHAPTER EIGHTEEN

LANCE HAD PRAYED HE COULD SOMEHOW GET TREY AND KENDRA to church today. But Trey didn't come home last night, and Kendra woke feeling nauseated and went back to bed. As he drove, he thought more about it, how hard it would be. Trey hadn't been in over a year, and Kendra in over a decade, plus her sickness made it that much harder. But by the time he got to Living Word, his mind had begun working in reverse.

Why not bring church to them?

He walked into the youth building with that one thought, unsure what to do with it. What did it mean? Was it something he'd come up with? Or was it God? When Pastor Lyles had raised the idea of starting a church plant in Clayton, he hadn't felt led to take it on. He couldn't see himself at the helm of a new church, trying to fill pews in a building. And he cringed at the thought of his name circulating around Clayton as pastor of a new church. Given his former reputation, the only thing *that* would start was a boycott.

But what if they did something in the home?

Maybe Molly would even come.

He entered the auditorium where the students had service. The worship band was rehearsing, and he stood there a moment, processing. What if he didn't think of it as church at all? He was known for meeting friends and strangers alike at the Bread Company, hearing their hearts, talking about life, studying, and in the midst of it all, sharing the gospel. Why couldn't the same thing happen at home?

But how would Mr. Woods feel about that? And what would it look like? Who would even come?

He thought about the circles Trey and Molly ran in, the friends who were a little wild, or troubled, bucking the conventional side of life. They wouldn't flock to pews in a building anyway. But maybe they'd come for a meal and fellowship.

Lance felt a churning inside. He needed to flesh this out with Pastor Lyles, and—"Cyd!"

Lance didn't know why he called out to her, but as soon as he saw her walking through the auditorium, the idea popped into his mind. *Cyd London lives in Clayton.* Her parents had been members of Living Word for three decades. Now in her forties, Cyd had become known herself for a love of discipleship. Nothing was framed in his mind, and yet he already knew he'd be more excited if she were part of it.

Cyd came near, smiling. "Hey, Lance, we were talking about you last night."

"Uh-oh."

She laughed. "You know it was all good. We had dinner at my parents', and Pastor Lyles was raving about you as usual. Then he said something curious—'Pray about whether the Lord would open a door for Lance to minister in Clayton.' I wondered what that was about, since you don't live in Clayton."

"Actually, I'm staying at Marlon Woodses' home," he said.

Her eyes lit up. "Really? That's awesome. Should be really good for Trey."

"You're familiar with the situation?"

Cyd nodded. "From the Living Word side of things and also, I'm a professor at Wash U. So I know Marlon, and I know Trey's professors. They're concerned."

"I forgot you teach up there," he said.

Lance's wheels turned all the more.

"Listen," he said, "are you and Cedric busy after church? I'd love to talk to you about something."

❦

Once Lance and Cyd got talking, the ideas flowed. They'd been sitting at the kitchen table in the Woodses' home for over an hour. Cyd's husband, Cedric, had bailed before it started.

"I know how my wife is when she gets going with something like this," he had said. "I'm taking the little man home for a nap."

The plus was that they lived only three blocks away. Cyd had kissed her toddler son good-bye, and she and Lance got to it.

"So what are our next steps?" she said.

"Prayer, talk to Pastor Lyles to see if he green-lights it, talk to Mr. Woods to get his okay, and more prayer." Lance looked at what he'd written down. "I want to be sure we're hearing from God about what to do, how to do it, and even when to start."

Cyd nodded. "I'm really excited about this, Lance. I've always had a heart for younger people, which I guess is no surprise. I think this could have a huge impact."

"It's exciting to me, too," Lance said, "mainly because I feel like it's God, the way it came out of the blue and—"

They both looked up as Kendra walked into the kitchen, slowly, hand to her stomach, hair unbrushed.

She straightened when she saw Cyd. "Professor Sanders, I didn't know you were here."

Cyd rose from her chair. "I didn't know you were here either." She hugged her. "Two things, though—it's London now. I got married three years ago. And please call me Cyd. I'm not *that* much older than you." She smiled.

"Sorry, old habits die hard," Kendra said. "I remember meeting you just after you became a professor at Wash U. My dad introduced us. I must've been about fifteen, and I totally looked up to you." She smiled. "And congrats on getting married."

"Thanks," Cyd said, "and didn't I hear you have a wedding upcoming?"

Lance winced a little.

"It was supposed to be this weekend actually, but . . . it got canceled."

Cyd looked at her. "How are you, Kendra?"

Kendra tightened her robe. "I'm fine."

"No, sweetie, really . . ." Cyd took her hand. "How are you?"

Kendra glanced at Lance. "He told you?"

"Lance hasn't mentioned you at all," Cyd said.

"I guess you could say I've been better, Profess—Cyd." Kendra stared downward several seconds, then looked at Cyd. "I've been diagnosed with breast cancer, Stage IV."

Cyd's hand went to her mouth. "Oh my Lord." She brought Kendra close, embracing her. "I'm so sorry. I had no idea."

"I know," Kendra said. "Can we sit down? I'm feeling tired."

"Absolutely." Cyd pulled out a chair for her. "I'm glad you decided to come home. I imagine your dad's on his way back to the States."

"No." Kendra paused. "I haven't told him. I've hardly told anyone."

Cyd leaned in. "Why, sweetheart? If you don't mind my asking."

"I don't know," Kendra said. "When the wedding was canceled, I kind of shut down. Didn't want to talk to anyone. Didn't want to have to explain. Didn't want pity . . ."

"I can understand that," Cyd said. "So you've started treatment? The cancer center at Barnes-Jewish?"

"Yes," Kendra said. "Right now, it's chemo every three weeks. I had my first session last Thursday." She attempted to smile. "Some days are better than others."

"Probably some *moments* are better than others," Cyd said. Her eyes filled with compassion. "I don't know you that well, Kendra, but I hope I can say this."

Kendra waited.

"I've never walked this road personally, but I've walked it with others, and I know it's a hard one." She grabbed Kendra's hand across the table. "You'll have people who will sincerely want to help you through this. Please . . . let them on your team."

Kendra glanced at Lance. "I'm learning that."

"One more thing."

"What's that?"

Cyd squeezed her hand. "I'm on the team, whether you like it or not."

CHAPTER NINETEEN

July

KENDRA STOOD IN HER SIDE YARD, HOLDING THE CAMERA STEADY, trying to remember f-stops from apertures so she could set her dials just right before the cardinal flew away. Lance had given her an assignment—and his camera—to work on depth of field. She had to photograph an object in perfect focus, with the background blurred. When a cardinal flew into the yard, it was the perfect challenge.

"Don't move," she murmured.

The bird had perched itself on a tree limb, checking out its surroundings.

Kendra turned the lens this way and that, but everything in the picture stayed in focus. Didn't he say something about backing up if that happened? She tried it, eyes trained on the bird. "Don't move . . . don't move . . ."

Click. Click. Click.

She checked the shots right away on the back of the camera. "Yes!" The bright red cardinal was in the foreground, focused beautifully, and the trees in the background were blurred.

She couldn't wait to show Lance and to see it more fully on his big computer screen.

The sound of a car got her attention. It was Trey, by himself for once, at midmorning. As he parked, she headed inside the garage entrance. She'd been waiting for this opportunity.

They hadn't had a real conversation since the blow-up last week. Well, no. She didn't know when they'd last had a real conversation, if ever. He was eight years old when she left for college, and their interactions since then were best characterized as brief. Shallow. How's it going? How's school? You playing a sport?

She was hard-pressed to think of a single conversation they'd had about their mom's illness. Maybe she'd asked him how Mom was doing. But an actual conversation about the illness or the dynamics of the situation or, "Trey, how are you weathering all of this?" No. Until he brought it up last week, she hadn't given it a thought.

They hadn't talked about their dad either, not in any depth.

Kendra set the camera on the kitchen counter and got a bottled water from the refrigerator. She needed to be doing something, holding something. How weird to be nervous with her own brother. But Trey had been so hostile, so *different*, she didn't know what to expect.

The front door opened and closed. Kendra expected the footsteps to go up, since he came through the front, but they moved toward the kitchen. She moved into his line of vision as he was about to open the door to the lower level.

"Trey, hey, you got a minute?"

His hand stayed on the knob. "I came to talk to Lance real quick, then I'm heading back out."

Something about him right now, in his camouflage shorts and T-shirt and Miami Heat hat, touched her heart. This was her little brother.

"Just a few minutes, Trey? We haven't had any time to talk."

"Talk?" He said it as if he'd never heard the word. "When do we ever talk?"

"That's part of what I wanted to talk about," Kendra said. "I wanted to apologize."

He looked skeptical, but his hand came off the knob. "All right, I can take a sec." He walked into the kitchen and opened the refrigerator door.

Kendra sat at the table and swigged her water, feeling drained from the heat.

Trey cut a slice of chocolate silk pie—a treat Lance had brought home after she'd said chocolate was the one thing she didn't seem to gag over. Trey poured a glass of milk and brought his slice to the table.

He forked up a bite. "So what's up?"

"I've been thinking about what you said, and you're right." Kendra's hands rested on the bottle in front of her. "I was in a busy season at work, and to be honest, it seemed like Mom's illness took a nosedive at the worst possible time." The irony. Was illness ever timely? "I offered to come home and help care for her, but frankly I was relieved when she said there was no need. I figured you were here. Dad was here. I could do what I needed to do at work."

He stared at her while he took his next bite.

"But I should've asked you how it was going. I should've scheduled more visits, just to be here. For support. Because we're family. When your nose is to the grind, it seems like it's the most important thing." She sighed. "I'm sorry, Trey. I'm sorry I wasn't here for Mom, for you, for the family."

He ate the last piece and tipped the glass to his mouth, taking a long drink. "That's what you wanted to say?"

Kendra looked at him, ready to take it all back. But she had to keep going. "Not all of it, no." She gathered her words. "I just feel like I haven't been the sister I should've been. I haven't taken the time to call and talk to you. I mean, *really* talk. I don't know you like I'd like to, and that saddens me. Trey, I'm sorry for the kind of sister I've been. I hope you can forgive me."

"Where is all this coming from?" He finished the glass and wiped a milk stain from his lip. "I mean, for real, you act like you're on your death bed or something."

Kendra stared at him. "And you wouldn't care if I was." She pushed back and got up from the table, apparently too fast, because at once she felt woozy and dropped back down, half missing the chair.

Trey came around to her side. "Ken, are you okay?"

"Keep your fake concern, Trey. Just . . . go talk to Lance."

She put the bottle to her lips, but when the water hit her mouth . . . *Don't. Don't.* She dry heaved twice, then ran into the first-floor bathroom and vomited. Thankfully, it wasn't a lot.

Kendra flushed the toilet, washed her hands, and splashed water on her face.

Trey appeared in the bathroom mirror. "What's going on? Are you pregnant?"

She closed her eyes, feeling her stomach working its way up again. "No, I'm not pregnant."

"Are you sick? The flu or something?"

"Yeah. Or something."

He leaned against the doorjamb. "Well, what is it?"

She turned to face him. "I was planning to tell you, but when you didn't care one iota about anything I was saying, I said forget it."

He spread his hands in defense. "I only asked where it was coming from."

"You know what? I'm done." Nausea was rising, and she needed to make it upstairs so she could get sick in private. "Do what you came to do. I need to lie down."

Kendra brushed past him and started up the stairs, making it a third of the way—and lost total strength. Her legs gave way and she missed a step, stumbling partway down.

She heard Trey shouting for Lance as he came to her, lifting her up. Seconds later, Lance had bounded up and met them on the stairs as Trey helped her to her room.

"What happened?" Lance said.

Trey lowered her to the bed. "That's what I'm wondering," he said. "Kendra got faint and vomited downstairs, then got weak on the stairs. Somebody tell me what's going on."

Lance looked to Kendra.

"You can tell him," she said, closing her eyes.

"Trey, Kendra was diagnosed with something called inflammatory breast cancer," Lance said. "It's already spread to her neck. The doctors say it's terminal, and she's started chemo."

Seconds passed, and Trey hadn't responded, so Kendra opened her eyes. He'd fallen to a crouch against the wall, his head buried in his arms.

"Why is life such a freaking joke?" His shoulders shook with tears. "It's a *joke*. You know?" He looked up at them, wiping his nose. "First God takes my mom. Then my dad is gone, and was never who we thought he was anyway. And now my sister is *dying*?"

He stood suddenly. "This is how much of a joke life is." He laughed his pain. "My sister is dying, and I'm the one who wants to die." He looked up. "You got it backwards, God! I'm the one who's supposed to have the terminal diagnosis. Just take it from her and give it to me!"

"Come here." Kendra reached her hand to him.

Trey came and hugged her so tight she could barely breathe. "I'm sorry," he said. "I'm so sorry, Ken. I'm so sorry. If I could switch places with you, I would."

"Shh." She rubbed his back. "Stop saying that, Trey."

His tears wet her face, and he held her in his arms until she drifted to sleep.

CHAPTER TWENTY

"TREY."

Trey looked toward the doorway, where Lance stood. He'd left Trey and Kendra alone, but now he was back and Trey knew why. It was time to talk.

He eased his arms from Kendra, laying her head on the bed, and met Lance in the hall. "We can talk in here," he said, "in my room."

Trey motioned for Lance to take the desk chair, and he sat on the bed, pushing aside dirty and clean clothes. His eyes floated past the shelves—Awana trophies, Bibles in different translations, journals. They reminded him why he spent little time here.

"I was glad to get your text this morning." Lance leaned forward, forearms on his thighs. "You said you wanted to talk."

"I'll be straight with you," Trey said. "I only came because I made a deal with Molly. But after that"—he pointed to Kendra's room, shaking his head—"I don't even see the point. Everything is just crazy."

Lance's gaze penetrated. "You said some things in Kendra's room that were troubling."

"What, that I want to die? That's nothing new."

"How long have you felt that way?"

"Eight, nine years."

Lance seemed taken aback by that. "Why, Trey?"

"Why not? Life is too hard. I figured it was easier to just go be with Jesus."

"But you looked so . . . I don't know, *happy* when you were younger."

"I was naive," Trey said. "I believed what I was taught, that God loved me, that He cared. I had hope. I really thought God answered prayer."

"You don't think so anymore?"

"Not mine," Trey said. "And what more could I do?" He gestured at the shelves. "I was going hard after God—reading my Bible, trying to fill myself with it, to push out everything else. Man, I memorized whole *books* of the Bible." He threw up his hands. "It's like I've been at war, by myself. I'm not doing it anymore."

Lance was quiet a moment. "What made you want to talk? Why today?"

"Friends in Atlanta called," Trey said. "They've been trying to get me to come down, and the timing seems perfect. I'm moving next week." He paused. "But I told Molly a year ago that if I ever planned to move, to make sure I talk to someone first." He shrugged. "I was trying to put accountability in place, back when I cared about it."

"I'm confused," Lance said. "Why would you need accountability regarding a move?"

Trey sifted his words . . . It was about to get real. "Being here, being with Molly . . . It's been a form of protection for me." He shifted his gaze downward. "But for a long time I've felt this temptation to leave. Like, if I got away from everything I've known, it would be easier to embrace who I really am."

"What are you saying, Trey? Who are you?"

Trey's heart began pounding in his chest. He was suddenly afraid. Of rejection. Condemnation. Of every painful thing he'd ever read or heard about people like himself. He got up, paced a little. Why did he have to be different? Why did he have to be the outcast? All he ever wanted was to feel loved by God. Accepted. To not feel like a reject. He'd pleaded with God for years, his journal filled with one request—*Lord, change me.*

Why wouldn't He?

He looked up. *Why wouldn't You answer that one prayer, God?*

Stop pleading with Him. You already know He doesn't care.

Trey closed his eyes, hands fisted in frustration. *But I want Him to care. It hurts that He doesn't care.*

"Trey." Lance turned him around. "Whatever it is, I love you, man. I love you."

Trey broke down in his arms. Years of pain, years of guilt, years of silence . . . all of it washed up on Lance's shoulder.

"I don't know what to do," Trey said. "I don't know what to do."

Lance stepped back, held his shoulders. "Trey, what is it?"

"I'm . . ." He swiped the tears. "I'm gay."

Lance kept looking at him. "Okay."

"What do you mean *okay*?" Trey looked dumbfounded. "You're a pastor. Now's when you say I'm going to hell."

"I said okay because I'm still listening."

"Listening to hear what?" Trey said.

"I don't even know what you mean by gay."

Now Trey was exasperated. "You don't know what it means?"

"I don't know what *you* mean. Are you referring to an inclination? An attraction? Or have you entered into it and acted on it?"

"I haven't acted on anything," Trey said. "That's what I've been fighting. That's what my prayers have been about."

"Okay," Lance said again, sitting back down. "Do you mind telling me what you've been praying?"

Trey took a breath, sitting as well, thinking back to those first prayers. "From the time I hit puberty"—he couldn't believe he was sharing this—"it was clear I had no interest in girls. Other guys, that's all they talked about. I wanted to be like them. Thought I would grow into it, but it didn't happen." He sighed. "Meanwhile, I start seeing what the Bible says about it, and I'm saying, 'Lord, I don't want to be this way, but I know I can't change myself. I see all these miracles you've done from Genesis to Revelation. This is nothing for You. Please, change me. Make me heterosexual." He looked at Lance. "That's been my ceaseless prayer."

"So in your mind, if God doesn't give you a desire for women, He hasn't answered your prayer. And if He doesn't answer that prayer, your only other option is to embrace the gay lifestyle."

Trey gave him a look that said it was evident. "Right."

"And temptation gets crazy overwhelming because you're trying to suppress this urge that's in you, and you get these thoughts that say, 'It's not worth the fight. Just do it.'"

Trey's eyes got a little wider. "How do you know?"

"Because I'm single, Trey. Temptation comes hard at me, too, toward women. I've prayed for God to take away the desire for sex outside of marriage. It gets overwhelming at times. I've had women at church invite me over, and it's clear what they have in mind—and I want to go. I think to myself sometimes that if I never get married, this will be a lifelong struggle."

Trey wasn't sure where Lance was going with this, but his heart and mind clamored to understand. "What are you saying to me, Lance?"

Lance took his time, looking at him. "I'm saying, you've prayed to be heterosexual, as if that's the gold standard. The opposite of homosexuality isn't heterosexuality—a whole heckuva lot of people are sinning with the opposite sex." His voice had equal parts warmth and strength. "God didn't call you to be heterosexual, Trey. He called you to be holy, like Him."

Trey let Lance's words settle, words that looped over and over in his head. Heterosexuality *had* been the gold standard as far as he'd been concerned. Those who were attracted to the opposite sex were the blessed ones, the normal ones. In his mind, they lived several rungs above, in space he longed to occupy.

But why did he think that? Suddenly he realized—that wasn't in the Bible.

"I have the same battle as you," Lance said. "The battle for holiness. We're pursuing the same standard. We're in this together."

"But what if God never changes me? What kind of life would I live?"

"I wish I could tell you all the plans God has for you," Lance said. "But I know He'll show you. And what kind of life? Any life lived in Christ is an abundant life."

Trey stared into the distance, his thoughts like scattered puzzle pieces trying to find shape and structure. He felt a pressing need to pray, but what would his prayers look like now? *Could* he pray with any feeling of closeness to God? It had been so long.

"Something else . . . ," Lance said.

Trey looked at him.

"When something is in our lives that brings affliction or suffering or any struggle we can't control, we're more aware of our need for God. We're more aware that this is not our home, that we have a greater hope." Lance paused. "It might seem that God doesn't care because He won't remove the struggle. But when you start looking

107

to Him in the midst of it, you get to see His love and care in deeper ways than most."

"I could see that, actually," Trey said. When he did feel good about praying again, he thought, he would pray that for Kendra.

A smile broke onto Lance's face. "I just thought about something you said. So God used Molly as protection for you, huh?"

"I hadn't thought about it being something God did." Trey smiled with him at the thought. "Molly and I met freshman year and became best buds. I helped her through some things and was kind of trying to lead her to the faith. But my own issues popped up when Mom got sick and the stuff with my dad came out." He sighed. "We ended up both going down the partying road."

Lance nodded. "I know a little something about U-turns on wrong roads."

CHAPTER TWENTY-ONE

KENDRA ALIGHTED FROM THE CAR AT THE WORLD'S FAIR Pavilion, smiling at a gorgeous sunrise. She glanced around, scoping the possibilities for scenery and lighting, then bent back down through the window. "I think this'll work, Lance. Come on."

"Oh, you think so?" He looked amused. "It's your shoot. Let's do it."

Kendra marched up the tiny incline with her equipment. She'd treated herself to a new camera yesterday, so she wouldn't have to pester Lance for his. Every day she'd taken a few shots to learn something new. It only took minutes, which she could find even when she felt mostly crummy.

She'd planned to do the same today to play with her new toy. But when she woke up feeling good, she took it a step further, asking Lance if he'd join her on a little trip to Forest Park. She wanted to learn more about shooting people, and he would be her subject.

"I can't believe you got me out here this early." Lance trudged behind her.

"But it's so beautiful this time of morning, and we beat the heat." She glanced back. "And didn't you say something about seizing the moments when I feel good?"

"Try seizing them midmorning," he said, "or when I haven't been up late editing photos."

Kendra paused, assessing the location. "Oh yes, Miss Adrienne's photo shoot."

"Her pictures turned out really nice."

"You know she likes you."

"Adrienne?" He shook his head. "I don't think so."

"Lance, get a clue." Kendra looked through the lens, framing the shot. "You get home from the photo shoot, and minutes later she's ringing the doorbell with Maggiano's?" She looked over at him. "She likes you."

"She felt bad because the shoot ran late."

"Then she could've dropped it off. She brought carryout for two and wanted to eat with you."

"Well, I hope she wasn't disappointed when I had you come down to make it three," Lance said. "It's my policy not to be alone with a woman in the house like that."

She eyed him. "How does that work, given that we're in the house alone most of the time?"

"That's an unusual circumstance, the way it happened," he said. "And with your situation being what it is, and me wanting to help, it's just a different type of thing."

"Although I'm now thankful for your help"—she smiled—"you need to live your life. Why don't you ask her on a date?"

"Where is this coming from?" Lance said. "You're planning my love life now?"

"I saw the way she looked at you, plus she's pretty, seems nice, church girl. Why not?"

"Your light is moving." Lance cast a quick glance at the sun. "Are you paying attention?"

"Fine, I'll leave it alone for now." Kendra wagged her eyebrows. "Okay, what if you stand by this column right here, inside the portico?" She walked to it and looked up, checking the direction of light. "And I'll stand over here, with the sun behind me. I want to get a few shots, close up and at a distance. How does that sound?"

"Try it and see what happens."

"What about poses?"

He smiled. "What you got?"

"You're not planning to make this easy, are you?" She bit her lip, trying a couple. "Maybe lean against the column, with one foot kind of like this."

Lance got in position while she backed up, checking her settings. It would take awhile to get beyond the basics and develop style, but she'd perused enough photography blogs now to know what she was aiming for.

She brought him a little closer with the zoom lens and adjusted the settings. "Ready?"

"Whenever you are."

"On three," she said. "One, two—three!"

She checked the back of the camera immediately.

"Well?" Lance said. "How is it? Am I in focus?"

"You're in focus. Framing looks good—got the rule of thirds going. The background is even blurred a little, but not as much as I'd like."

She kept studying it, drawn by something else. Something about his pose, the angle of his head, maybe the lighting . . . and the way it shone on his honey-brown skin. She blew out a breath. The man was *fine*.

Kendra shook the thought away. "Okay," she said, "I'm going to take a few in rapid succession."

Lance carried Kendra's camera bag across the grassy field, back to the car. They'd been all around the grounds of the pavilion and adjacent areas of the park, as Kendra saw one location after another that would make a good backdrop. But it became one too many when fatigue overtook her. Always, she was reminded of her limitations.

Lance slowed a little, looking at her. "I talked to your father last night."

Kendra kept walking.

"I needed to ask him something. But it was weird because he's your dad and doesn't know you're sick, doesn't even know you're home."

She saw his gaze trained on her. "Am I supposed to comment? You know what happened."

"But from what I understand," Lance said, "that's all in the past. He's apologized and tried to reconcile."

"Which might've worked had it been an affair only." Kendra stopped. "He had a child and kept it secret. And for it all to come out in my mom's last months . . ." She continued on. "This from a so-called godly man committed to his family."

"I know it was devastating." Lance pulled her to a stop. "But Kendra, it's not just a cliché—nobody's perfect. We're all vulnerable to sin. We do things we regret. Did you ever hear his side of things?"

"No," Kendra said. "What I heard were my mother's tears, and the pain of dealing with an illness and betrayal simultaneously. Plus having to deal with his lover."

"What?" Lance said. "I didn't know that."

"That's how my mom found out," Kendra said. "This woman showed up at the house one day and decided to tell all."

"Why?"

"Who knows? But I'm telling you, I think the stress of it all worsened Mom's condition."

They walked on to the car and got in.

Kendra fastened her seat belt. "So what did you have to ask Dad anyway?"

Lance started the car and backed out. "It's what Cyd and I were meeting about last Sunday. We're starting a weekly Bible study, thinking of it as food, fellowship, and faith. And I wanted to make sure your dad was okay with having it at the house."

"What made you start it?"

He wound his way through the park. "Well, Pastor Lyles has been talking to me about a church-plant idea for Clayton, which I'm not feeling. In the midst of praying about it though, this came to me."

"Why weren't you feeling the church plant?"

He shrugged. "A lot of reasons. But for one, how would it look for me to pastor a church in Clayton, given my past?" He glanced at her. "And to be honest, I always felt like an outsider here. I couldn't get my mind around the idea."

Her eyes rested on him, and he glanced at her again. "What?"

"I think you would be an awesome pastor."

His brows knit. "Why do you say that?"

She shrugged. "A lot of reasons."

"You're funny. Give me one."

"The way you care about people."

Lance seemed to think on that. "I've never asked you . . . Why did you stop going to church?"

"Probably because it was easy," Kendra said. "Being away at college, then law school, I never took time to find one. Then I started working all the time."

"Did you miss it?"

"I'm sure this is the wrong answer, but not really. I'd been going to youth group, and the lessons were boring to me." She nudged him. "See, you should've been the youth pastor back then. I'm sure I would've had a whole different experience."

Lance pulled up to the house. "I was waiting for you to say you hated church or had a problem with God. But okay, one, you were busy"—he ticked it off on his fingers—"and two, youth group was wack."

Kendra laughed. "It's not that simple." She stared vaguely. "I did some soul-searching after Trey confronted me. It kind of rocked me, which was why I had to go back and apologize." She looked at Lance. "I realized how selfish I've been, how life's been all about me. Even as I think more about your question, the main reason I probably didn't go to church was because I wanted to live my own way. I could always return to God later." Her own self-reflection grabbed her. "I guess my later is suddenly my now."

Chapter Twenty-Two

Lance walked into the local Starbucks, looking for Adrienne. She'd called after he returned from Forest Park to see if her photos were done, since he'd promised a rush job before the holiday. He spotted the waving hand, but he couldn't have missed her regardless. She had a presence that drew the eye. He moved toward her table.

"Hey there." He handed her the disc. "Your photos are on here. I focused my edits on the ones you wanted, but I also did light edits on the rest, just in case. I really think they turned out great."

He meant it. Adrienne worked for a boutique public relations firm that wanted to feature her in a marketing package about the city, and he could see why. Her mocha skin; thick, coily, natural hair; and athletic shape made her an engaging subject.

Adrienne looked up at him, smiling. "I was so excited about your work that I told one of my friends to call you. She needs engagement photos."

"I appreciate the referral," Lance said. "Thank you."

"Seriously, you're amazing," Adrienne said. "I forwarded the preview shots you sent last night to the team. They said it captured the exact mood they wanted." She was hunched forward, animated.

"Thanks again for your willingness to drive all around the city for the shoot."

"No problem at all," he said. "I'm glad everybody liked them."

"I hope you're not in a rush," she said. "You should get some coffee or a cold drink and join me."

"Thanks," Lance said. "I was actually planning to head right back though."

"Oh, come on, the holiday's almost here." Her smile was infectious. "Take a few minutes to relax."

Lance relented, smiling. "I guess a few minutes won't hurt."

He ordered a tall latte and returned, sitting across from her.

"So we talked about my work at the PR firm yesterday," Adrienne said. "What about you? Is photography your main job?"

"It is," he said, "and I'm on staff part-time at the church."

"I love Living Word," she said. "I moved to St. Louis last year, and my roomie told me about it. How long have you been there?"

"About ten years."

"And you're from St. Louis?"

"Born and raised."

She leaned in with a pause. "I was trying to figure you out yesterday."

"How so?"

"You're like, all business," she said. "You answer a question and won't volunteer much more. But I know there's a lot more, because a person with that much creative passion is usually a deep thinker and a deep feeler."

"Wow. All that, huh?"

"See." She pointed at him. "See how little you said. You're a mystery to me now." She laughed. "'How to unlock Lance Alexander.'"

He chuckled. "I'm really not that deep. Trust me."

She sipped her berry drink. "I hope you don't mind my asking, but the woman you share a house with . . . Are you two in a relationship?"

"Kendra? It's complicated, but no."

"Not the 'complicated' thing."

"Not *that* kind of complicated."

They laughed together.

"I'm sorry," she said. "That question was probably way out of line, but I was wondering."

"Nah, it's cool."

"It's just refreshing to meet someone who's God-fearing, passionate about what he does, handsome but not full of himself . . . I'm sure that tells you the type of men I've come across."

"I'm sure I've been those men."

A brow went up. "Aaand he stops right there."

Lance sipped, offering a faint smile. It wasn't the first time a woman had charged him with being cryptic. It was his default setting.

"What are you doing for the Fourth?" she asked.

"I'm not sure yet." It depended on how Kendra was feeling, which was unpredictable, and what Trey was doing, also unpredictable.

"Well, my roomie has this big cookout every Fourth of July," Adrienne said. "You may have heard about it. A lot of people from Living Word come."

Lance nodded. "Darrin told me about it."

"I hope you can come by for a little while at least. I really do think you're an interesting person to get to know."

"Thanks for the invite," Lance said. "I'll definitely keep it in mind." He stood, extending his hand. "Pleasure doing business with you, Adrienne."

She shook it, holding his gaze. "Likewise, Mr. Alexander."

Questions flooded his mind the minute he left. What *was* wrong with him? Yes, he was guarded. Yes, he aimed for propriety. But he usually had to fight himself to do it, especially with a beautiful woman—a beautiful woman who, he now knew, was clearly interested. Temptation would do its dance, and the old Lance would show up, with old memories of what it was like when he had no boundaries. Why did he feel none of that, not even an urge to flirt?

And why, as he hopped into his car for the short ride home, were his thoughts so quickly shifting to Kendra?

Chapter Twenty-Three

Kendra wrestled through the night with shooting pains in her breast—her dimpled, hard, reddish-pink breast. Sleep was hard every night, impossible on the swollen side. But the pain last night drove her mad. Mad at her breast. Mad at cancer. Mad at Derek. Mad that she wasn't in Paris. And mad that she had to be mad in bed alone.

Sometime around seven she woke again, mad still when she saw her camera across the room and had no energy to use it. And mad when she realized it was the Fourth of July, and she couldn't enjoy it. Eight days out from her first chemo treatment, and it had to be really working—because parts of her felt on fire.

Tears slid down the sides of her face. *I can't do this. God, I can't do this. I've never been in this much pain. I've never felt so alone. I'm supposed to be married right now, and it still hurts that I'm not. Everything is wrong.*

Kendra reached for a tissue, and her hand hit against something. Shifting a little, she opened her eyes and squinted at it. A Bible? She brought it near and, in the soft light of morning, saw a sticky note on the cover.

Got you this gift. Three a.m. seemed the perfect time to give it.

She'd texted Lance in the night, when the pain had become unbearable, asking him to pray. But she didn't think he'd get her message until morning. She stared at his handwriting. He'd not only gotten it but sneaked this in without her knowing. It was pretty, too, with a soft cover of olive-green leather.

Moving from her back to her good side, she propped herself on an elbow and flipped through. When had she last opened a Bible? She'd Googled popular wedding verses and read them online as she planned the ceremony. But Bible in hand . . . It had been so long.

A pain shot through her breast, and she curled up, wincing. She kept turning pages until she got to the Psalms. Then she skimmed and stopped at the beginning of Psalm 5.

Give ear to my words, O LORD,
Consider my groaning.
Heed the sound of my cry for help, my King and my God,
For to You I pray.
In the morning, O LORD, You will hear my voice;
In the morning I will order my prayer to You and eagerly watch.

She could cry to God for help. That's what struck her. Would He hear her, though?

Kendra kept reading, of souls dismayed, of the need for refuge, of grief and distress. She saw herself, her pain, in the pages.

Psalm 18 stopped her next.

"I love You, O LORD, my strength."
The LORD is my rock and my fortress and my deliverer,
My God, my rock, in whom I take refuge;
My shield and the horn of my salvation, my stronghold.

I call upon the LORD, who is worthy to be praised,
And I am saved from my enemies.

The words reached to her core. She closed her eyes, suddenly aware of how far she was from God. She didn't know Him like this—as her strength and rock and fortress and deliverer. What did it even mean? What did that look like?

She read those three verses again, and words jumped out at her: . . . *the horn of my salvation . . . my stronghold . . . and I am saved . . .*

She read the entire psalm, seeing those words repeated, and words like *blameless* and *pure* and this—*For I have kept the ways of the LORD . . .*

Kendra's heart was pounding. She hadn't kept God's ways. She hadn't even thought much about Him. Was she saved? She'd grown up in church, but suddenly she wasn't sure what that meant.

So many questions pressed through her mind. On impulse, she grabbed her phone and texted Lance.

R U UP?

Seconds later she read his reply.

YEP.

Her thumb typed again.

U MIND COMING UP?

A moment later Kendra heard his footsteps. He knocked on the door.

"Come in," she said, pulling the covers up gently. It hurt when they rubbed against her breast.

Lance entered her room in long gym shorts and a faded Cardinals World Series Champs tee. "I thought you might need help this morning," he said. "Sounded like the pain got really bad."

"It did," she said, "but that's not why I texted." She raked a hand through her hair. "I'm sorry, I must look a complete mess."

"Kendra . . ."

"I know." She sighed. It was hard being needy and vulnerable . . . and messy.

He came closer, waiting.

"First, thank you." She lifted the Bible from under the covers. "I didn't realize how much I needed this until I started reading." She glanced down at it. "It really hit me."

"Yeah," he said. "It does that. And you're welcome."

"You can sit down." She moved over in the queen-size bed, giving him space. "So . . . I feel really stupid right now."

"Why?"

"I feel like there's so much I should know, but don't . . . about the Bible, I mean." She stared at the page, still opened to Psalm 18. "And I feel like you could probably answer every question I have."

"I highly doubt that," he said.

Kendra curled inward again, groaning at the pain, then took a breath when it passed.

"I'm almost sure you can," she said. "It's about salvation."

Kendra sat in the living area of the lower level, laughing at photos with Lance. He'd pushed the chair over so she could sit beside him at the computer in comfort as she learned to edit.

"I see you," Kendra said, "thinking you got swag. Look at that pose."

They'd taken that one by the water yesterday.

"That's how you told me to pose."

"Yeah, but you threw a little extra in there."

"And what do you mean, 'thinking you got swag'? Don't get confused. I *gots* swag."

Kendra laughed. "Oh, it's a fact, is it?" She cut him a side-glance. "Okay. I didn't know."

Lance was laughing with her. "I got that getting-old-thirtysomething swag."

She shook her head at him as she played with the tools in Lightroom, the software Lance was training her on. By early afternoon she'd grown sick of her room and needed a change of scenery. This way, she could rest and indulge in photography at the same time.

Lance's phone rang, and he answered it.

"Darrin, what's up? . . . Y'all are over there now? . . . Yeah, she invited me . . ."

Kendra lessened the exposure on a photo of Lance, then cropped it a little.

"I don't know, man. I'll have to see . . . I know. I know . . . All right, later."

Kendra kept her gaze on the screen, testing levels of sharpness. "Go."

"Huh?" Lance said.

"Go to the cookout."

"How do you know there's a cookout?"

"It doesn't take rocket science. It's the Fourth." She looked at him. "Lance, seriously, you shouldn't be stuck in the house on a holiday. You need to be outside in the sunshine with friends, having a good time."

"I'm not stuck," he said. "And I thought I was already having a good time."

Kendra twirled a finger. "Woo, what a party. Doing what you can do in your sleep, with a woman who's too sick to stand." She looked back at the screen. "You don't have to feel sorry for me. I keep telling you—live your life."

She moved the mouse, maneuvering another tool, and he covered her hand with his.

"Did it occur to you that I might be living my life right here . . . right now?"

An unexpected flurry of . . . something . . . shot through her. They held each other's gaze, then she looked back at the screen, silently exhaling.

"Hey, where is everybody?"

Footsteps bounded downstairs.

"Trey and Molly, with grocery bags?" Lance asked.

"When I called and y'all weren't doing anything," Trey said, "I figured, hey, we can have a cookout."

Kendra was smiling. "Aw, I haven't had a cookout at home in forever."

"You said *we*," Lance said. "Does that mean you'll be grilling?"

"By *we*, I meant *you*." Trey laughed. "But I can get the grill ready."

"That's good stuff, man," Lance said. "Let's get it going."

The guys went upstairs, but Molly stayed behind. She looked over Kendra's shoulder. "What are you working on?"

"I've been bitten by the photography bug," Kendra said. "Learning how to edit photos."

"You took these?"

"Well. Yeah. It was my first location shoot, so I've got a lot more to learn."

"They're cool, though." Molly took Lance's seat. "Mind if I sit down?"

"Not at all."

Molly dug into a grocery bag she had with her. "I made you something," she said, pulling out a pan covered with foil. "Brownies."

Kendra turned to her. "Really? Why?"

"Trey said chocolate helps you, so . . ." She shrugged.

Kendra looked at the girl she'd never really focused on, beyond her clothes and hair, which today was purple and spiky. "Thank you. I really appreciate that." She eyed the pan. "Can I taste one?"

"Absolutely!" Molly rolled back the foil.

Kendra picked one and tasted it. "Oh my gosh, so good." She took another bite, a big one.

Molly did a head bow. "Why, thank you."

Kendra paused before her next bite. "Molly, for what it's worth at this point, I apologize for saying Trey couldn't bring you to the wedding."

Molly shrugged. "No big deal. I get it. I don't fit in most places." She paused. "And sometimes I try too hard to fit in, and I get myself in trouble."

Kendra looked long at her. "I want to get to know you, Molly. Just as you are."

CHAPTER TWENTY-FOUR

IT FELT LIKE THEY WERE HAVING A PARTY. LANCE MOVED ABOUT the house, cleaning, excited about their first gathering, and doubly excited that Trey was there, helping him.

"How many chairs should I bring up?" Trey shouted from below.

"I don't know," Lance called back from the kitchen. Initially at least, they wanted to keep the group small, comprising mostly people who weren't churched. Trey had invited some of his circle, including Molly, of course. "Maybe bring four or five," he shouted back.

The doorbell rang, and Lance shouted in that direction. "Come in!"

Cyd walked in with a huge baking dish, Cedric behind her with Chase in his arms, fighting to get down.

"The Londons, how are ya?" Lance went to greet them. "Aw, why are you keeping him captive, Cedric? Let the little man down."

Cedric laughed. "Remember you said that when you're begging for me to pick him up."

Cedric set him down, and the two-year-old ran behind his mother to the kitchen. "I want a cookie, Mommy. I want a cookie."

"Not yet, baby." Cyd put the pan on the stove. "Cookies are still in the car, and you're eating dinner with vegetables before you get one."

He stomped a foot. "I don't want veggietables."

She eyed her son, then looked at Lance. "My life. Never a dull moment."

"I'll get the rest of the food," Cedric said.

Lance looked at Cyd. "How much did you bring?"

"Baked chicken is in the pan," she said. "Cedric's bringing in a sweet potato dish, green beans, homemade rolls . . ."

"Are you serious? Homemade rolls?"

". . . macaroni and cheese, German chocolate cake, and cookies."

He blank-stared her. "What if we don't get many people beyond us? And whoever we do get, I hope they don't think we're rolling like this every week. Next week might be beans and franks."

Trey came up carrying folding chairs, two in each arm. "Hey, Professor London."

"Hey, Trey, it's good to see you." She hugged him, then looked him in the eye. "How are you?"

"I'm . . . good." He nodded slightly, almost to himself, maybe convincing himself.

Lance nodded with him. In the past week they'd had a couple more extended conversations, one spontaneously as they grilled on the Fourth, another when Trey had come downstairs looking for him. They'd prayed together, looked at Scriptures together, and wrestled together with questions. Trey hadn't stopped hanging out—but he'd been home more. And when he said he'd be here tonight, Lance was overjoyed.

"I'm glad to hear that," Cyd said. "I've been praying for you."

"I appreciate that," Trey said, and seemed to mean it.

"Where's Kendra?" Cyd asked.

"Lying down," Lance said. "She's had some rough days. But she wants to come down when we get started."

Cedric brought in the rest of the goods, and the group worked to get set up. Less than an hour later they were ready and wondering who would show.

Lance knocked on Kendra's door and poked his head in. "It's seven," he said. "Do you want to come down now or wait awhile?"

"I'll come now," she said.

She raised herself slowly and moved her legs over the side of the bed, slipping on flip-flops. Lance helped her up.

"I'm okay," she said.

Twice, nausea and fatigue had made her legs go wobbly on the stairs, so Lance wasn't taking any chances. Arm around her waist, he supported her down as the doorbell rang.

"I'll help her to the kitchen," Trey said.

"Good grief." Kendra cut her eyes at both of them. "Y'all stop treating me like an invalid."

Lance opened the door and smiled. "Moll, what's up?"

"Dude." Molly raised her hands, launching them into a complicated series of slaps, fist pounds, and snaps, all of which ended in a hug.

A young woman with black-rimmed glasses and sandy hair stood behind her. "Did you just call him dude? Is that the pastor?"

Lance chuckled. He'd gotten to know Molly better on the Fourth, when everybody's silly side seemed to come out, and they'd ended up creating their own secret shake.

Molly turned to her friend. "Jess, meet Lance, pastor and, yes, cool dude."

Lance shook Jess's hand. "Nice to meet you, Jess. Welcome." Then he half bowed to Molly. "Cool dude is a high honor."

She bowed in return. "An honor most due."

Trey saw them from the kitchen. "You two bring out the weirdness in one another."

Lance went to close the door but saw someone straggling near the foot of the walkway. He recognized him and walked out to greet him. "Hey, Timmy, you coming in?"

Hands in his pockets, Timmy stared into the street. "Still deciding."

"You can always eat while you decide."

Timmy turned slightly. "I probably won't stay."

Lance shrugged. "That's cool."

They all congregated in the kitchen, four women at the table, four guys standing nearby. The younger ones, all Wash U students, had piled high their plates.

"I haven't had a meal like this in a long time." Trey paused with a roll in his hand. "This is on point, Professor London."

Molly nodded. "I don't think I've *ever* had a meal like this. It's delicious, Professor London."

"Thanks, you guys." She smiled. "And I think I'll be Cyd off campus."

"Cyd!" Chase pointed at her. "Mommy!"

Cyd laughed. "If everyone wants to call me Mommy, that works too."

"Is it appropriate to get seconds?" Timmy asked.

Molly twisted in her chair, looking at him. "What, you got the munchies, Timmy?"

Timmy cocked his head at her. "I can't believe you said that in front of Profess—Cyd."

"It's a Bible study," Molly said. "They expect us to have issues."

"And on that note," Lance said with a chuckle, "while we're eating, we're going to start with an icebreaker, where we introduce ourselves—but this is an unconventional icebreaker."

Heads turned, giving attention.

"I'll start. My name is Lance Alexander. I'm a photographer and a youth pastor. I'm also an ex–drug dealer and ex-convict."

Timmy turned from the mac and cheese with a look suggesting he hadn't heard right.

Lance gestured to Cedric.

"My name is Cedric London. I'm a husband and father, and VP at an executive search firm. I'm also an ex-womanizer."

"And I'm Cyd London. Wife, mother, and professor." She paused. "I almost said ex-worrier and ex-doubter, but I still struggle with those things at times. So I'll say ex–people pleaser."

Molly seemed to soak in that one.

"We don't always introduce ourselves this way"—Lance smiled—"but we're calling this Wednesday night gathering The Shadow for a reason. We tend to live in shadows—shadows of doubt, fear, shame, secrecy."

Lance was surprised to see Jess nodding.

He continued. "Sometimes we *want* to operate in the shadows. I wanted to keep my activity hidden from the police." He draped an arm around Cedric. "My man here had to make sure one woman didn't know about the other."

Cedric nodded knowingly.

"We shared that about ourselves so you'd know that we know what it's like to live in shadows, dark shadows," Lance said. "And tonight we want to begin talking about what it's like to dwell in a different shadow. Instead of fear and shame, it's a place of refuge and blessing."

Lance looked around the room. "But first, let's continue introductions." He saw a couple of nervous expressions. "And no, you don't have to introduce yourself the way we did!"

"Right." Molly wagged her eyebrows. "We'll share all our issues later."

Chapter Twenty-Five

Kendra took a midmorning shower, still focused on the shadow. It was on her mind as she awoke through the night and when she finally got up. Lance had explained what it meant, but she had to see for herself. With a Bible app she'd downloaded to her phone, she searched the word and looked up the relevant verses as she lay in bed. Once again, the Psalms were nurturing her soul.

She closed her eyes, remembering the words as water cascaded down her back.

Hide me in the shadow of Your wings.
My soul takes refuge in You; and in the shadow of Your wings I will
take refuge . . .
For You have been my help, and in the shadow of your wings I sing
for joy.

That place. She could picture it, nestled under the wings of the Almighty. Sheltered from the raging storm. She was protected there. She could sing there. Or so it said.

How do I sing there, Lord? How do I sing for joy in the midst of pain?

She'd been talking to God a lot lately, questions more than anything, and she had a lot of time to do it. It helped to talk through the pain.

She finished showering and stepped out, wrapping herself in her towel. She removed her shower cap and fluffed out her hair—and a clump came out in her hand. A big clump. Her heart constricted.

Dr. Contee had said that two weeks after the start of chemo, her hair would begin to fall out. A couple of days ago, her scalp had felt a little tingly, but her hair was fine. Now here it was in her hand, like clockwork.

Turning to the mirror, she saw the spot missing the hair. She laid the clump on the sink and carefully touched a different side of her head. Tears welled when another clump filled her hand.

Kendra knew this would be a hard day. Her hair had always been the first thing people noticed about her. She'd worn it various lengths over the years, but mostly long. Although for the past weeks she'd only had energy to let it dry naturally and ponytail it, she liked to wet-set it and sit under the dryer for full, bouncy curls. What would she do now? She could watch it fall out, or cut it all off.

Kendra thought about it as she dressed, wondering whether she had the nerve to do it herself. A barber could do it, but she didn't want the questions.

She sighed to herself. The questions would come whether she wanted them or not, once her hair was gone. Would she wear a wig? Scarves or hats?

She wasn't ready to think about all that. It was enough that cancer marched over her breast, growing it, deforming it. Would any aspect of her being go untouched? Would she become a shell of herself? Her arms began to shake as new realities bombarded her. New pain. New emotions. New fears. New awareness of something else about her life that would never be the same. She closed her eyes and held herself.

In the shadow of Your wings I will take refuge.
In the shadow of Your wings I will take refuge.

Her heart repeated it until tears wet her cheeks—and a knock on the door startled her.

She wiped her eyes. "Come in."

Lance showed himself. "Spinach omelet?"

"I guess," Kendra said, only because she probably wouldn't taste it. "But first, can you . . ." She swallowed. "Can you help me cut my hair?" She'd seen him shaping up his own.

Lance came closer, looking at her.

"It's coming out, and I . . ."

The words caught in her throat. This was harder than she thought. Who would she be without her hair?

"You sure?" Lance said. "You're ready?"

That was all the trigger her emotions needed. "No . . ."

He hugged her. "It'll be okay. I'll be right back."

Lance returned with scissors and clippers, and even a broom and dustpan. "Let's go into the bathroom," he said.

Kendra's arms wouldn't stop twitching as she followed him. He put a towel around her shoulders.

"How much are we cutting?" he asked.

She stared in the mirror, her hair hanging below her shoulders, and took a breath. "Cut it to less than an inch."

When he reached for the scissors, she took a quarter turn away from the mirror and closed her eyes. The scissors closed on a chunk of hair in back, and her eyes closed even tighter. A second later, she could feel it, a weight of hair gone.

Lance moved to another area in the back, and another, then the sides, snipping, snipping. When he moved in front of her and lifted her hair, tears began to fall. *Snip. Snip.* She heard buzzing next as he took his time, shaping it down to a teeny 'fro.

The buzzing ended finally, and Kendra's heart beat fast. She turned to the mirror, wanting to see one of the cute fly cuts she'd seen on other women. One of her law school classmates had cut her hair off and gone natural, and though Kendra hadn't had the nerve to do it, it looked fabulous on her friend. Maybe that . . . *please*, at least that.

But when she opened her eyes, it wasn't cute or fly. It was a close cut induced by cancer, a cut that said her hair would keep falling out, and she'd soon be bald.

She stared at herself, unable to move.

Lance turned her around. "You look beautiful."

She only shook her head. If she spoke, she'd surely cry. And she was sick of crying.

"You said I looked intimidating in high school." Lance spoke softly.

Kendra looked curiously at him. Where was this coming from?

"You were intimidating to me too," he said. "You were the girl who had everything—beautiful, smart, popular, family had money, and actually lived in Clayton. I was the poor boy who got bused in."

He held her with his gaze.

"All these years later," he said, "part of me still saw you as that. Untouchable. Unreachable. With your hair gone . . . I don't know . . . It's like, I see you. And you're beautiful. Not the beauty I saw before. Deeply . . . beautiful."

Slowly they moved closer, and the same arms embraced her, the ones that had been helping her, comforting her. But now she was feeling them, melting into them.

"I'm sorry," he said, backing up. "I don't want to . . . I shouldn't have . . . I should just . . . sweep up the hair."

He went for the broom, and Kendra hastened out of the bathroom to her room. And cried.

Chapter Twenty-Six

Trey stood outside the reddish-brown brick duplex apartment, wondering if it could really be true. Did he have a little sister who'd been living here all this time, right around the corner?

He'd never bothered to investigate. Thoughts of his dad's other woman only made him angry. He knew she was a professor at Wash U who worked with his father—which made the weeks on campus following the revelation difficult. But he hadn't cared to ask questions beyond that. His mother had been his concern, and once she passed he didn't want to deal with any of it. It'd been a relief when his dad decided to take a sabbatical and spend time at the University of Ghana, far from the scandal.

But he and Lance had talked about it earlier this week, and he realized he had no answers to the questions Lance asked about his sister. Trey hadn't given her much thought. She'd been a package deal with her mother, a symbol of his dad's betrayal. But the more he thought about it, the more he realized he needed answers . . . for himself.

And they were easy to find. He knew the woman's name, and though her information was unpublished in official directories, nothing was sacred online. It wasn't surprising that he found her within a few clicks. The surprise was where.

Trey had been so shocked that he'd jotted down the address, closed the laptop, and walked directly here, in seven minutes. But he wasn't sure of his next move. Go ahead and knock? Write a letter? Maybe it was an old address, and they'd moved.

He went with his first instinct, walked inside, and found the door. When he heard nothing on the other side, he suspected no one was home. But moments after he knocked, the apartment door opened.

The woman was shorter than his mother, maybe five four. And younger. And white. If he was honest, he admitted to himself that it had added to the hurt—that his dad cheated with a white woman.

"Hello," he said. "My name is Trey. Actually, Marlon Woods III."

"I know who you are, Trey." She tucked a strand of her chin-length bob behind her ear. "I'm Ellen Patterson. What can I do for you?"

"Well." Awkward was an understatement. Trey was suddenly glad he'd shaved and gotten a haircut over the weekend. "I guess it's simple. I'd like to meet my sister, if that's all right."

"She's at a day camp," Ellen said. "But does your dad know you're here?"

"No, he doesn't," Trey said. "Does it matter?"

"I was hoping he'd sent you, if you want to know the truth." Ellen's arms were folded, her mouth tight. "Brooklyn hasn't heard from him in months."

"Brooklyn? That's her name?"

Ellen nodded.

"How old is she?"

"Just turned eight." She eyed him. "Tell you what, if you want to come in, I can show you a picture of her."

"I'd like that."

Trey stayed for an hour, looking at picture albums of Brooklyn Renee Patterson. It was weird, the way she came to life in his heart. Her laughing smile and big brown eyes seemed to grab him from the page.

He looked at Ellen. "It's crazy that Brooklyn lives around the corner, and we've never met. Do you think you could bring her over one day, to spend time with Kendra and me?"

"Kendra's here?" Ellen said. "I thought she lived in DC."

"She's in town, yes, for a little while."

Ellen thought a moment. "I don't have a problem with that," she said. "Maybe it's time."

Chapter Twenty-Seven

Lance tried his best to stay engaged in conversation. The Bible study had ended, and everyone was still there—those from last week plus a friend of Timmy's and another friend of Molly's. He loved that they wanted to hang out, and really loved that they had tons of questions, which had veered off onto wild tangents. Any other time he'd be all over the current debate about the best rappers of all time. But he couldn't get his mind off Kendra.

She'd gotten nauseated a little while ago, as she reclined with them in the living room. And Lance had gotten up to help her to the bathroom. But she looked to Trey instead, which was cool . . . except it had happened a lot lately. And not just Trey, but Molly or Cyd or anyone on the planet, it seemed, but Lance.

Ever since their bathroom encounter almost a week ago, Kendra had been acting different. Lance didn't know what had come over him, telling her she was beautiful, holding her the way he had. It was out of line. Kendra had been especially vulnerable after he'd cut her hair, and she was probably upset with him for taking advantage. He hated that he'd lost the little trust he'd gained with her.

Lance looked up as she and Trey returned.

"I'm about to help Kendra up to her room," Trey said, eyes on Molly.

"Oh yes . . . wait!" Molly hopped up and scurried across the entryway to the dining room, emerging seconds later with a gift box.

Cyd and the other women had gotten up and joined her. They presented it to Kendra together. "Surprise!"

"For me?" Kendra said. "What for?"

"For Chemo Day tomorrow," Molly said. "Come on. I'll help you open it."

She set the box on the coffee table, and together they tore off the glittery paper. Kendra fished through tissue paper and pulled out a package of Saran-wrapped fudge cookies. She held it up, smiling. "Who made these?"

Cyd raised her hand. "Guilty."

"Oh my goodness, thank you."

Lance could tell Kendra was laboring, trying to show excitement, but she could barely get through this. He wanted to interject, get her upstairs, let her open gifts while lying down. But he checked himself. Who was he to be so protective of her?

"Aww," Kendra said, "I love these plush pink socks."

"Yeah, you said it got cold in there last time," Molly said.

Kendra swished more tissue paper. "Wow, and fun magazines and more snacks—"

"I had to throw some healthy stuff in there to offset the cookies," Cyd said.

"Ooh, and a movie."

"Yep," Molly said. "When you said animated movies were a good escape afterward, I had to get you one of my faves, *The Incredibles*. I can't wait to watch it with you."

"Oh good, that'll be fun," Kendra said.

Lance glanced downward. Movie nights had been their thing.

"Hey," Trey said, "we should Netflix some stuff on the laptop while we're there. That'd be a good way to pass the time."

"Dope idea," Molly said. "I didn't know you were going."

"I asked Kendra about it today," Trey said.

Kendra glanced briefly at Lance. Two days ago, he'd checked with her to confirm that he was still going with her to chemo, something they'd talked about shortly after her first treatment. She'd said it would be good to go alone, maybe work on her photo blog, something new she'd taken up.

"I think I'd better head upstairs," she said.

A flurry of good-byes and hugs followed, as everyone else got up to go. But when the door closed, Molly lagged behind.

"Can I ask y'all something?" she said.

Kendra hadn't yet gone up, so she, Lance, and Trey waited.

"I know this is really an imposition, which is funny coming from me since I've been an imposition around here for weeks—sorry." Her eyes turned sheepish. "Buuut, I was wondering if I could crash here for a little while to join that 'regular rhythm of life' quest thing."

Trey had coined the term, saying he'd be home more to reclaim that rhythm.

"I feel like I can't do that at my apartment right now," she continued. "It's more normal over here."

"You must mean, now that Lance and Kendra are here," Trey said.

"That goes without saying."

"Molly, of course you can stay," Kendra said. "Take the guest bedroom upstairs, right next to mine."

"Awesome," Molly said. "I'll pack some things and be back tomorrow after chemo." She rubbed her hands together. "I'm excited."

Kendra smiled. "Me too. I get to watch you mix new hair colors."

Molly hesitated, glancing at Kendra's head. "I'm sorry. I can tone down—"

"Don't you dare," Kendra said. "I'm living vicariously through you."

Molly opened the door. "I'm glad I'll be around to help you, at least for a little while."

Molly left. Trey helped Kendra to her room. And Lance went to clean the kitchen, talking back to himself.

It's a blessing that Kendra has so much help now . . . a real blessing.

CHAPTER TWENTY-EIGHT

KENDRA LAY STRETCHED ACROSS THE SECTIONAL SOFA IN THE lower level, laughing at *Despicable Me*. She and Molly had gone Netflix crazy today, watching one movie after another, though Kendra had fallen asleep during parts of them.

She thought they'd get kicked out by now. Lance had a photo shoot late morning, and he liked to edit his pictures right away. She'd warned Molly they'd have to take a break once he got back. But it was early evening, and she hadn't yet seen him. In fact, she hadn't seen him much yesterday either. As much as she'd coaxed him to get out and live his life, she didn't think it would feel so weird when he actually did.

"That's so sad," she said, back into the movie. "All those little girls want is to be adopted."

Molly lay on the other end of the sectional. "I remember I wanted that too."

"Wanted what?"

"To be adopted."

Kendra paused the movie. "Were you in foster care or something?"

"No, nothing like that," Molly said. "But we didn't have much, and I used to dream that a rich family adopted me."

"Where did you grow up?" Kendra asked.

"Near the Ozarks," Molly said.

Kendra had read about the high poverty in that part of Missouri, but she'd never met anyone from there. "So what did you dream of having?"

"A car that didn't break down all the time, for one," Molly said. "New clothes, that kind of thing."

"Did you live with both your parents? What about siblings?"

"Yeah, Dad did odd jobs to make ends meet. Mom ran a home day care. I'm the oldest, with a younger brother and sister."

Kendra was silent, taking in what she'd said. "So, I'm curious how you got to Wash U. I mean, clearly you're smart, but there are a whole lot of smart people who want to go there. And it's stupid expensive."

"Life was hard," Molly said, "but school was easy. I had a teacher who really got behind me, wanted me to succeed. She said I tested at 'genius level,' whatever that means. She and the principal helped me get an academic scholarship." She paused. "But if I had it to do over, I wouldn't come."

"Why not?"

"Too much pressure to have things," Molly said. "I took out loans the first two years to buy clothes and a car, lied about my background. I wanted so badly to belong. Even dyed my hair blond—which I don't even like—to fit in." She saw Kendra's eyes graze her current shade. "I know. You're thinking, okay, you like electric blue over blond?"

"Nope," Kendra said. "Just listening."

"The thing is," Molly said, "when my little charade blew up, it was my way of acting out, saying I'm just going to be me."

"Well, what happened?"

"Everything unraveled when my parents came up to visit. I told them not to, but they just had to surprise me." She shook her head. "One of the girls in my dorm—I couldn't stand her—talked to them like she was my best friend. Then she told everybody I was a fraud."

"Oh, Molly . . ."

"Trey knew my story from the beginning though," Molly said. "If it weren't for him . . ." She lapsed into thought. "He's really been there for me."

"You've been there for him too," Kendra said.

During chemo on Thursday, she and Trey had done none of the things they'd planned. Instead they simply talked, and Kendra had been grateful to her brother for opening up and entrusting her with the things he'd been going through. She'd never felt closer to him.

Kendra continued. "When Trey didn't trust anyone else, he trusted you. You're a true friend."

"I told him we need shirts that say 'Dynamic Duo' or something." Molly got a text and looked at it. "Speaking of Dynamo Man, he's back from the grocery store and wants me to help cook." She looked at Kendra. "Be afraid. Be very afraid."

Kendra laughed. "I'm more afraid of Trey's cooking than yours."

"Will you be all right down here?" Molly said. "I can help you up."

"Thanks, I'm okay," Kendra said. "I'll upload some photos I took this morning and take a look at them."

Since apparently I have time to use the computer . . . since Lance is who knows where . . .

"I'll help you over there then," Molly said.

Molly helped Kendra stand, knowing she'd been woozy and fatigued, and Kendra grabbed her camera from the coffee table.

"Thanks, girl," Kendra said, sitting in Lance's chair.

Kendra shook the mouse to wake the computer, then took the

media card out of her camera. Ready to upload, she looked at the screen and paused. Lance must've been editing earlier, from yesterday's engagement shoot. But why was there a picture of Adrienne on the screen?

Curious, she started scrolling, seeing dozens of shots of a woman and, presumably, her fiancé in an area of Forest Park. Then she came to one of Adrienne with the woman. Okay, they're friends—and Adrienne just *had* to go to the engagement shoot. No need to wonder why.

Lance had taken four or five of the two women, which wasn't a lot given the total. There was another of Adrienne alone, a close-up. But Kendra's heart stuttered when she saw the next—of Lance and Adrienne. They each had an arm around the other's shoulder, laughing, and in the next, were making funny faces at the camera.

Kendra's hand came off the mouse, a mixture of emotions swirling. Why was she feeling this way? *What* was she feeling? Hadn't she told him to ask Adrienne on a date? That's probably where he was right now, again today, out with Adrienne.

She chided herself. Of course he should be out with Adrienne. Why *wouldn't* he be out with Adrienne? The sky was the limit. They could hang all day, plan exciting ventures. Shoot, they could plan months and years out, no problem. They could plan their lives together. And Lance deserved nothing less.

So why the need for this little conversation with herself? Why was she feeling so—

The back door opened, and Kendra wished she could sprint upstairs. She did what she could though, switching the computer window to photos she'd already uploaded.

Lance came around the corner. "Oh. Hey."

"Hey." Kendra gave him a glance and saw he had on a nice pair of jeans, ones she hadn't seen. Nice top too. "I'll be out of your way in a quick sec," she said.

"No rush."

"I was headed up anyway."

"Okay." He paused. "When you're ready, let me know. I'll help you."

Kendra exited from her photos. "It's okay," she said, pulling out her phone. "Molly's right in the kitchen."

Molly was down in a flash, and Kendra moved as quickly as she could back up the stairs.

CHAPTER TWENTY-NINE

TREY HAD NEVER FELT HE WAS MEANT TO BE AT A PARTICULAR place at a particular time more than right now. He awoke with Living Word on his mind and knew he had to go to church, suddenly aware that the rhythm he needed to reclaim was deeper than he thought. Walking into the youth building with Lance brought a ton of memories, of a strong relationship with God, a deep connection to Jesus.

He stayed through the youth worship service, watching, remembering. And when Lance gave his message, it was as if Trey were a teen again, hanging on every word, wanting nothing more than for the Lord to use him . . . and wondering how He would.

But it was the message in the main sanctuary that rocked him. Trey and Lance sat in a pew near the front and listened to the guest speaker, a missionary sharing about his time in Burkina Faso. But then the speaker turned a corner, from talking about himself to talking about them.

"We live in our comfortable homes with our comfortable jobs and our spouse, kids, dog, and cat—all of whom are probably comfortable too," he said.

The audience chuckled.

"If we think of doing anything outside the box, it's either when we're young and don't know much or when we're old and retired. Right? And I'm old and retired, so I can say that." His eyes twinkled. "But those middle years are spent *in* the box. We're raising a family, climbing a corporate ladder. Things are predictable. Settled." He walked across the platform. "And let's face it, for many of us, it's hard to live outside the box when we've got toddlers. It's hard to say, 'Hey, let's go live in a hut in Ouagadougou, learn the native tongue, and win souls for Jesus!'"

He smiled at them. "But some of you are called to live outside the box. You might not realize it yet, but your life is not meant to be ordinary. You're not meant to have the comfortable spouse, kids, cat, and dog. Maybe you won't marry at all." He stopped, eyeing them. "And guess what? That's okay. In fact, it's wonderful. Singleness is not a second-class gift. It's a true gift. And if that's your gift, embrace it. Have a ball with it. Go wild for Jesus in ways your comfortable friends and family members could never manage to do . . ."

Trey was almost fidgety. This man was talking to *him*. For years he'd felt he didn't want to marry. But whenever he mentioned it, to his mom especially, she'd bat it down.

"Trey, of course you'll get married. Don't be silly."

Marriage was a given, a mark of adulthood. As he thought about it, he realized what had driven his prayers all these years—this idea of needing to be married to be complete. It hadn't been driven by personal desires, but by outside pressure to pursue what he was supposed to pursue—marriage.

Yet this man was affirming singleness. And not only that, but Trey's mind was racing with answers to questions he'd had about the type of life he could live. There was no end of options. He'd be free to go anywhere in the world, wherever God would send him. He could live out of the box.

He leaned over. "Are you hearing this, Lance? I mean, really hearing this?"

"I'm hearing this." Lance smiled. "And I've been thinking about you the whole time."

Pastor Lyles came up at the end, encouraging people to check out the missions table. Trey had passed it a thousand times over the years. Today he would linger.

They made their way up the aisle slowly after the service.

"I'm gonna stop by the missions table," Trey said.

"Absolutely," Lance said. "Take your time."

Trey scooped up a handful of pamphlets and even applications for long-term and short-term mission trips. He had no idea if such a thing was in his foreseeable future, but he already knew he'd be praying about it.

He found Lance in the main lobby area, talking with a woman.

"Trey, this is Adrienne," Lance said. "Adrienne, Trey."

Trey shook her hand. "Nice to meet you."

"Likewise," Adrienne said. She turned to Lance, smiling. "Just wanted to tell you how much fun I had. I feel like the key turned to unlocking you, just a little."

"As long as it was only a little," Lance said. "I'd be off my game otherwise."

"You know what I'm learning?" she said. "That you're a piece of work." She laughed and gave him a hug. "I'll talk to you later."

Trey followed her with his gaze as she walked away, then turned back to Lance, brow raised.

"Don't ask," Lance said, heading out the door. "I'm not even asking myself."

CHAPTER THIRTY

KENDRA SET HER TRIPOD TO THE RIGHT OF HER BED NEAR A BIG window, where she'd discovered perfect late-morning light in her very midst. At least she hoped it'd be perfect. But that was the fun in experimenting. She could snap tons of photos with various settings and angles, and if only a few came out well, it was great. She could study them, see what settings she used, and hopefully replicate the best ones next time.

Photography was becoming an even bigger part of her existence. Although she'd never been active in social media herself, since her diagnosis she had realized how helpful blogs could be. She was grateful to the women who'd taken the time to chronicle their journeys, the highs and the lows, letting her know what each step was like. Kendra couldn't see herself writing daily about her journey, but the idea came to set up a blog nonetheless—and post pictures.

She challenged herself to post a picture daily that reflected God's goodness, as an encouragement to herself and to others who might be going through a hard time. This morning her goal was twofold, though. She was also trying self-portraiture.

Kendra fixed the height of the tripod and secured her camera on it. She'd been reading about self-portraiture, how it provided practice and developed skills both in composing shots and in post-process-ing. But what intrigued her most was self-portraiture as a journey of personal discovery, even healing of sorts, as it exposed aspects of the self buried deep inside.

When she realized no one was home this morning, she forced herself out of bed. Taking her own portrait seemed weird enough. She certainly didn't want anyone watching. This way, she had the freedom to work out the kinks.

Her camera set, Kendra positioned herself against a spot on her bedroom wall for a few test shots. She clicked with her remote and checked for framing, focus, and exposure. Then she took a big breath. *Lord, if there's something I can learn from this about myself, about You . . . let me learn.*

She'd gotten a big, beige, floppy hat from her closet, probably from some silly high school event, and set it on her almost-bald head. She'd already put on makeup and dressed in a loose tunic top to try to mask her uneven breasts. She stood against the wall again with a simple pose, clicked the remote, and checked it.

A little too much space up top. She'd lower the camera a tad. But she liked her position, to the left of the frame, her purple wall filling most of it, the entire shot cast in a soft, almost shadowy light.

She adjusted the camera and took another. Yeah! She loved this one, loved how she looked in it. She wasn't smiling, but the floppy hat gave a cosmopolitan feel, as if her hair was pinned up in the back. It reminded her of her old self.

She took a few more with different poses, then grabbed a base-ball cap she'd found. She tried it in the mirror first and wasn't too happy with the look. She was used to long curls falling from the cap, or a ponytail. Now she could see the baldness.

She snatched it off and in that moment knew this was the photo she needed to take of herself . . . with an almost-bald head.

Kendra closed her eyes. She couldn't. She didn't want to see herself like that. She heard herself say it in her heart—*it's ugly.*

She opened her eyes again. Wasn't this part of the photography journey, to face herself? Could she somehow see God's goodness in this?

She walked back to her spot, head uncovered, and took the picture. It looked different from the others. Her countenance was different. Her eyes were different. With the hat, there was a little spark. Without, they were lifeless.

She sighed and decided to take another. But first she considered God and His goodness, on purpose. And after she took the picture, she saw a difference yet again. It was as if her gaze had moved off herself. Her soul was in it.

As hard as it would be to post a picture of herself like this, she knew she had to do it. And she would caption it: *Today's goodness—His life in me. I am so much more than what my eye can see.*

Kendra was debating whether to take more when she heard footsteps on the stairs. Trey or Molly probably, heading to their rooms. Lance hadn't been up here since the day he cut her hair.

But seconds later she heard a knock, and Trey stuck his head in. "Oh good, you're up."

"You can come in," Kendra said.

Trey opened the door wider and walked in—with a young girl beside him. She had pretty brown eyes and thick, dark-brown curly hair gathered in a long ponytail.

"Well, hello," Kendra said, half-eyeing her brother.

He'd gotten fired up after the message he heard Sunday, researching various ministry pursuits online. Kendra might have thought he was starting an in-home camp for the disadvantaged if the little girl didn't look like a Gymboree model, in her picture-perfect shorts, shirt, and matching socks.

Trey took the child's hand, leading her farther inside. "Kendra, this is Brooklyn," he said. "Brooklyn Patterson."

Fatigue began to wash over her. Kendra sat on the bed. "Hi, Brooklyn, it's nice to meet you. My name is Kendra."

"I know, Trey told me," Brooklyn said. "He said you're my sister. I always wanted a sister."

Kendra raised her gaze slowly to Trey.

Trey cleared his throat. "Her mom is Ellen Patterson. I got to meet Brooklyn this morning, and I wanted you to meet her too."

Brooklyn walked closer, her little head angling to the side. "Are you sick? Because my teacher last year got sick, and she had to cut her hair off, like yours."

Kendra nodded. "Yes, Brooklyn, I'm sick. And the medicine made my hair come out, so I cut it."

The little girl stared at Kendra. "Can I say a prayer?"

Kendra stared back at her. "Sure, yes, I'd love that."

Brooklyn clasped her hands tight and closed her eyes. "Dear God, could you please, please heal my sister? Amen."

Tears sprang to Kendra's eyes. "How old are you, Brooklyn?"

"Eight. Well, eight and two-twelfths, to be precise."

Kendra smiled. "Where'd you learn to pray such a beautiful prayer?"

"My dad prayed with me when I was a little girl." Brooklyn played with her fingers. "When I used to see him sometimes."

Kendra and Trey exchanged a glance.

"Brooklyn, come sit next to me." Kendra patted the bed. "When was the last time you saw your dad?"

Brooklyn shrugged. "A year and a half ago."

"Have you talked to him?"

"Once or twice."

Kendra struggled to understand. Despite his failures as a husband, Marlon Woods had always been a doting, very present dad. If Kendra and Trey hadn't distanced themselves, he'd still be a regular part of their lives.

Kendra smiled at her. "So you always wanted a sister?"

"And a brother," Brooklyn said. "Now I have both. Can you believe that?" She shook her head. "You appeared out of nowhere."

"I know what you mean," Kendra said, eyes on her brother. She couldn't wait to hear how Miss Brooklyn had appeared.

$\approx$

Evening Bible study was in full swing—the meal part anyway—and Brooklyn hadn't yet left. Whenever her mom phoned Trey, Brooklyn would plead for a little while more.

"There's nothing to do at home," she would say. "I'm having fun with my brother and sister and Molly."

It was easy to grant Brooklyn's request since they only lived around the corner—a fact that blew Kendra's mind.

Had Ellen lived there during the affair? Was it that easy for her dad to step out on his marriage? Kendra tried not to dwell on that. She had no desire to think about, let alone meet or talk to Ellen. But Brooklyn—that little girl had stolen her heart.

She'd stolen Chase's too. Cyd's toddler had a playmate now, as Brooklyn played hide-and-seek and tag with him.

"Today is her first time here?" Cyd asked, watching them run around the kitchen. "She's so comfortable already."

Trey laughed. "I think she's pulled out every game we had in storage. If I'm not mistaken, she moved in when we weren't looking."

"I saw the Twister game on the dining room floor," Cyd said. "Brought back memories."

"Oh, that was a blast." Molly crunched into her taco and chewed a second. "Brooklyn and I were all about that."

"Brooklyn, you didn't finish your taco," Kendra said. "Take a break from playing and finish eating, sweetheart."

Brooklyn scooted into her chair next to Kendra's and took a bite, as she'd done several times before.

"Where's your food?" Brooklyn asked, looking at Kendra.

"Right here." Kendra lifted her glass. "Trey made me a drink with vegetables and fruit because the sores in my mouth make it hard to eat food right now."

Brooklyn's brows bunched. "You're still sick?" She pointed behind her. "That was all the way this morning when I prayed."

Kendra pulled her into a hug. "God's making me feel better because you bring a smile to my face." She made a pouting face. "But I still wish I could have tacos. This drink is really nasty."

"Don't blame me," Trey said. "Lance was the one who suggested it and told me what to put in it."

"Where did Lance go anyway?" Cyd asked.

"Downstairs," Trey said. "Cedric wanted to see his camera equipment."

"Oh no," Cyd said, "not another hobby in the making."

"Look out," Kendra said. "It's addicting."

The guys came back up as the doorbell rang.

"I'll get it," Lance said, "probably Timmy."

"Mmm. Smells like a Mexican restaurant in here," Timmy said, walking in with another guy at his side. "I hope it's okay to bring someone else. This is David, a friend of mine from SLU."

Jess and Molly's friend from last week showed up next, and a contingent went to the dining room to eat.

The doorbell rang once more.

"It might be this other girl I invited," Molly said. "I'll get it." Seconds later she called, "Trey, it's Brooklyn's mom."

Kendra quietly called him over and whispered, "Please make sure you handle everything at the door. I can't take that woman coming into Mom's house."

"Brooklyn, your mom's here," Trey said. "You have to get ready to go."

Brooklyn folded her arms. "But I don't want to go. Can I stay the night?"

"Brooklyn," a voice called. "Let's go, honey."

"Give me a hug, sweetheart," Kendra said. "It's okay. You can come over anytime you want."

The little girl's eyes lit up. "Really and truly?"

Kendra smiled. "Really and truly."

Brooklyn followed Trey out, and Kendra could hear her telling her mother all the things she'd done.

"Tell Trey thank you," Ellen said.

"Thank you, Trey."

Kendra heard the front door close and for the first time wondered about her dad's side of the story.

CHAPTER THIRTY-ONE

LANCE TOSSED HIS BOSE HEADPHONES INTO A BOX OF PERSONAL belongings on the bed. It was probably full enough. He'd pack his books next and take them and the boxes to the car, then his clothes, leaving the computer and camera equipment last. He'd be out of here by evening.

He put an empty crate on the bed and began filling it with heavy theology books and commentaries. With every move he considered giving away the texts and reading them online with Bible software. It would lessen his load considerably and free up much shelf space. But there was something about holding them in his hand, flipping the pages.

One crate filled, he decided to start loading. He lifted a box and turned—and saw Kendra at the door.

"How'd you get down here?" Lance said.

"I walked."

"But you know you shouldn't be taking a chance—"

"You're leaving, and you weren't going to tell me?"

Lance set the box down. "I was going to tell you."

"When?" Kendra asked. "With the car packed and the motor running? And why did Molly know before me?"

"She came down to get a DVD and saw me packing."

Kendra winced, though she tried to cover it.

"Come sit down," he said, leading her to the sectional.

She reclined slightly, looking at him. "Why are you moving?"

He sat near her, on the edge. "It's time."

"What does that mean, 'it's time'?"

"I think I was meant to be here for a short season, to help you and Trey, but . . . the season ended. And that's a good thing. I thank God for how He's leading Trey, and you have a great community of helpers around you."

"So that's what you were, part of the 'community of helpers'? One of many interchangeable parts?"

"I don't know what to call it, Kendra," Lance said. "I just know I started feeling like I was in the way." He looked at her. "To be honest, I felt like you didn't want me here anymore. And you shouldn't feel uncomfortable in your own house. When you want to watch a movie, you should be able to come down and watch a movie, without worrying whether I'm here."

She stared into her lap. "Where are you going?"

"Darrin's," Lance said. "His roommate moved out, so it was perfect timing."

Kendra nodded, letting several seconds pass. "For the record, it's not true," she said finally. "I don't know why you thought I didn't want you here."

"Maybe because whenever I came into a room, you'd leave. Whenever I'd offer to help, you'd refuse it." His eyes spoke his hurt. "It was like you couldn't stand the sight of me."

Kendra stared away from him now, hand swiping a tear. "I couldn't *bear* the sight of you."

He lifted his hands. "What's the difference?"

"After you cut my hair and held me . . . then apologized and picked up the broom . . . I knew I could never be someone you . . ." She waved away the rest of her thought.

Lance moved closer. "Kendra, I'm not following. What are you saying?"

She looked upward with a sigh, fisting tears away. "I'm saying I wanted you to hug me. Okay? But it was selfish to want that because *look* at me." She gestured at herself. "It was selfish to want you to care about me."

"I do care about you."

She tossed her eyes. "Right. Part of the community of helpers."

"Can we be real here?" Lance asked. "Can you handle real? Or would you rather talk in circles?"

Kendra looked at him. "I'm all for being real," she said. "Why not? It can be our parting gift to one another."

"Here's my *real*, Kendra Woods: I love you."

"Don't do that." Kendra shook her head back and forth. "Don't tell me you're being real and then say what you think will make me feel better."

"Kendra, stop." His gaze penetrated. "I love you."

"But how is that possible?" she asked. "How could you love me? *Why* would you love me?"

He moved closer. "I can't explain it any more than I can explain why you have cancer," he said. "We've only spent a few weeks together. You were supposed to marry someone else just last month. I've told myself I'm crazy." He paused. "When we hugged in the bathroom, I apologized because you were vulnerable, and I didn't want to take advantage. But the last thing I wanted to do was stop holding you."

Her brown eyes met his gaze. "I told myself I was crazy, too, that it made no sense. For the same reasons."

"What are you saying?" It was almost a whisper.

Kendra let a tear roll. "I'm saying I love you too."

He brought her to himself, holding her, his heart beating a pattern he'd never felt.

"It's not right though, Lance," Kendra said. "It's not fair for you to love me because nothing can come of this. I already saw it with Derek—"

"Wait. Whoa." Lance rubbed her arm. "I'm not Derek. And whatever you two had, this is not that." He looked down at her. "Can we agree on that much?"

"We can definitely agree on that much."

"I want to ask one thing of you."

Kendra waited, looking up at him.

"Will you let me love you?"

"Why do I feel like that's a trick question?"

"Not at all," Lance said. "It's just, if we don't establish this now, you'll keep telling me what you think is right or fair or what kind of life I could or should be living." He met her gaze. "Just . . . let me love you. Can you do that?"

Kendra twisted her mouth as if thinking. "I'll try?"

"I'll take it," he said. "For you, that's good."

She shifted suddenly, eyeing him. "Does this mean you're staying?"

"Only if you want me to."

She sank into his embrace, answering his question. And he held her.

CHAPTER THIRTY-TWO

KENDRA HAD NEVER SEEN THE WOMEN OPEN UP LIKE THIS. THE guys usually had the questions and comments, most of them skeptical, which made for interesting dialogue. But it took up most of the time, and often not even Molly seemed willing to interject.

Lance must've noticed. Tonight, at the fourth meeting, he announced that the men and women would break into smaller groups for discussion after the main study. Since Kendra was lying on the sofa, the women stayed in the living room, and the guys took the lower level.

Darla Reyes, a neighbor from a few houses down, was speaking now. She'd lived there over twenty years and was universally regarded around the block as nosy. In that vein, she'd asked Lance why people were coming to the house Wednesday nights. When he told her, and followed with an invitation to check it out, she'd said she just might. Still, they were surprised to see her show up, and chalked that up to nosiness also. But no matter her initial motive, she seemed moved to share.

"I don't know. Is this too personal?" Darla asked. "I've never been to anything like this."

"You can say whatever's on your heart, Darla," Cyd said. "It sometimes helps just to get it out into the open."

"The first thing I thought about when Lance said people disappoint, that they will never be everything we want them to be . . ." She paused, thinking. "No. He said they *can't* be everything we want them to be. That's what struck me, that they can't. And I thought about Bernie, my husband of twenty-four years, and how plain unhappy I am." She glanced around the room. "This won't get out, will it?"

"We have a code of confidentiality," Cyd said, "and I can only hope everyone adheres to it."

"So, as I was saying, I'm forty-six, and I have needs, you know? I mean, I'm not in the grave yet. And I'm not even talking about sex necessarily, but will I never get that fluttery feeling when we kiss or—no, wait—how about, we don't even kiss!" She threw her hands in the air at the travesty. "I used to love kissing more than sex, and we don't even kiss anymore."

The young women looked at one another, probably wondering if this would be their fate.

"So, what I want to know is, how would Jesus fulfill that longing? Because didn't Lance say Jesus is the One we look to, to satisfy our needs?"

"Darla, I love your comment and your question," Cyd said. "I know I needed to hear that because I'm in my forties, but I've only been married three years. And by age forty, I had built up so many ideals of marriage that I thought my husband would satisfy all the longings of my heart. It's just not possible."

"I had a lot of ideals about marriage too," Kendra said. "Ideals that were shattered *before* the marriage." She looked at Darla. "You probably don't know. I was engaged, but my fiancé broke it off when I got sick."

Darla nodded. "I knew it was broken off but didn't know why. I promise to keep it secret. But be glad, honey," she continued. "Think what would have happened if you'd found out what a schmuck he was after you married him."

"Oooh, that was good, Darla," Molly said, "but now I'm waiting to hear Cyd's response too. How does Jesus fulfill these basic longings we have as women, whether married or single?"

Cyd blew out a sigh. "These are not easy questions," she said. "I'll answer from the standpoint of looking to Jesus as a single, since I spent so many years with those basic longings." She thought a moment. "Jesus became my pursuit; meaning, I focused on knowing Him, growing in Him, walking with Him. And whenever those basic longings began to overwhelm me, it was because I had taken my focus off of Jesus." She paused. "I don't know if that makes sense, but I can honestly say Jesus became my everything. He was enough." Her eyes brightened. "Wow, it just clicked that I need to incorporate that same mind-set into my marriage. Jesus should still be my pursuit. He's still my everything, because Cedric can never be that."

"So I'm guessing I'm out of luck if I don't believe in Jesus," Darla said.

"Not at all, Darla," Cyd said. "This isn't an exclusive club. You can get to know Him too."

Darla seemed to ponder that.

"So, I found out very recently that people disappoint," Jess said. Everyone shifted her way.

"I was a virgin when I came to Wash U. I wanted to save myself for someone special, and I thought I'd found him. He said he loved me." Jess spoke evenly, not a hint of emotion, yet her words were clearly coming from a deep place. "On Monday I told him I was three weeks late, and he stopped taking my calls."

"What is it with these schmucks?" Darla muttered.

"I got my period this morning," Jess said, "but I didn't bother to tell him."

"I know that was painful," Cyd said. "It hurts when we hope in someone, and those hopes are crushed. And here's the hard question to ask ourselves—whom have *we* hurt? Because we've all hurt someone. We're all flawed."

Heads nodded reluctantly.

"But Lance said it well," Cyd continued. "Jesus is the hope that never disappoints. He *can't* disappoint. It's not in His nature. He's the Way, the Truth, and the Life."

Kendra thought about the person she'd hoped in, whom she wanted to be perfect—her dad. But he was flawed, just as she was flawed. He was on her mind more and more. And for the first time, she decided to pray about it.

CHAPTER THIRTY-THREE

August

"ARE YOU SURE YOU'RE UP FOR IT?" ARM AROUND KENDRA'S waist, Lance helped her down the stairs. "We can do this another time."

"I don't even know what 'this' is," Kendra said. "But you told me you had a surprise, and I want to see it."

"That was before you started having those spasms."

Kendra had had her third chemo session yesterday, with Lance accompanying her for the first time. Since she usually didn't get hit with the worst effects until two to three days after, he thought it would be safe to plan the surprise for today.

"It's not like we're leaving the house," Kendra said. "I'll just lie down if it gets bad."

Lance looked at her, wishing he could take away her pain. "Have I told you how much I admire you?"

She looked surprised. "For what?"

"For the way you're dealing with such a horrible disease," Lance said. "I know there are times when the pain is excruciating, but you don't give up."

"Someone once told me I could live in the midst of this." Kendra paused. "I've never forgotten your words. I might've started falling for you that day."

"Oh, you might've, huh?"

"Maybe."

He smiled, helping her past the last stair. "Now. Close your eyes."

"Really?" Kendra smiled, closing them.

Lance led her a few feet into the dining room. He wasn't the most romantic guy. He knew that. His mind didn't work like that, to come up with creative ways to romance a woman. He just wanted this to be special for her.

"Okay," he said. "Open."

Kendra's hands went to her face. "Oh, Lance . . ."

He'd set the dining room table with two place settings. Cyd had helped him pick everything out—the place mats, chargers and matching plates, cloth napkins, even the floral centerpiece. But the rest was his doing. Around the room were select photos Kendra had taken over the past month, blown up to poster size. The images were stunning.

"I can't believe you did this." She moved from picture to picture. "Did I take these? I don't remember them looking like this."

"Yes. You captured these. You can really see the beauty when they're cropped and blown up. I wanted to encourage you to keep going with it. You're really talented."

"It's almost therapeutic." Kendra stared at one she'd taken of a blue sky with swirling clouds and a bit of rainbow bursting through. "You see things—everyday things—you didn't see before. You see life you didn't see before, so much of God's creation." She turned to him. "I see why you said it's a form of worship for you."

"This is my favorite, Ken," Lance said, "the close-up of this daisy." He low-whistled. "Look at that. And this wasn't me cropping it; this is how you shot it. Look at the droplets of rain on the petals."

"That was right down the street," Kendra said. "Before, I would've passed it like it was nothing."

"We get to enjoy these beautiful images while we eat dinner," Lance said, "so let me pull out your chair and seat you."

She smiled. "Thank you, sir."

"I'll be back with the first course."

Kendra called after him. "It's not your famous green drink, is it?"

Lance chuckled, moving around the mess he'd made in the kitchen. He stirred the soup he'd left on a low simmer, then ladled it into bowls that matched the plates. He walked them piping hot to the dining room.

"Mmm . . . ," Kendra said. "I love your soups."

Lance loved that she loved them. It motivated him to try different recipes. But his main motivation was that they were easy for her to eat.

"What kind is it?" She watched as he set down the bowls.

"Cream of broccoli," he said, smiling. "I know you're not crazy about broccoli, but it's good for you."

She narrowed her eyes at him. "I feel like a kid being forced to eat my veggies." She leaned over the bowl. "Smells good though."

Lance sat next to her and took her hand, and they bowed their heads together.

"Lord, we praise You because You are good. In the midst of sickness and disease and so much we can never understand, You are good, and we pray to keep our focus on You. Thank You for Your beauty in creation and for giving Kendra an eye to capture it and a spirit to enjoy it. And thank You for our time together this evening. I pray You bless it, and bless the food for the nourishment of our bodies— double nourishment for Kendra's. In Jesus's name."

"Amen." Kendra looked at him. "Where did you come from?

You're like, this amazing man who dropped into my life, and I'm still trying to figure out how it happened."

"I'm not amazing, Ken." He looked at her. "Don't even think it, because I'll disappoint you."

She gave him a look as she lowered her head, tasting. "Can I say this soup is amazing?"

He smiled. "The soup can be amazing."

"What's in here?" she asked. "There's a nice kick to it."

He had a spoonful. "Can't tell you my secrets."

Kendra ate in silence a moment, then said, "So why do you always knock down compliments?"

He semi-frowned. "The 'amazing man' thing? That wasn't a compliment; that was fantasy."

"See what I mean." Kendra ate more of her soup.

He rested his spoon. "Kendra, I really want you to have a clear view of me. I'm not trying to be extra humble when I say I'm nothing. I'm just a guy who has to stay desperate for God." He lifted his spoon, but lowered it again. "And don't forget, in society's eyes, I'm a low-life ex-convict. Have you thought about that?"

"What do you mean, have I thought about that?"

"It's so far from who you are and what you've known," Lance said. "Never in a million years would you have seen yourself in a relationship—or whatever we're calling this—with a former inmate."

"And never would you have seen yourself with a terminally ill patient."

"That's different," he said. "You can't help that." He paused. "I'm just saying, my past bothers me sometimes still, so it has to bother you on some level."

"No, it doesn't have to bother me on some level, because it doesn't."

Kendra stared at him. "It's not who you are." She ate more soup. "But now I see why you're not so amazing."

He smirked at her. "Why is that?"

"Because you let the past plague you."

"It doesn't plague me."

"It tells you that you're not good enough, like you're the same Lance Alexander who walked into Clayton and thought it was everything to live in Clayton. Or the Lance Alexander who made wrong choices and got locked up." She cocked her head at him. "You need to put that guy to rest."

Lance sat back in his chair, giving it thought. "I think, around you especially, it's easy to lapse into the past and see myself as the high school boy who would've never been good enough for you."

"As you say to me . . . stop. Whoever you thought I was, that was a fantasy too. I think you know by now that I'm—what in the world?"

The doorbell was ringing . . . and ringing and ringing.

"I don't think Trey and Molly could be back from the movies yet," Lance said. "And they have a key anyway."

He got up and opened it.

A snaggletoothed little girl stood on the step, waving. "Hi," she sang.

"Is that Brooklyn?" Kendra called.

Brooklyn darted inside, straight to Kendra's voice.

"Brooklyn . . . ," Lance said, following her.

She smiled sweetly. "Yes?"

"Did you walk down here by yourself?"

"Yes."

"Does your mom know you're here?"

"I . . . think so," she said, sweetening her answer with a grin.

Kendra eyed her. "Brooklyn . . ."

"Okay, no. But she went to the store, and I got scared by myself."

Lance and Kendra exchanged a glance. Brooklyn wasn't scared. She just saw an opportunity to visit.

Lance looked at his watch. "It's seven thirty and still light out, but I'm not comfortable with her walking back alone."

"Me either," Kendra said.

Brooklyn spread her hands and offered a solution. "I don't have to go home. I can stay until my mom gets back from the store." She spied the plates. "What's for dinner?"

Chapter Thirty-Four

Kendra retired to the living-room sofa, felled by a wave of nausea stemming from the chemo—or, more likely, from the call that Brooklyn's mom was on her way. She'd called Lance's phone after he had let her know Brooklyn was there. And she'd asked if Kendra was home, saying she'd like to talk to her.

"And there you are, Miss Woods. Your pedicure is complete." Brooklyn capped the nail polish, sighing with satisfaction at her work.

"Beautiful job, Brooklyn. Wow, lime green." Kendra had been instructed not to look down while she did it. "Where'd you get that?"

"It's Molly's." Her palm went out. "That'll be a hundred dollars."

"A hundred dollars?" Kendra's mouth gaped. "You said it was free."

"I changed my mind."

"And they say to watch out for lawyers . . ."

Brooklyn's nose wrinkled. "Huh?"

Kendra chuckled. "You better get ready. Your mom'll be here shortly."

"Can you ask if I can spend the night? Please?"

"No, ma'am."

"But why? I haven't gotten to stay over yet."

"You can ask yourself," Kendra said, "but since you sneaked out, she might not be feeling generous."

Brooklyn folded her arms in a huff, then jumped up. "She's here," she said, looking out the window. She ran to the door and opened it. "Mom, can I spend the night?"

Kendra heard, "Brooklyn Renee, you're not staying anywhere. You and I will have a little talk about your behavior when we leave."

Lance came from the kitchen to the front door and greeted her. "Ellen, how are you?" he said. "Come on in."

"I'm fine, thanks, Lance." Footsteps entered the foyer. "Is this a good time to talk to Kendra?"

"She's here in the living room," Lance said.

Kendra shifted on the sofa as they approached. Introductions felt weird.

"Ellen, this is Kendra," Lance said. "Kendra, Brooklyn's mom, Ellen."

Ellen wore jeans and a solid-colored tee, and her hair fell straight and blunt, stopping below the ear. With no makeup, she had a plainness about her, yet an attractive plainness.

Kendra's stomach felt tight. "How are you?" she managed.

"I'm good. How are you?" Ellen asked. "Well. Sorry. Brooklyn told me you were sick, and I see now myself. I'm very sorry you have to go through this."

"I appreciate that," Kendra said.

"Is this . . . the same cancer your mother had?"

Okay, really? Kendra sighed inside and tried to think about the pep talk Lance had given her.

"No, it isn't."

"If you're feeling up to it, I wondered if I could talk to you a minute."

"I guess it's fine."

"Brooklyn, let's get some cookies and milk, if your mom will let you," Lance said.

"Sounds good," Ellen said. "Thanks."

When Lance and Brooklyn were gone, Ellen gestured toward the chair. "Mind if I sit?"

Kendra shook her head.

"First, I've heard a lot about you—"

"Ellen, seriously," Kendra said, "you're telling me you heard a lot about me, from my dad, in the midst of your affair?"

"Actually, I worked with your dad"—she cleared her throat—"before . . . Look, this isn't easy for me either. I only wanted to talk to you because of Brooklyn. I'm trying to understand what's going on."

"What's going on with what?"

"Out of the blue, my daughter never wants to be home. She only wants to spend time over here."

Kendra frowned. "I don't see that it's out of the blue. It's because she found out she has a brother and sister who live around the corner, and she enjoys spending time here."

"I'm wondering if there's more to it, though," Ellen said.

She sat forward and kept eye contact. But then, Kendra shouldn't be surprised. You'd have to have a direct nature to confront the wife, as Ellen had.

"I don't expect you to like me," Ellen said, "but I hope you won't poison Brooklyn's mind against me."

"What? I would never do that," Kendra said. "I don't believe in coming between parents and their children, by word or deed."

Ellen's mouth tightened. "I had to ask." She stood. "So you don't have a problem with Brooklyn coming over here?"

"Of course not," Kendra said. "I love Brooklyn."

"Well. Thank you for your kindness to my daughter."

"You don't have to thank me," Kendra said. "She's my sister."

Ellen started toward the entryway and paused. "I do the Susan G. Komen Race for the Cure every year. I hope you beat this thing."

"Thank you."

"And can I say one last thing?" She didn't wait for a response. "There are two sides to every story." Then she called to her daughter. "Brooklyn, let's go."

Brooklyn ran into the living room and hugged Kendra. "See you tomorrow," Brooklyn sang.

"You don't know that yet," Ellen said.

"Love you, Brookie," Kendra said.

"Love you too."

Lance came in after they'd left. "So how'd it go?"

"She wanted to know if we were poisoning Brooklyn against her, since she'd rather be here than home."

"What?"

"That's what I said. But just before she left she said something curious: 'There are two sides to every story.'"

"You might get to hear the other side sooner than you think."

Kendra looked at him. "Why?"

"I got an e-mail from your dad," Lance said. "He's planning a trip to the States. He'll be here by the end of September."

CHAPTER THIRTY-FIVE

KENDRA HADN'T HAD SUCH A FUN EVENING IN WEEKS. SHE'D BEEN out of the house many times, but the outings were usually medical related—chemo, blood draws, appointments with Dr. Contee. And she'd gotten out on short photography excursions. But this was *out* out. A date. With Lance. And after several days spent mostly in bed or on the sofa with stiffness and pain, she felt good. Well, good enough.

They hadn't gone far, just a mile up the road to the Cheesecake Factory. But just being in the mall was nice. Sitting in a booth in a dimly lit corner was nice. Dressing a notch up was nice. And now that her hair had fallen out completely, she felt stylish in her head scarf, tied with guidance from a YouTube tutorial.

Dr. Contee had given permission for her to eat more than normal, since she'd been losing weight, and tonight Kendra obliged fully. She'd eaten much of the huge serving of shrimp pasta and was now savoring key lime cheesecake.

Lance had his chin in his hand, smiling at her.

Kendra slid her fork slowly from her mouth. "What?"

"I love you."

Her heart double flipped every time he said it. "I love you more."

"No way."

"Way."

They laughed together.

Kendra forked up another piece. "Is it my imagination, or have you been doing fewer photo shoots?"

Lance sipped his cappuccino. "It's not your imagination."

"Why?"

He shrugged. "I'd rather be with you."

Her fork came down. She didn't know what to say.

"When you're lying down," he said, "dealing with the pain, I don't want to do anything other than sit with you, talk with you, watch you sleep."

Hearing that made her heart inch even closer to him. "I caught you praying over me when I woke up one time."

"I pray over you all the time," Lance said. "I pray for you as I go about my day. Praying for you is like breathing."

She let his words soak into her soul. "I've never been loved like this."

"I've never loved like this."

Moments like this brought exhilaration and sadness. "Why can't I spend a lifetime with you? Why can't we have years and years to look forward to? It's not fair, to have something like this, but only for a little while."

"We wouldn't have it at all if it weren't for this circumstance. You'd be in DC, married." He reached for her hand across the table. "If we were both in perfect health, tomorrow still wouldn't be promised. Years and years together wouldn't be guaranteed. We don't know how long of a 'lifetime' God will give you or me. But wow, what if we intentionally make the most of every day we receive?"

"I like that," Kendra said. "Being intentional about it." She drank some of her water. "That's in line with the conversation I had with Grace today."

Kendra had spoken with Grace and others on the litigation team somewhat regularly, as questions arose about different cases on which she'd worked. But this conversation was different.

"I made the break," Kendra said. "I told her I wasn't coming back."

"That's huge," Lance said. "I'm surprised you didn't mention it earlier."

"I guess it's huge." Kendra shrugged slightly. "But the break had basically been made. Now it's just official."

He lifted his cup. "How do you feel? That was your dream, to work there."

"I feel . . ." Kendra thought on it. "Surprisingly okay. The firm feels so removed from me now, part of another time and place. I'm thankful, though, for all the support they've given me."

"That box of—what did they call it, pink madness?—was awesome."

Kendra nodded. "That was so cool. Pink shirt, pink hoodie, pink baseball cap, even pink Converse." She smiled, thinking how they must've planned that.

"What about health insurance?" Lance asked. "I'm sure you're taking care of that."

"That was my main concern," Kendra said. "The premium is higher, but I'll have continuing coverage."

"So, do you think you'll look for a position at a firm here in St. Louis at some point?" Lance asked. "You were telling me about women with inflammatory breast cancer who continue to work."

"Yeah, it depends on treatment and how they're feeling," Kendra said. "There's no way I could've continued working at the same pace, if at all, given the pain and fatigue." She contemplated it more. "When I think about my life now, I really want to focus on enjoying every day God gives me, and photography helps me do that. I would love to keep developing my skills, with your help of course."

"You'll surpass me soon," Lance said, "the way you research every tip and trick online." He smiled at her. "But I'm glad it's official you won't be returning to DC to live. But what about all your stuff?"

Kendra sighed. "I know. I'm paying on a month-to-month lease for no reason. But who knows when I'll feel well enough to take a trip out there to pack up and move out of the condo as well as my office."

"What if Trey and I handle it for you?"

"How would you do that?"

"Drive out there with a U-Haul, throw your stuff inside, drive back."

Kendra laughed. "That simple, huh?"

"Maybe a tad more involved, but not much." Lance pulled out his phone. "I can text Trey right now. He starts classes in less than two weeks, so we'd need to get on it."

"I'm so happy for him," Kendra said. "Back on track with school, planning a short missions trip for Christmas break . . ."

"He's got me fired up," Lance said, "looking at my life, wondering how I can live more out of the box."

"Seriously?" Kendra said. "You've been thinking about that?"

"Absolutely. I don't want to miss God in some way because my mind is thinking too 'ordinary'—you know?"

"Hmm," Kendra said, "maybe we all need to start praying about that. I can't see being intentional and making the most of each day . . . inside a box."

CHAPTER THIRTY-SIX

LANCE AND TREY PULLED INTO WASHINGTON LATE THURSDAY night. They'd hit the road at six a.m. and driven straight through, making quick stops for food and gas. In the rented U-Haul, it took longer than the estimated twelve hours, but they still reached Kendra's condo in good time and sacked out.

They awakened early, ready to go. The hardest part was packing the kitchen, making sure Kendra's dishes, glasses, and other breakable items were protected. But the rest she'd told them to pack crudely. If they could throw it in a box, throw it in a box. If it worked better to throw it loosely in the truck, throw it in the truck. The plan was to get everything loaded by afternoon, stop by the firm and grab what was there, and get right back on the road.

"I wish I had time to see the city." Lance spoke from inside Kendra's closet, as he and Trey packed up the last room. "I've never been to DC."

Trey stripped the bed and added the comforter and sheets to a pile by the door. "I've been here twice," he said, "but never got to see all I wanted to see."

Lance lifted another armful of items from the rack and brought

179

them to the empty bed. "Your sister's got a serious wardrobe. We might've needed a bigger truck just for her clothes."

"And shoes."

"True." Lance paused. "I should probably call to check on her."

"Didn't you call an hour ago?"

"Yes. But that was an hour ago. Anything can happen in an hour."

Trey gave him a look. "Molly's there. Cyd said she'd stop by. Brooklyn's coming after school. If anything happens, they've got it covered."

"You might have a point. I'll call next hour."

Lance cleared off a shelf in the closet and saw three picture frames facedown toward the back. He turned them over—Kendra and Derek. They were obviously engagement photos, and the photography was stunning.

In one, her back was against an outdoor wall as Derek leaned against her, arms to her waist, lips against hers. The Washington Monument stood in the distant background, against a cloudy sky. In another they were walking along the river hand in hand, the focus on gorgeous sunrays breaking through the clouds overhead. He stared at it, at the way she smiled at him, head tossed to the side with long, beautiful curls. Took him back to the Kendra who had always seemed beyond him. He gazed at the third—

"I forgot about those," Trey said, taking them from his hands. "Ken told me to toss them in the trash. I already got rid of the album."

Lance stared vaguely, lost in thought.

"Hey," Trey said. "You're the best thing that ever happened to my sister. Don't you forget that."

Lance shook it off, emptying the rest of the closet. There was no wedding dress. Her maid of honor took care of that early on, so she wouldn't have to see it. Lance could appreciate that himself now.

Two hours later, they'd loaded the furniture, boxes, clothes, and miscellaneous items into the truck. Lance picked up the phone, with good reason this time.

"Hey, Ken," he said, "we're headed to your office. What do we need to do?"

"My legal assistant already transitioned the files and all that and boxed up my personal things," Kendra said. "All you have to do is pick it up. She'll meet you at main reception and show you where to go."

"Cool," Lance said. "How're you feeling? Any better than this morning?"

"A little."

"I hate being this far from you."

It wasn't his nature, but Lance wanted to be open with Kendra about his feelings. What was the point of holding back? Making the most of every moment, living out of the box, meant he couldn't be guarded.

"I didn't think I'd miss you this much," Kendra said.

"I'll call you when we get on the road. Love you."

"Love you more."

Trey leaned against the truck outside her condo. "Think we can keep moving with the task at hand?"

Lance smiled. "I'm recharged, ready to keep moving."

❧

Kendra's assistant, Jennifer, had shown them into her office, where a box was sitting atop her desk, good to go. But she realized she'd overlooked some knickknacks on the shelves and a few things inside the desk. Lance and Trey waited for her to return with a smaller box so they could pack those.

Lance leaned against the desk. "I see why this is one of the top firms in the world," he said. "It *looks* high-powered, from the interior design to the designer suits people are wearing."

Trey nodded with a chuckle. "We got some looks in our ratty jeans, didn't we?"

"They've been nice though."

Before they could get up to her office, they'd been stopped several times by people asking about Kendra and sending their love. Others had stopped into her office as they waited. She'd clearly been missed.

A knock sounded on the door, and Lance turned. He recognized the man at once from the pictures.

"Hey," Derek said, hand extended. "Trey, right?"

Trey looked at him. "That's right." He shook his hand.

He moved to Lance next. "Derek Richards."

Lance shook his hand. "Lance Alexander."

Derek stepped back, looking like the other attorneys in his blue power suit. "I heard you two were here and, uh . . . I wanted to ask how Kendra's doing."

Trey looked annoyed. "Have you called to ask her yourself?"

"I'm . . . almost positive she doesn't want to speak to me."

"Even so, the attempt might've shown you cared, at least a little."

"Trey, I know I'm not your favorite person," Derek said. "I understand that. I'm just genuinely wondering . . . How's Kendra doing? How are the chemo sessions going?"

"Lance can answer that," Trey said, motioning to him. "He's with her more than anyone."

Derek looked at Lance, brow raised a little.

"Honestly," Lance said, "I don't know what you want to hear. It's a hard road. But you already anticipated that, right?"

Derek's gaze fell off.

"If you want me to help you feel better by saying she's doing great, I can't do that." Lance was focused on him. "What I can tell you is she's surrounded by people who love her, and her faith is strong."

Derek gave a bare nod. "That's . . . that's good."

Jennifer breezed in. "Sorry it took me so long. I had to hunt one down in the mailroom."

"No problem," Lance said, taking the box. "Thank you. We'll get it packed quickly."

When Lance glanced back, Derek was gone.

Chapter Thirty-Seven

"I can't believe he had the audacity to ask about me."

Kendra tossed her phone down. She'd spoken to Jennifer, who'd told her about Derek, which prompted a call to Trey—who said he hadn't planned to tell her about the convo with her ex, but reluctantly did.

Whatever sluggishness she'd been feeling had been overridden. She sat up on the lower-level sofa, mentally stoking it.

"I mean seriously, the audacity," she said again, looking at Molly.

Brooklyn looked up from the movie she was watching, brow furrowed. "What's audastity?"

"Au*dac*ity." Kendra kissed her forehead. "It means someone has a lot of nerve."

"Darla already said it." Molly sat lotus style on the floor, shaking her head. "Schmuck."

"Why pretend you care? You obviously don't care." Kendra spoke to the air, turning now to Molly. "He only went up to my office because others asked about me, and he would've looked like a schmuck if he didn't. Well, guess what? Now he's a double schmuck." She rolled her eyes. "Ugh!"

Molly cracked up.

"What?" Kendra said.

"That face you just made," Molly said. "You need to capture that on camera. It can be your God's goodness photo of the day."

Kendra had to laugh. "Right. Caption: *He gives muscles with which to contort the face into maniacal expressions.*"

Molly's eyes lit. "I dare you."

"Seriously?"

"Double dare."

Kendra moved faster than she should have and groaned when she got stabbed by a shooting pain.

"I'm sorry," Molly said. "I shouldn't have goaded you to get up, especially for something dumb like a schmuck photo."

"I need it," Kendra said. "Instead of lying down focused on what hurts, I can do something fun and silly."

She moved to get up again, waiting for Molly's help this time, and was glad her camera and tripod were already downstairs. She set up the tripod in the backyard for good lighting and positioned the camera.

Molly watched. "What are you gonna do, run it through your mind again and get mad all over?"

Kendra stood a little ways from the camera. "That's exactly what I'm gonna do."

"Okay, cool, I'll help," Molly said. She paused, clearing her throat. "Can you believe Derek's audacity? I mean, the nerve of him stopping by to ask, 'Hey, how's Kendra?' after he dumped you the week before your wedding. Who *does* that?"

"Exactly!" Kendra said. "Who does that? Who has that much nerve? Every time I think about it, it's just—ugh!"

Kendra clicked, several times, making even more faces at the camera.

They moved back inside and uploaded the shots on the computer. When the thumbnails of Kendra's face appeared on-screen, they couldn't stop laughing.

Brooklyn paused the movie and ran over to see. "Look at your face," she said, joining the laughter. "Can I make some silly faces for the camera too?"

"You sure can, as soon as I'm done with this."

Brooklyn ran back, and Kendra and Molly continued surveying the choices.

"Make that one bigger," Molly said, pointing.

Kendra brought the thumbnail to life on-screen. She'd never noticed the cleft between her brows when she frowned, or the way one eye narrowed more than the other.

"You know," Kendra said, "jokes aside, it *is* kind of amazing that God made our faces to move and stretch and dimple like this. It could've been a flat, immovable surface."

Molly made a face herself, stretching it long, which made her laugh. "That's true. We can do all sorts of things with our faces."

Kendra brought up her blog and uploaded the picture with a slight change of caption: *Today's goodness: When news that provokes bitterness turns into laughter at funny faces.*

Chapter Thirty-Eight

KENDRA COULDN'T STOP SHAKING IN THE CHEMO CHAIR.

Lance reached into the duffel bag and pulled out a blanket. "Ken, let's put this around you."

"Thanks, I'm okay." She tried to smile reassurance. "I've already got on a hoodie, hat, and thick socks."

He rubbed her IV-free arm. "But you're shaking."

The complications this morning had unnerved her. A new tech—new to Kendra, anyway—drew her blood and used a bruised vein from last time, which hurt. Then in the chemo ward, she did get her favorite nurse, but the nurse somehow missed her vein and blew another one, which *really* hurt. But her mind was mostly burdened by what happened in between.

"I'm a little depressed about my white cell count," she said. "I almost couldn't get chemo today because it was so low."

"But from what the doctor said, that'll be helped by the shot you'll get later."

"In the stomach. Yay."

"I know, Ken." Lance held her hand. "We'll keep counting down. This is your fourth session; only two more to go."

"Then surgery for the mastectomy, then weeks of radiation, then more chemo. It's so much." She sighed. "I'm sorry. I don't want to whine. It doesn't help."

"It's a lot, Ken. No doubt about that. Whenever you need to vent, let it out."

She stared at the medicine going through the vein, into her blood. "I'm looking forward to my appointment with Dr. Contee end of next week," she said. "She'll be assessing the treatment regimen, how it's impacting everything." She thought about it. "Maybe that's why I'm nervous. What if there's no improvement?"

"We're not going there, Ken. You can't add speculation to the mix. You'll go crazy."

Kendra thought about it anyway. She'd thought about it for some time.

She turned to Lance. "So what do you think about Darla coming to Bible study?"

"From one speculation to the next, huh?" Lance asked. "You're asking because of last night?"

"I just thought it was strange to see Darla and Ellen talking outside."

Lance shrugged. "Why strange? They're neighbors."

"I don't know . . . I was surprised Darla showed up to Bible study to begin with. I hope she's not there to spy for Ellen."

"Spy?" Lance said. "Kendra, come on."

"I don't mean a planned covert operation," Kendra said. "I mean she may be checking us out, reporting back. I'm just not totally comfortable with her being there. Plus, she made a comment last night about how unforgiving people can be."

"Could it be your own conscience that's bothering you?"

"What do you mean?"

"With Brooklyn there all the time and Ellen dropping off and picking up, you can't help but think about what happened between her and your dad. It'll eat you up if you hang on to it, Ken. Maybe it's time to forgive."

"Then what? Ellen and I can be friends? It would feel like betrayal to my mom."

"Nobody said you have to be friends," Lance said. "Forgiveness is about your heart."

Kendra was silent for a while. "Why is all this coming up right now? Brooklyn and Ellen in the picture, Dad coming to the States . . ."

"Answer's pretty simple to me," Lance said. "Your sickness."

She looked at him, questioning.

"Trey was motivated to find Brooklyn partly because you made him think about life and how short it is for all of us." Lance spoke softly, mindful of others in the room. "And I could almost guarantee your dad was motivated to come because of you."

"How would he know about my sickness?"

"How wouldn't he know, the way word travels?" He squeezed her hand. "Your dad loves you. Surely you don't doubt that."

Kendra allowed herself to ponder that.

"And remember," Lance said, "you and Trey aren't the only ones affected by all of this. Brooklyn might be the one most affected. She's not growing up with her daddy."

Chapter Thirty-Nine

Kendra couldn't get Lance's words off her mind. She knew Brooklyn's situation, but somehow it broke her heart to hear it that way—"She's not growing up with her daddy." Lance had been right. That sweet girl was the most affected. Kendra and Trey had had the benefit of their dad's presence. He'd cultivated a close relationship and set the bar high as to what it meant to be a father. That's why they'd been so disappointed in him, because their expectations of him were high. At this rate, Brooklyn would have no expectations of him at all.

Throughout the night, as Kendra wakened with her usual discomfort and pain, she thought of Brooklyn. She prayed for Brooklyn. And by morning she couldn't shake what she needed to do. Trey and Molly had early-morning classes, so she showered and dressed without questions. And she left a note for Lance.

At nine in the morning she was knocking on Ellen's door. The lock turned, and Kendra took a breath.

"Kendra." Ellen wore comfortable slacks and a top. She looked past Kendra to see who was with her. "How did you get here?"

"I drove," Kendra said.

"Well, please, come in and sit down."

Ellen led Kendra to a sofa in the living room, gesturing for her to sit. Ellen took the chair.

"What can I do for you?" Ellen asked.

"You're one who gets to the point," Kendra said, "and I appreciate that. Do you mind if I do the same?"

"I'd prefer it."

"You told me there are two sides to every story," Kendra said. "Actually, in this case, there are three. I'm wondering if I could hear your side."

Surprise showed in Ellen's eyes. "I wouldn't feel comfortable," she said. "It's between you and your dad."

"To an extent." Kendra had addressed the same within herself. "If this were an affair only, I wouldn't be here. But with Brooklyn . . . I just want to understand why she doesn't have a relationship with her dad."

"Again, your dad is best suited to tell you that," Ellen said. "I don't know the answer myself."

Kendra sighed within. She'd felt so sure that this was what God wanted her to do. But she couldn't make the woman talk to her. And Ellen had a point. Her dad was best suited to address issues between—

Her thoughts shifted. What about between Kendra and Ellen? Wasn't there an issue with them?

"You said it was no secret that I didn't like you," Kendra said, "which was true. In my mind, you were the worst of the worst, coming between my parents, having his baby . . ."

Ellen stared head-on.

Kendra was grappling for the right words. "So maybe . . . maybe it would help me to hear your side of the story, to see you as human. If that makes sense." She sighed, moving to get up. "This was a dumb idea. I'm not sure what I'm even saying. I'm sorry I wasted your time . . ."

"Kendra, wait." Ellen leaned forward slightly. "In a weird way, I understand where you're coming from. And even weirder, I kind of want you to see me as human, as maybe . . . not so evil, if that's possible. But I do want to be careful not to tread on areas that are uniquely between you and your dad."

Kendra settled back a little, prompted by minor pain spasms.

"What can I get you?" Ellen asked.

"Water would be great, thank you."

Ellen got water for both of them, returned to her seat, and hesitated only briefly before she began.

"I'm not sure where to start . . ." Ellen paused. "I don't want any of this to sound self-serving. I want to say off the bat that I was wrong to get involved with a married man."

Kendra held the bottle, listening.

"I started my career at the University of Kentucky, and Marlon recruited me to come here twelve years ago. I was familiar with his research in sociology, of course, and had met him at conferences." Ellen spoke as if presenting a paper at a conference. "I was in my early thirties—about your age—not yet tenured, and knew I could learn a lot from him. We ended up working on research projects, co-authoring papers, and traveling."

Kendra's mind put an emphasis on *traveling*.

"We became friends. And on one trip in particular, he drank a little too much and—"

"Dad was drinking?"

"I knew it was out of character," Ellen said. "And when I asked if he was all right, he began to . . ." Her lips pressed together. "I'm moving from my territory to his. I won't continue with that part."

"It's no big mystery," Kendra said. "He was drinking too much and made moves on you."

"Not true. At that point, nothing would happen between us for another year."

"I'm confused," Kendra said.

"Suffice to say," Ellen said, "that over the course of that next year, we became close friends. Mostly him sharing, me listening." She paused, took a breath. "I won't get into hows or whys, but the affair began. It only lasted a few months. Marlon loved his wife—that much was obvious throughout."

Kendra wasn't sure how much more she could bear.

"So. Affair was over by mutual agreement. We would both move on, no problem."

"And then you found out you were pregnant."

Ellen nodded. "And then, again by mutual agreement, I would have an abortion."

Kendra's eyes almost popped out of her head. "My dad would've never suggested an abortion."

"All I will say, Kendra, is you don't know what people will do when their backs are against the wall."

Brooklyn almost wasn't here. Kendra thought she might be physically sick. "You didn't do it, obviously."

"I couldn't," Ellen said. "I just couldn't. But I told Marlon that since it was my choice to have her, he could choose whether to be involved in her life." She sat forward. "And I said, 'If you choose to be involved in her life, you have to stay involved. You can't float in and float out.'" She shook her head in disgust. "Which is exactly what he did—floated in for a few years, then floated out."

"But why?" Kendra said. "That's what doesn't make sense. It's not like my dad."

"The dad you know is part of a nuclear family," Ellen said. "He woke up in your house, ate dinner at your house, mowed the lawn. That's not Brooklyn's dad. Her dad stole an hour here or there to see her. He was her father in secret. If you think about it that way, it'll make more sense."

"But it doesn't," Kendra said. "Why did he stop stealing hours here and there? Why did he float out?"

"When your mom got sick," Ellen said, "he started coming less and less. I understood. Your mom needed him. But I think it was more than that." She stopped. "I'll leave that to him."

Kendra asked the question she'd always wanted to ask. "Why did you come to my house—when you knew my mom was sick—and drop the bombshell about you and Dad and Brooklyn?"

Ellen looked away for several seconds. "That was difficult for me, believe it or not." She paused again. "Marlon hadn't seen or spoken to Brooklyn in months. It was as if he had cut her off, not financially but in every other way. And . . ."

It was the first break in Ellen's story, the first time she'd shown emotion.

". . . the day I came, it had been ten nights straight of Brooklyn crying, asking what she did wrong to make her daddy not love her anymore."

Kendra imagined what that must've been like. No little girl should have to hurt like that.

"I went to talk to Marlon," Ellen continued, "since he wouldn't take my calls. But when your mom answered, things were said that shouldn't have been said. I regret that day immensely."

"But it had to come out." Kendra had never thought of it like that. "I hate that my mom found out the way she did and when she did. But the fact is, Brooklyn existed. What if she was still hidden in the shadows? What if I didn't know her?"

"It's quite unexpected, the bond that's developed between you all," Ellen said. "You know I had my reservations at first about her spending time there, but know that I trust you completely with Brooklyn."

The pain began to shoot more intensely. "I'd better make my way back home while I can."

Ellen helped her up and walked her to the door.

"You didn't have to invite me in, and you didn't have to tell me your part of the story. Thank you." Kendra turned to her before she opened the door. "You're human to me now."

Ellen gave a tight nod. "That means a great deal."

"And I should tell you so you can be prepared," Kendra said, "since Brooklyn is at the house all the time, and there's no way to really avoid it . . . It could actually get sticky, I guess."

Ellen frowned a little. "What is it?"

"My dad—Brooklyn's dad—will be here in a month."

CHAPTER FORTY

September

LANCE DIDN'T KNOW HOW HE'D GOTTEN ROPED INTO THIS. A small cookout at home turned into a fun hangout for the Bible study group, which morphed into a Labor Day bash that included friends from Living Word. And Lance had been designated host and grill captain.

Darrin was supposed to help, since he'd invited himself and the LW gang, as he called them, but he hadn't arrived yet, and over two dozen others had. So Lance got started on the basic plan, hamburgers and hot dogs, while Trey and Molly worked on the sides.

He walked inside now through the kitchen. People were everywhere—outdoors, kitchen, dining room, hunched over plastic plates, talking. Lance glanced around for Trey to help get more chairs but, not finding him, headed down by himself. He was halfway down the stairs when he heard voices.

"You can't fire that up in here, man," Trey was saying.

"Since when?" a guy said. "We always roll like this at your parties."

"First, it's not my party," Trey said, "and second, I don't roll like that anymore."

"You need to put it out," another voice said. "Now."

Is that Timmy?

"Whatever, man, I'm out of here."

The guy swept past him on the stairs as Lance continued down.

"I'm proud of you guys," Lance said, pulling each to a handshake-hug. "Seems like yesterday you were partying and trashing the house. Now you're cleaning up behind the last guest and picking up in the yard, from napkins to paper plates to soda cans."

Timmy looked from Trey to Lance, confused. "What?"

"I think he's saying that's what we're doing tonight," Trey said. "As payback."

"Payback?" Lance put his hand to his chest in disbelief. "Never. Just life lessons in responsibility."

"That party, though . . ." Timmy's eyes brightened with the memory. "In terms of sheer volume of attendance juxtaposed against how late in the day we put the word out . . . killer."

Lance patted him on the back. "To the last stray paper cup in the living room." He went to the stacked chairs. "I need you guys to help with these too."

On the way up with folding chairs, Lance heard Darrin's voice. "Finally decided to show up?" Lance called.

At the top of the stairs, he saw him in the entryway—with Adrienne and her roommate. Darrin hadn't said he was bringing them, but Lance wasn't surprised. He set the chairs down to greet them.

"Hey, stranger." Adrienne hugged him, then gave his shoulder a playful hit. "I thought we were friends. You're a hard person to keep up with."

He smiled. "I guess I can't deny that."

The group of them settled outside as Lance and Darrin put more meat on the grill. Adrienne and her roommate pulled up chairs close by.

"Did I hear someone say there's a Bible study here on Wednesday nights?" Adrienne asked.

"There is," Lance said. "We started it earlier this summer, for people in the area."

"So that means my roomie and I can't come?" She gave him a playful glance. "Would you deny us entry to a Bible study, Pastor Lance?"

He flipped a burger. "If you don't know the secret password, you will indeed be denied admittance."

"Seriously though, I'd love to hear you teach," Adrienne said. "I happened into part of your message at one of the youth services and got a lot from it."

"So I'm assuming," Darrin said, tongs in hand, "that if Lance planted a church, you'd visit?"

"Oh my goodness, is that a possibility?" Adrienne tipped her can up and sipped some soda. "I love Pastor Lyles, but if Living Word plants another church with Lance as pastor . . . I'm there."

"Darrin's just talking," Lance said, giving him the eye.

A line began forming, Molly among them, as sizzling hot burgers came off the grill.

Lance scooped a burger onto Molly's bun. "Hey, Moll, how's Kendra? Still in bed?"

"Yeah," Molly said. "She took some pain medication and went to sleep."

"Okay," Lance said. "I'll check on her in a little bit."

Trey brought his iPod outside. "We got some requests for line-dance music," he said.

Lance made a face. "Are you serious?"

"You got a problem with that?" Cedric came over, laughing, with his wife in tow.

"Cedric thinks he's the line-dance king," Cyd said. "Something he can still excel at in his forties."

"Aw, that's cold." Cedric grabbed her hand. "But can you still hang with me? . . . That's the question."

Trey cued up the "Wobble," and in seconds the grass had filled with people. Cedric and Cyd took the lead to show the others what to do, and in no time everyone was leaning side to side with their arms in the air.

Brooklyn had been playing games inside with a few of the younger kids but ran out when she heard the music. She pulled Lance from beside the grill. "Come on. Let's dance," she said.

Lance resisted. "Go out there with Trey, Brooklyn. That's not my thing."

"Oh, stop being a fuddy-duddy." Adrienne got up and took his other hand. "It's painless. Come on, just once."

Lance followed them out there. There were four rows of line dancers, and he made sure they took the back row.

He got a kick out of Brooklyn. "I didn't know you could dance like that," he said.

She wobbled left, then right, grinning. "We did this in day camp."

Adrienne knew it, too, dancing smoothly, coaching Lance with her movements. "See, you're getting the hang of it!"

"I wasn't worried about getting the hang of it," Lance said. "I just think it's silly."

She pushed his shoulder. "Oh, stop."

Everyone quarter-turned, and Lance's line became the front. Cedric shouted from the back, "Go, Lance! Go, Lance! Go, Lance!"

Lance waved him off, laughing. Then his eyes caught a glimpse of someone watching from the upstairs bathroom window.

CHAPTER FORTY-ONE

THIS HAD TO BE ONE OF KENDRA'S HARDEST WEEKS YET. Nausea and vomiting had become the morning and evening ritual. Her upper left side was stiff, arm and chest muscles perpetually fatigued, likely from hauling a heavy cancerous tumor that once was her left breast. Bruises like tattoos covered her arms from the needle sticks and IVs. Her gums were sore. Fingernails discolored. And to match her bald head, her eyebrows were almost gone.

Still, she'd ventured down for Bible study, thankful it was right here at home. She was learning that when her body felt the worst, her soul gained the most from this time. From the lesson to the inevitable laughter, she didn't want to miss it.

The meal had concluded, and everyone had found a spot in the living room, many on the floor. Kendra felt bad taking up the sofa, so she curled up while others shared the space with her. It had gotten more crowded now that classes had started and students were back. Kendra wouldn't be surprised if Molly had been passing out flyers for the study in the student union.

"Welcome, everyone, to The Shadow." Lance sat in a folding chair on the perimeter of a makeshift circle. "For those who don't know why we have such a mysterious-sounding name, it's about coming out of the dark shadows that imprison us and into the shadow of the Almighty, through His Son, Jesus."

Kendra always thought someone might get up and walk out when they found out the study revolved around Jesus, but so far, people at least took time to listen.

"We've talked about God's shadow in various ways," Lance continued. "As a place of truth, light, and protection, for example, always incorporating Jesus and who He is. In our discussion groups, Cyd and I have had enough questions that I want to spend our time tonight just talking about salvation." He took in their faces. "Some of you have questions like 'How can Jesus be the only way to heaven?' and those are good questions. We welcome those—"

The doorbell rang, and Molly jumped up from the floor.

"Sorry we're late," a voice said.

"Oh, you're cool," Molly said. "Come on in."

Kendra glanced up—and her evening tanked. *What are Adrienne and her roommate doing here?*

A couple of people scooted over, making room on the floor, which happened to be by Lance's chair. Adrienne took the floor space beside him—of course—and set her Bible in her lap like a dutiful student.

"Hey, you two," Lance said. "So first," he continued, looking around the room, "let's look at who we are before we're saved. Turn to Ephesians chapter 2."

Kendra could see Adrienne turning, head angled down, with a full mane of thick, gorgeous hair. Eyebrows perfectly plucked. Two healthy, same-size breasts. And a bundle of energy.

Kendra shifted, searching out a comfortable position, touching the scarf that now seemed poorly tied. She'd forgotten what passage Lance said to turn to. Tonight even her soul couldn't find relief.

Most everyone had cleared out except Darla, who'd cornered Lance with more questions; Timmy, who seemed to be in line behind Darla, if there were a line; and Adrienne and her roommate—obviously angling for last in line. Trey and Molly had just mentioned going to clean the kitchen.

"Molly," Kendra whispered.

Molly bopped over. "What's up?"

Kendra motioned for her to sit next to her. "Don't leave me in here by myself."

Molly raised a confused brow, glancing around the room. "How would you be by yourself?"

"Take my word for it."

"Want me to help you upstairs?" Molly asked.

"Not yet."

Molly leaned in. "You trying to see what Adrienne is up to?"

Kendra cocked her head. "How'd you know?"

"Girl . . ." She gave Kendra a look. "Is there such a thing as pastor groupies? Because she's one."

Monday night, Adrienne had stayed late at the cookout, dancing and playing Spades in a card tourney. Kendra, too sick to come down, had missed it all. She was tired of sickness driving her from the fun, or in this case, from plain curiosity.

"Molly, where'd you put the trash bags I bought?" Trey called.

"Be right back," Molly said, heading to the kitchen.

Darla waved at her. "Bye, Kendra, I'll see you next time."

"See you, Darla," Kendra said.

Timmy engaged Lance next. And seconds later, Adrienne hopped over and sat on the floor beside Kendra.

"I haven't had a chance to really talk to you," Adrienne said, "other than that time I brought Maggiano's."

"How've you been, Adrienne?"

"I've been good, but . . . I didn't realize you were sick when we first met." She paused. "You still had all your hair."

"Oh. Yeah. I guess I did."

"I'm so sorry." Adrienne looked sincere. "Is it breast cancer?"

"It is," Kendra said, preferring to leave out specifics.

"I'll definitely be praying for you," Adrienne said. "Now I understand why Lance said it was complicated."

"What do you mean?"

She looked a little embarrassed. "I kind of asked if the two of you were in a relationship, since you lived here together, and he said no, but it was complicated."

Kendra's arms twitched. They'd apparently had time for a late-night convo in the midst of everything else on Labor Day. And this was what he said? "Yes, complicated is . . . a fair assessment."

Molly returned, stopping midstride at the view.

"Can you help me up now, Molly?" Kendra's nighttime nausea was coming on strong. "I'm not feeling well."

CHAPTER FORTY-TWO

LANCE WAS GLAD ADRIENNE STAYED UNTIL THE END, SO HE wouldn't have to delay what he needed to say. He walked Timmy to the door.

"I love your excitement, Timmy. I hear the wonder of discovery."

"I didn't realize faith could be such an intellectual pursuit," Timmy said. "I was raised in a family of scientists and always thought religious people were hokey. No offense."

Lance chuckled. "I didn't grow up in a family of scientists, and I thought they were hokey too."

Timmy tucked his hands in his pockets. "I really thought science and God lived on opposite poles. But after reading those books you recommended, by scientists . . ." He lapsed into thought for a moment. "I'm seeing what science shows us about God." He opened the screen door. "I'd better go. I've got class in the morning."

"See you, Timmy."

Lance left the door ajar as he returned to the living room.

"Hey, Lance," Adrienne said, "we were wondering if you wanted to catch a movie with us tonight." She looked at her watch. "Starts at 10:10. Darrin's meeting us there."

"I can't make it," Lance said. He moved closer to Adrienne. "Can we talk a minute?"

Adrienne got up and joined him in the entryway.

Lance paused, desiring the right tone. "I want to apologize, because I think I must've given you the wrong impression."

"I don't know what you mean," she said.

"Maybe I'm mistaken," Lance said. "But I think you may think there's an opportunity for us to build something beyond friendship. And that's not the case." He added quickly, "But again, if I'm wrong, I'm sorry, and I'll just be greatly embarrassed."

Adrienne smiled faintly. "I did think there was some chemistry between us," she said. "And I debated hard about whether to come tonight, especially after being here so late Monday. But . . ." She sighed. "Now *I'm* greatly embarrassed."

"Don't be," Lance said. "I just wanted to make sure there were no misunderstandings between us."

"So . . . did I do something to turn you away?" she said. "I thought we enjoyed one another's company."

"It's not that you did anything," Lance said. "I just don't want to do anything to hurt Kendra."

"Kendra? I thought you told me you two weren't in a relationship."

"We weren't at the time you asked," Lance said. "Things have changed."

Adrienne hesitated. "Really? I guess that surprises me."

"Why?"

"Well, given that she's sick . . ."

Lance wasn't sure how to respond. "I understand that that matters to some." He shrugged. "Bottom line is: I love her."

Adrienne's eyes widened a little. "I feel bad then," she said.

"I was just talking to Kendra tonight and told her I didn't know she was sick, but that now I understood why you said things were complicated—"

"I'm sorry. I have to go," Lance said. "Trey," he called, "can you see them out, please?"

Lance took the stairs by two, understanding now why Kendra looked the way she did on her way up. Actually, she hadn't been herself all week. Lance suspected it had to do with Adrienne's visit Monday, but Kendra hadn't wanted to talk about it when he asked.

He knocked lightly and, hearing nothing, peered in. The covers were pulled almost over Kendra's head.

"Kendra," he whispered.

She usually lay in bed for more than an hour before falling asleep, especially if she'd rested most of the day. But she didn't budge.

Lance leaned against the doorjamb, sighing, wishing he could clear this up tonight. He knew what would happen. Kendra would wake through the night, keep it steeping in her mind, and by morning, she'd feel that much worse.

This was the last thing she needed before her appointment with Dr. Contee in the morning.

CHAPTER FORTY-THREE

KENDRA ALMOST WISHED SHE'D LET LANCE COME TO HER doctor's appointment, to help her understand. Dr. Contee was talking, but the words landed sparsely, as if choosing for themselves whether to reach Kendra or stop just short. And what did land, landed hard. She was reminded of June 17, a date seared on her brain, when she sat in Dr. Watson's office. Her life before that bore no resemblance to life after. She had that feeling right now, like life was taking another big hit.

"It's not working?" Kendra said. "That's what you're basically saying, right? The chemo's not working."

It was too much to comprehend. Weeks of industrial-strength chemo pumped into her body and knocking her flat on her back, with one thought pushing her through—that something was getting better, and then finding out it wasn't . . .

"It's not that it's not working," Dr. Contee said. "We're seeing some positive change. Just not to the extent we had hoped."

"Which means it's not working." Kendra's head fell in her hand as more words sailed over and around her. *Lord, why? This road is hard enough. Why can't I get good news on the hard road? Why is everything on this road hard?*

"Kendra," Dr. Contee said, "I know this isn't what you wanted to hear. It's not what I wanted to hear. This is an aggressive cancer, and as we discussed at the outset, I can't give any guarantees." She eyed Kendra with compassion. "But by changing your chemo cocktail for the next two sessions, I'm hoping for excellent results."

"Dr. Contee, I don't even know what that means anymore—'excellent' results. What's excellent? If it extends my life by two more months?"

Kendra stood to go. She knew the answer.

Dr. Contee rose as well and came around her desk. "You told me last month that you were praying regularly." She hugged her. "I'm praying too. Keep the faith, Ken."

"Thank you, Dr. Contee." Her voice was bare. "I know you're doing the best you can."

Kendra's phone vibrated as she left. Looking at it, she saw three text messages and as many missed calls from Lance, starting early this morning. She'd left the house at six, before anyone was up, tired of lying in bed under an avalanche of thoughts. But the thoughts buried her still as she drove around and ate at a breakfast spot. Now, with this latest news, it was hard to see daylight.

She walked to her car, envisioning long stretches of highway to drive so she could think for as long as it took to make sense of her life—but it would never make sense. And she barely had the strength to make it three miles to home.

Her next-best scenario was to sneak into the house and up to her room, close the door, and shut out the world. But when she walked through the garage door and into the kitchen, Lance was the first thing she saw.

Now late morning, she was getting hungry again, but she kept moving. "I don't want to talk right now," she said.

"Kendra, we need to talk." Lance followed. "I want to hear how the appointment went, and I need to talk to you about last night."

She turned before she reached the stairs. "Oh, about Adrienne? Or about our complicated non-relationship?"

"That's why I need to talk to you," Lance said. "Adrienne told you about a conversation we had almost two months ago. I told her last night that you and I *are* in a relationship . . . and that I love you."

"It doesn't even matter."

"What doesn't matter?"

"Whether we're in a relationship. What does that even mean? I don't know what anything means anymore." She went up a stair and turned back. "No, here's a better way to say it. Nothing means what it used to anymore."

"So you're saying it doesn't matter to you if we're in a relationship?"

"I'm saying the relationship doesn't matter, period. How could it?" She threw up her hands, forgetting it hurt her arms to do so. "There's no future. And the little future I thought I had is dwindling."

He stepped closer. "What did Dr. Contee say, Ken?"

Kendra took a breath, feeling the weight of the doctor's words again. "She said we're not getting the tumor shrinkage they hoped we'd get. My interpretation: I've had four cycles of aggressive chemo, four cycles of intense pain . . . for nothing."

"No way it's been for nothing," Lance said. "I know Dr. Contee didn't say that."

"She'd never say what the real deal is. You have to read between the lines." Tears came. She couldn't hold them any longer. "What she might as well have said is that I'm part of the statistic for whom the 'treatment regimen' doesn't work. Somebody has to be in that statistic, right? Why not me?"

"What is she going to do?" Lance asked.

"Change the chemo cocktail. Use different drugs."

"That sounds positive," Lance said. "I'm sure it'll work much better."

He pulled her to himself, but she backed off.

"I really need to plant myself in reality." Kendra dried her tears. "I can't do the fake optimism of 'this'll work great' and 'hope for the best.' I can't." She flinched when he tried again to hold her. "And I can't tell myself this 'relationship' can work and then look out the window and see what a real relationship for you could look like."

Lance's eyes welled up. "Don't do this, Ken. You're tired, probably hungry, and you got less than favorable news—"

"And none of it means I can't think clearly," Kendra said. "I was thinking about this before today. The appointment only sealed it."

"Sealed what?"

Kendra looked into his eyes. "You asked if I would let you love me, but I can't, Lance. It would be selfish of me." Her tears were back, because of his. "It's all one-sided. You give, and I take . . . of your time and your energy and your strength. You were having so much fun outside dancing, just loose and . . . unburdened. I want that for you. You don't have to shackle yourself to my illness."

He wiped her tears. "That's not what this is at all. I love you, Ken. That was just one dance, mainly because Brooklyn—"

"See, now you're justifying why you were having fun." Kendra shook her head. "No, Lance. *Have* fun. *Please.* You shouldn't be worrying about me. You're not even working like you used to."

His eyes held a sadness she'd never seen. "I'm going to let you rest," he said, "and we can talk about this later." He took her arm to help her upstairs.

Kendra stiffened. "I drove to a breakfast place and to the doctor's this morning," she said. "I can walk up the stairs."

Lance let go and she could feel him watching as she made her way up. Going ahead with her next-best scenario, she closed the door and shut out the world.

CHAPTER FORTY-FOUR

"THIS IS SO LIKE A FIELD TRIP."

Lance looked at Molly. "It does feel like that, doesn't it? Except, who takes a field trip to church?"

"Hokey people like us," Timmy said.

Lance laughed as he walked into Living Word with Trey, Molly, and Timmy. Molly couldn't remember the last time she'd been to church. For Timmy, it was never. But they'd been hanging at the house last night, asking questions about what Living Word was like and the kinds of things they did, and Lance suggested they come check it out.

"But seriously, do I look all right?" Molly smoothed her ripped jeans and plucked at her platinum-red hair. "I look too crazy, don't I?"

"Since when do you care?" Trey asked.

"Oh, Moll, I forgot . . . ," Lance said. "Actually, they won't let you in the service without a skirt and brown, black, blond, or naturally red hair."

Molly stopped, eyes wide.

Lance pulled her along. "Girl, get in here."

She trudged forward with a side-glance at Lance. "Dude. Seriously."

Lance had told them they could drive separately and meet him for second service in the main building, but they wanted to check him out, too, as he led the youth. Their field trip would span the entire morning.

Timmy watched the people filing in. "I find it fascinating that scores of teens fill this building every week," he said. "They've probably heard Bible stories and messages all their lives. And others like me have heard nothing. I want to tap them on the shoulder and say, 'Don't take this for granted. Soak it up.'"

Lance nodded. "It'd be nice if we could pour the knowledge and wisdom we've gained into the next person so they'd get it and run with it." He eyed a particular circle of teens who'd grown up at Living Word and gotten caught up in bad behavior. "But God has to do an individual work in each heart. It's amazing, really, how personal He is."

"I've seen it this summer more than ever," Trey said. "I didn't think I could experience God in such a personal way."

Lance noticed Molly was quiet. "You okay, Moll?"

A couple seconds lapsed, and she nodded. "I'm cool."

"All right, guys," Lance said, "I have to make sure everything and everybody's set for service. I'll see you after."

Lance couldn't help praying for them as he walked away. He cared for them as if they were his own kids. *Lord, I pray right now that they would each know You in an intimate way.*

The service kicked off with worship, then Lance had everyone sit to hear a testimony from a young woman named Heather who'd started a ministry for women dealing with heart issues surrounding sexual immorality. Lance didn't mind the guys hearing, since they needed to know those issues, too, and would hopefully think about it next time they were tempted to lead one of these young women astray. Next week, a guy would talk to them about the same issues from a male perspective.

Heather took the stage. In her twenties, dressed in faded jeans with blond hair in a high ponytail, she looked as youthful as the teens.

"My name is Heather Anderson, and I want to talk to you about sex. And don't look embarrassed because I know among this very group of high schoolers, some of you nice, Christian kids are having sex." She walked to the edge of the stage and looked from side to side, scoping them out. "Uh-huh, and I know exactly which ones."

They laughed, pointing at one another.

"How many of you have heard that sex before marriage is wrong?"

Almost every hand went up.

"How many of you have heard that you should be striving to remain pure?"

Hands went up again.

"How many of you have heard these things from a fornicator and adulterer?"

The room went quiet as the kids exchanged glances, looking as if they weren't sure they'd heard correctly.

Heather raised her hand high. "I'm that person. I didn't make the right choices. In fact, I made terrible choices. But I'm not here to talk about the rightness and wrongness of those choices. You all already know right from wrong." She took her time, letting her gaze crisscross the audience. "I want to talk about the heart behind those choices. What's going on in the heart of a young woman who gives herself to guy after guy? Why would she so freely give her body to someone who's given her, not a wedding ring, but a few crudely strung together words in a text message?"

Hoots and hollers sounded around the room now, from girls affirming the lame communication efforts by the guys.

Heather waited until the noise died down. "I'll tell you what's going on, more often than not, in the heart of that woman . . ."

Lance, Trey, and Timmy were ready to head over to the main building, but Molly was still talking . . . to Heather. Heather had told the young women she'd love to talk or pray with them afterward. Lance knew from experience that many of them wouldn't, self-conscious as they were about what others thought. But to his surprise, Molly had gone right up to Heather as soon as the group was dismissed, and the two were now sitting down and talking.

"I'm wondering if we should wait," Lance said. "Molly won't know how to find us."

"I'll text her and tell her to come to the main building when she's done," Trey said. "Then she can text me, and I'll go get her."

"Sounds like a plan."

The three of them walked across the parking lot and into the main building, where it was always crowded as first-service people left and second-service people arrived.

"Lance!"

He turned to see Cyd coming toward him and walked to meet her. "Cyd, Heather was awesome, just like you said. I'm glad you told me about her ministry."

"I wanted to be there," Cyd said, "but I got held up with Kendra when I stopped by with a breakfast casserole."

"Did something happen?"

Cyd looked perplexed. "Did she say something to you about changing her treatment regimen?"

"Yes, the doctor told her the chemo cocktail will change."

"No, not that," Cyd said. "Kendra says she researched alternatives online, and she's no longer doing aggressive chemo."

"What do you mean, no longer doing it?"

"That's what she said. That it didn't make sense to go through all the pain for nothing."

Lance was ready to run out the door to talk to her. "The thing is," he said, "she doesn't know it's for nothing. It could extend her life significantly."

"You know," Cyd said, "I had a friend who opted not to do aggressive chemo and radiation because she preferred a better quality of life for the time she had remaining. But she'd really prayed about it and consulted with her doctors and family."

"That's the problem," Lance said. "I'm worried because Kendra's not herself right now, and she's not listening to the people around her." He sighed. "I'm praying she doesn't make a life-altering decision in this state."

CHAPTER FORTY-FIVE

"SO, THIS MUST BE AN INTERVENTION."

Kendra watched as Trey, Molly, and Cyd filed into her room.

Trey nodded without apology. "That's exactly what it is, Ken. You're saying you're not going to do chemo."

"I'm not," she said. "I'm talking to Dr. Contee about it today."

Her friends positioned themselves at various spots on her bed. Lance had tried yesterday, but he didn't get farther than the door.

"It sounds like you're giving up," Trey said, "and we want you to fight."

"You want me to fight." Kendra had been on a low boil for days, and it didn't take much to turn it up. "Do you even know what that means?"

Trey sat closest. "Ken, I know how hard this is. I know—"

Kendra raised a hand partway. "All of you are here out of love, and I appreciate that. But please don't tell me you know how hard this is. You can't know. I don't even tell you because I'd be talking about it 24–7." She looked away. "You have no idea."

"Can you tell us?" Molly asked.

"Tell you what?"

"Help us understand what you go through," Molly said. "We see you wincing and commenting here and there, and even getting sick sometimes. But what's it actually like for you, going through chemo?"

Kendra gave it some thought. Not to search for words—she had the words. But she wasn't sure she wanted to talk at all, let alone about her illness, especially when the stated intent of the visit was to change her mind. But maybe she could help them see where she was coming from . . .

"Right now," Kendra said, "it hurts to talk to you. It often hurts, but I've just gotten used to talking through it. The inside of my mouth has sores that get so painful, sometimes it hurts to swallow water. The other day a pill got stuck in my throat. Wouldn't go down, couldn't spit it back up. After several minutes of panic, it finally moved."

Cyd moved up quietly and rested a hand on Kendra.

"And speaking of my mouth," Kendra said, "most of what I eat tastes like a metal ashtray. I don't complain because I don't want you all to feel bad when I can't enjoy the food you cook. And everything I eat gives me bad acid reflux and burning indigestion, plus other issues that send me to the bathroom. And speaking of the bathroom, it hurts to pee, hurts to brush my teeth, hurts to get in and out of the shower, hurts to look at myself in the mirror . . ."

Kendra took a big breath. No one said anything to fill the space.

"My breast . . . ," Kendra continued. "I don't talk about that. You can see it's swollen to a size much bigger than the other, but it's also hard and uncomfortable, and it hurts. And it's ugly. And whenever I look at it, I'm reminded that cancer is ravaging"—she closed her eyes, waited—"ravaging my body. I have pain spasms that wake me from sleep. They hurt so bad. Something always hurts. Always." She showed her discolored fingernails. "I didn't know fingernails could hurt."

Molly's eyes started to fill. She stuck her fingers in their corners.

Kendra shifted positions. "Stiffness," she said, since she was feeling it. "Much of my upper left side feels stiff at times. And you already know about the constant fatigue and weakness." She sighed. "The hospital side of things is its own beast"—she lifted her arms from under the covers to show the tracks of bruises, then let her head rest on the pillow propped behind her. "There's more, but that should give you an idea."

"Kendra, that was the physical side," Cyd said. "And as horrible as it is to go through, I can only think that the mental and emotional aspects are just as rough." Her hand lay still on Kendra's leg. "Can you tell us about that too?"

Kendra stared at the ceiling. "I can't even describe that," she said, letting silence enfold them several minutes more. "If it's possible, those aspects are even harder. When I got the diagnosis, devastating as it was, I kept thinking, 'I can get through it with Derek.'"

She took a steadying breath. She hadn't gone back to those emotions in a while. And never had she voiced them.

"He rejected me. He pushed me out into an Arctic blast to fend for myself and shut the door. I'd never felt so alone and scared in my life." Kendra let the old feeling pass, refusing to cry for him. "Coming back home, being around all of you, it's been amazing. You've been amazing. Cultivating a relationship with God . . . even more amazing. But there's still mental and emotional grief. You know?"

Her voice broke. "There's the grief of knowing what you'll never do or be or have. There's the grief of feeling completely robbed, like a cruel joke. All the things you grew up looking forward to . . . won't happen. There's the grief of watching everyone else live happy, normal lives, and wishing you could have problems like a bad cold or strep throat, like they do."

She played with the sheet, folding the top of it over her hand, then unfolding. "And there's the grief of . . . of loving a man like you never thought you could love, and knowing that can't be either."

Kendra crumbled. "And you tell me to *fight*?" She looked at her brother. "Fight to extend the physical, mental, and emotional pain? Why? Don't we believe things will be better on the other side?"

No one answered.

CHAPTER FORTY-SIX

KENDRA HEARD THE KNOCK ON THE DOOR BUT KEPT HER FACE to the pillow. "I'm lying down," she said.

"You're always lying down. The question is, are you asleep?"

Kendra laughed inside. "Come in, Brookie." She turned onto her back as the door swung open and Brooklyn skipped in.

"How was school today, sweetie?"

"Good. Guess what? I got a new bike, and Mom said I could ride it down here."

Kendra brought her arm from under the covers and high-fived her. "Pretty awesome."

"Can you come see it?"

"Your bike?" Kendra said. "Where is it?"

"Downstairs," Brooklyn said. "I brought it inside just for you."

Kendra eyed her. "You want me to get up and walk downstairs to see your bike?"

Brooklyn grinned, nodding fast.

"Only for you, Brookie."

Brooklyn knew the routine. She pulled back the covers and helped lift Kendra to a sitting position, then helped her stand.

Kendra walked barefoot in her tried-and-true yoga pants, thankful for the bright spot in her life that Brooklyn was.

She could see the bike from the stairs. "You didn't tell me it was pink and purple," Kendra said. "Those were my favorite colors as a girl."

"For real?"

Kendra took a step at a time. "Totally. But it looks so big. Are you sure you can handle a bike that big?"

Brooklyn paused on the stair, hand in Kendra's. "You're kidding, right? I'm next to the next to the next tallest girl in my class."

Kendra chuckled. "Next to the next to the next? How do you know? Did you all line up to see?"

"Yes!"

At the bottom stair Kendra moved to observe the bike, but something flickered in her peripheral vision. She looked left—and saw red candles of various heights and widths ablaze on the dining room table and dozens of red roses. Her heart slipped completely out of rhythm.

"What's going on?"

Lance appeared from inside the dining room.

"Brooklyn, did you know about—" Kendra turned, and the bike was there, but Brooklyn was gone. "Where did she go?"

Lance didn't respond.

"What is going on?" Kendra asked again. She wasn't sure she could hear if he told her, for the pounding in her chest.

He extended his hand, and she walked slowly toward him, taking it.

Inside the dining room, she could see three giant poster boards like ones he'd blown up before, facing backward. He led her to the one on the far right and, without a word, turned it around.

"This is beautiful," Kendra said. The lights were dimmed, but she could see clearly. "Is this the Missouri River?"

He nodded.

The shot was a close-up of the waters, with the sun setting behind clouds in the distance.

"You took this?"

He nodded again.

"When?"

"Last Friday."

Only now did Kendra notice a caption near the bottom. She bent a little to read it.

Many waters cannot quench love, Nor will rivers overflow it . . .
                                        —Song of Solomon 8:7

She looked at him, heart pounding all the more.

Lance didn't say a word. He led her to the next and turned it around.

She gasped softly at a gorgeous picture of an open field with wild purple and yellow flowers and a glimpse of sun overhead. "You took this the same day?"

Lance nodded.

She went straight for the caption this time.

Enjoy life with the woman whom you love all the days of your fleeting life which He has given to you under the sun . . .
                                        —Ecclesiastes 9:9

"Lance . . ." Kendra read it again and took in the picture, mesmerized.

He wouldn't let her linger. He led her to the third and turned it. Kendra had to figure out what it was. Outdoor shot. Close-up of an old, yellow, wooden chair in a grove of trees. And on the chair, it looked like . . . a ring?

She was shaking as she bent to read.

Husbands, love your wives, just as Christ also loved the church and gave Himself up for her.

—EPHESIANS 5:25

"Lance, what is—"

She turned around and stared in disbelief. Lance was on one knee.

He took a ring out of a box.

"Lance, what are you doing?" Kendra said. "You can't. We can't . . ."

"Kendra Woods, will you marry me?"

"*Nooo* . . ." Tears spilled from her eyes.

He stood, wiping them with a finger. "Is that your answer? You don't want to marry me?"

"I'm saying we can't. You can't . . . marry me."

"Why can't I?"

"What kind of marriage would that be? I can't be the kind of wife you need. I can't even be your wife for very long."

"That verse from Ecclesiastes says it all for me." His voice was soothing. "Your life *and* my life are fleeting. I want to enjoy life with the woman I love all the days that God gives us."

"That's what I'm saying," Kendra said. "You can't 'enjoy life' with me."

"Kendra, loving you is enjoying life for me." He took her hand again. "You said our relationship was one-sided, that I give and you take. That's not true, but . . . I want it to be."

"That doesn't make sense."

"I want to be your husband, the kind of husband who gives himself up for his wife. The kind of husband who sacrifices and serves and does any one-sided thing his heart desires for his wife because he loves her that much. I want you to take from me all day, every day, and we'll let Jesus replenish us both."

Her gaze locked with his, and all she could think was she loved this man so much it hurt. "But what if you leave me, Lance?" She wiped more tears. "What if you leave me?"

He brought her close, gently, and whispered in her ear. "I'm not going anywhere, Ken. Just let me love you. Let . . . me . . . love . . . you." He got back on a knee. "I know this seems soon. But when you're living life out of the box, you don't worry about the number of months or years. You go with your heart. Kendra Woods, will you—"

"Yes—"

"—marry me?"

Lance twisted his lip. "Now I'm not sure because you were talking on top of me. Did you just say—"

"Yes, Lance Alexander. I'm scared and overwhelmed, but I could never love anyone more. I would be honored to marry you."

He closed his eyes a moment, then took the ring out of the box. "I don't know if this will feel okay on your finger."

He slid the ring on, and Kendra stared at it. "It feels fine, and it's absolutely gorgeous." She covered her face. "Thank You, Lord. Thank You so much . . ."

Lance stood, drying her tears once more. "You're so beautiful," he said. "And if you try any more of that nonsense where you push me away . . ."

"I've never known this kind of love. I need God to teach me how to receive it." She looked at him. "But no. Whatever life I have, I'm spending it close to you."

"Well?" a chorus of voices yelled. "What did she say?"

"Come on in," Lance called back.

Brooklyn, Trey, and Molly hurried in. Kendra lifted her ring finger.

They pumped their fists and cheered so loud Kendra covered her ears. When the noise died down, Brooklyn had one question: "When's the wedding?"

CHAPTER FORTY-SEVEN

WHEN THE MINI-CELEBRATION HAD ENDED, LANCE AND KENDRA cozied on the lower-level sofa together, making plans.

"This is funny," Kendra said. "We got engaged an hour ago, and we're looking at dates within the month. This is the easiest wedding planning ever."

"Is this weird for you, Ken?" Lance had an arm around her as she leaned back on his chest. "You just planned an elaborate wedding, and a few months later you're marrying someone else."

"All of life is foreign to me now," Kendra said. "So in the grand scheme of things, it fits." She was able to laugh a little. "But really, I'm just blown away by God. As much as it hurt for Derek to dump me, I thank God he did. I mean, what if I had married that man?" She shivered at the thought. "God knew exactly what I needed . . . and *didn't* need."

Lance's face touched hers. "I love you. Let me know if you get tired of hearing it."

She snuggled closer. "I'll never ever get tired of hearing it."

He looked at his phone again and opened to the calendar app. "So, as we think about dates, should we wait to see how your body is reacting to the new drugs so we'll know which days are better?"

Kendra gave him a look. "I caught that. You're trying to see if I changed my mind about chemo."

"Nope. I'm *assuming* you changed your mind. You can't give up. I want as much time with you as God will allow. I need you to fight. We fight together."

Kendra played with his hand. "I think I needed to feel like I was in control of something. I needed to feel like I had a choice whether to scrape the bottom of the pain barrel or not."

"I understand that," Lance said. "I knew you'd hit a really low point. By the way, what did Dr. Contee say when you told her your plan?"

"She wasn't exactly jumping up and down about it," Kendra said. "So two more chemo sessions—September 18 and October 9."

"I'll be there." Lance waved his phone. "Already calendared it—you okay?"

Kendra doubled over with a pain spasm. "I'm okay," she said moments later, settling back in. "And if you can't make both, I'm sure Trey or Molly will be free."

"They can be free all they want," Lance said, "but I'm going with my baby to chemo and everything else."

Butterflies swirled inside. "You've never called me that."

"I'm sure I'll be calling you all kinds of names—good names." He smiled. "You're my fiancée."

"That's the first time you've said that too. I like the sound of it."

"Don't get used to it," Lance said. "I'm ready to get to calling you my wife."

"Now, I *love* the sound of that." Kendra sat up a little. "Okay, so dates. I don't know how my body will react to the chemo, but so far, the week before the next session has been better than the others."

"Let's do it *this* week then." Lance wiggled his eyebrows.

Kendra smiled at him. "I don't know if it needs to be *that* soon."

She checked dates on his phone. "How about October 4? Not a lot of time, but enough to put together something special, I hope."

She waited a few seconds, then bumped him. "Hello?"

Lance turned to her. "I'm sorry. I was just thinking about my mom. I can't believe she can't be at my wedding. I really want her to meet you."

Kendra looked at him. "If this drug works like they want it to and I get past chemo and surgery and radiation . . ." She sighed. "It's so hard to think past all of that . . . But if I can travel one day, that's where I want to go, to Tallahassee federal prison to meet your mom."

"What?" Lance was genuinely surprised. "If you're able to travel, of all the places you could go, you'd want to go there?"

"I do." Kendra was nodding. "I want to meet the woman who raised you." She paused. "It's really something that neither of our moms can be at our wedding. But thankfully, your mom is still with us. She can't come here, but we can go there. That is, if I can go one day."

It took a moment for Lance to respond. "You have no idea how much that means to me, that you'd even want to go." He squeezed her softly. "I love you, girl."

"So, October 4?"

"Sounds good, in more ways than one." Lance shifted a little, looking at her. "Between the two of us, we only have one parent who could possibly attend. And your dad will be here."

"He's coming end of September," Kendra said, "but we don't know how long he's staying."

"I don't think he'd come all this way and not stay a week or longer." He paused. "I think he should be at our wedding, Ken."

She hesitated. "I don't have a problem with that." Her own statement struck her. "I guess it highlights yet another difference between a few months ago and now. So much has changed."

229

CHAPTER FORTY-EIGHT

TREY HUNTED FOR A TABLE IN THE STUDENT UNION AT THE height of lunch hour. Spying a group that appeared to be done, he hung nearby until they stood, then commandeered the table before someone else could approach from a different direction. He texted to tell Molly and Timmy where he was and started on the pizza slice he'd bought.

He overheard a voice nearby.

"I'm not sure I want to work with Professor Patterson though."

Trey let his gaze drift briefly to two female students sitting at the table next to him.

"Because of the affair with Dean Woods?" the other woman said. "I don't see why that matters."

"She's not well respected in the field. Everybody knows she slept her way to tenure—"

"Are you serious? I didn't realize that."

"A letter of recommendation from her would mean nothing. I'm working too hard to earn a PhD and become a professor at a top university to have it tarnished by working with the wrong person."

"I see your point. If that's the case, who *would* work with her?"

"No one who knows any better. I was talking to—"

"Hey, you." Molly slid into the seat next to Trey. "What's wrong?"

"Oh. Nothing." Trey couldn't shake their words. "Well . . ." He leaned in, keeping his voice low. "The women to my left were talking about Ellen. About what happened with my dad. I knew his reputation had taken a hit, but I didn't realize Ellen's had too."

"Oh, yeah," Molly said. "I think hers took a worse hit because people feel she was promoted because of it."

"How did you know that?" Trey asked.

"I'm fairly sure we talked about it."

"I'm fairly sure we didn't," Trey said. "I would've remembered that."

Molly shrugged. "What's the big deal anyway?"

Trey pondered it. "I think it's sad that people are talking about her like that."

"Sad?" Molly deadpanned him. "I thought you couldn't stand the woman."

"That was before. But she's basically part of our lives now because of Brooklyn." Trey glanced at the women as they left. "Ellen has such a cut-and-dried demeanor, like nothing fazes her. But I wonder how she's really doing. You know? I wonder if she has people she can talk to."

"Okay, really?" Molly said. "She's a grown woman and university professor, and you're wondering if she has someone to talk to?"

"Sometimes people assume other people have someone to talk to, and all the while they're languishing," Trey said. "I know about things like that."

"Yeah, you're right," Molly said. "If I didn't have you to talk to, I would've been seriously languishing. And talking to Heather a couple weeks ago gave me an understanding I'd never had."

Trey sipped his Coke. "You know, I've never prayed for Ellen. Not once. I don't know if she knows the Lord or not. I've only focused on Brooklyn." He sighed. "I've got to do better. I've been praying to have the heart of a missionary, to really care about people's souls . . . and I'm not even starting at home, so to speak."

"Friends, Romans, countrymen . . ." Timmy plopped down beside them with a hoagie. "What say you this fine afternoon?"

"Sometimes I think you're still on weed," Molly said.

Timmy lowered his sandwich, looking at her. "Fairest one, why dost thou besmirch my good name?"

Molly looked at Trey. "Methinks the lad is ever and always delusional."

Trey shook his head at both of them. "You two are getting married one day. I just know it."

※

Trey took a chance stopping by her office. This was the building his dad worked in—and still had an office in. People knew who he was, and they talked. But that was just as well. Might be a good thing for them to talk about Trey being cool with Professor Patterson.

He knocked on her door and opened at her invitation.

"Trey." Ellen looked up from a pile of books and papers. "What's going on? Did something happen with Brooklyn?"

"No, nothing like that." He walked in farther. "May I have a seat?"

"Sure."

Trey dropped his backpack to the floor and sat on the edge of his chair. "I hope you don't take this the wrong way . . ."

Ellen laid down her pen. "You and your sister have a knack for starting interesting dialogue."

"But I'm a lot younger, and I'm a student here, so I'm sure it's out of place," Trey said. "I apologize in advance."

"What in the world is it?"

"I was just having lunch in the union and heard some grad students talking . . . about you."

Ellen glanced downward. "Certainly nothing new."

"Well. That's actually what I figured. I know people talk about my dad."

"Why are you telling me this?" Ellen asked.

Trey searched for the right words. "I just wanted you to know . . . only if you didn't already . . . that you don't have to live with the shame of what happened. I'm not saying you feel shame, but if you do . . ." He paused, regrouped. "You can move beyond regret and accusation and live a true life."

Ellen stared at him a moment. "Where is this coming from?"

"I care. That's all." He shrugged, standing. "As you know, we have Bible study at the house on Wednesday evenings. I want you to know you're invited."

"That's rich," Ellen said. "Wash U professor attends Bible study at family home of ex-lover."

Trey shouldered his backpack. "The only ones who would say that are the ones talking about you anyway." He started to the door, then turned back. "I don't know how well you know Cyd London, professor in the classics department. Even if you don't come to the study, she's always there on Wednesdays. She's a good person to talk to—not saying you need someone to talk to, but if you do."

He felt her eyes on him as he walked out the door.

Chapter Forty-Nine

Kendra stepped out of her car in front of Cafe Napoli in downtown Clayton, happy to let a valet do the parking and excited about lunch with two high school buddies she hadn't seen in years. They'd heard about her sickness and had offered to come by the house, but Kendra thought it would be depressing to see them like that. She wanted to get out, pretend it was old times.

Kendra saw Lisa and Audrey on the outdoor patio soaking in the seventy-five-degree day. Their hands waved wildly when they glimpsed her, and on impulse she started to respond in kind. But the girl who once did backflips in a cheerleader's uniform couldn't lift her arm. She smiled big instead as she made her way to them.

They got up to greet her, squealing.

"Oh my gosh, it's so good to see you!" Lisa said.

"It's been way too long!" Audrey added.

Maybe it was the head scarf or the slowness of her gait or perhaps they just knew, but their hugs were soft, as if handling a porcelain doll.

"I've missed you guys!" Kendra said, joining them at the table.

It was weird. The first thing she noticed about people now was hair. And Lisa and Audrey had lots of it, full and beautiful. The next thing Kendra noticed was energy. They had lots of that too.

"I can't believe you've been here since June and haven't called anybody," Lisa said. She seemed to catch herself. "Not that you weren't preoccupied."

"Definitely a little busy," Kendra said with a smile. "It's been a whirlwind really. I haven't had time to do ordinary life things like catch up with friends."

"I saw it with my sister," Audrey said. "Cancer supersedes everything." She eyed Kendra sympathetically. "Ken, I was so shocked when I heard. I mean, you're thirty-two."

Kendra had figured she would run into someone she knew at the hospital eventually, and it had happened last week when she saw another high school friend. She'd gotten an influx of calls since then.

"And what's it called again," Audrey asked, "the type of breast cancer you have?"

"Inflammatory breast cancer," Kendra said.

"I've never heard of it," Lisa said. "How did you even learn you had it?"

Kendra explained what she saw in the bathtub and how she researched it online, followed by the doctor visits.

"So this is a breast cancer where there might not be a lump?" Audrey asked.

"That's right," Kendra said. "There might be redness, a pitted-orange appearance, swelling. And for some reason, it affects a lot of women in their thirties."

"Oh my gosh." Lisa spoke in a hushed tone, as if contemplating it all.

Audrey was shaking her head. "It's so hard to believe. And are they really saying . . . it's terminal?"

"That's the nature of the disease, yes," Kendra said. "Some people live long with it, and by long, that could be five years."

"Five years?" Lisa said. "That's not long at all."

"Or it could be two or three," Kendra said. "Ultimately, it's in God's hands."

"Oh, Ken, it's almost too much to fathom," Lisa said.

"Ladies, how are we doing this lovely afternoon?"

The three of them looked at the server, and his question hung in the air for a moment.

"We're doing just great," Lisa said, smiling big, which made them release the heaviness.

Once they'd placed their orders and the server had left, Kendra said, "I'm determined that this lunch is one thing cancer won't supersede. Let's talk about you girls. What have you been up to?" She looked at Lisa. "You're still at the bank, right?"

"Yep, two blocks over," Lisa said. "Still in mortgage lending."

"What about Brady?" Kendra asked. "How's he doing?"

"Brady's good," Lisa said. "Packed on a few pounds since high school, so you probably wouldn't recognize him."

Kendra smiled. "I can't even picture Brady bigger."

"Ah, here you go." Lisa pulled out her phone and showed a picture of the two of them. "I tell him it just means there's more to love."

"Brings back memories of the high school sweethearts," Kendra said. "And Brady's looking stylish in that suit." She turned to Audrey. "And you, Miss Mom, I'm ready to gush all over again at your news."

"I almost feel bad talking about it," Audrey said.

"Don't be," Kendra said. "You're pregnant with your first baby, and I want to celebrate that with you. Life is so precious."

"It really is," Audrey said. "We saw the sonogram for the first time two weeks ago, and I cried when I saw his teeny-weeny toes."

"I did, too," Lisa said, "with both kids. I'm such a sentimental nut."

Kendra shooed away the sadness. She truly did want to celebrate the gift of life and being a mom, even if she might never experience it.

The server set their salads before them and freshened their waters. Kendra said a silent prayer as her friends dug in.

"So, wait"—Lisa lifted Kendra's hand—"are you still wearing the ring from your ex-fiancé?"

"I gave Derek his ring back the day we broke up," Kendra said. They'd talked about him briefly on the phone. "This is a very new ring," she said, smiling. "*This week* new."

They both gasped. "You're engaged again?" Lisa said. "No way!"

"How did that happen?" Audrey asked.

Kendra tossed the dressing in her spinach salad. "The way it happened was just . . . so unexpected . . . He's really been there for me since I returned."

"Well, who is it?" Lisa asked. "Do we know him?"

Kendra felt a little something inside. She almost wanted to say no and move on. But it wouldn't be true.

"You might remember him," Kendra said. "His name is Lance Alexander."

The brows of both furrowed. "Where would we know him from?"

"He went to high school with us, briefly."

It registered with Lisa first. "Not the guy who got in that fight—"

"And broke Mr. Magnetti's nose?" Audrey finished it for her. "And didn't I hear he was locked up for a while?"

Lisa looked at Audrey. "Seriously?" She turned to Kendra. "And you're engaged to him? What's up with that?"

"What do you mean, 'what's up with that'?"

"Well, to be honest," Lisa said, "I wouldn't think of him as your type. Derek, that was your type—successful attorney. But—"

"You see where my 'type' got me." Kendra's arm was shaking, and not from the illness but because she was getting upset. "What you know about Lance took place almost two decades ago. He's a man of God now. A youth pastor. And he loves me and treats me in a way that Derek isn't even capable of."

"I'm sorry," Lisa said. "I didn't mean to offend. Who knows what decisions I might make if I were in your situation."

Kendra paused her fork. "So my engagement to Lance can be excused because of my illness?"

The server approached. "Ladies, your entrees will be out momentarily. Are you still working on your salads?"

Kendra sat back. "I'm done, thank you."

The other two indicated the same, and the server cleared away their plates, refreshing their waters before leaving. All three seemed to need a sip.

"Ken, I'm sorry," Lisa said again, setting her glass down. "What I meant was . . . if I were in your situation, I'm sure I wouldn't be tied to what I would *normally* do. And that's a good thing, obviously. Life sometimes forces us to think outside the box."

Kendra had to smile. "That's actually been the mantra around the house, thinking outside the box." She sighed. "I'm sorry, you guys, for getting in a huff. If the shoe were on the other foot, I'd be surprised and asking questions too. It's just, I love Lance more than I've ever loved anyone. I hadn't realized I was so protective of him."

"Protect your man, girl." Audrey smiled. "He's got to be special to stand with you through all of this. And shoot, as I think about it, I'm sure none of us at this table would want to be judged based on our behavior in high school."

"Nooo," the others chorused, back to laughter.

The server returned with their entrees and began doling them out.

Kendra thought about Lance, how much he'd been there for her. She could never thank him enough. She slipped her phone from her purse and texted him.

I'M TAKING YOUR PIC WHEN I GET HOME.

Seconds later he replied. WHY?

She smiled as she typed. YOU'RE MY "GOD'S GOODNESS" OF THE DAY.

CHAPTER FIFTY

KENDRA AND LANCE WALKED INTO THE MAIN OFFICE OF THE local elementary school, looking like harried parents.

The front desk secretary acknowledged them. "May I help you?"

"We're here to pick up Brooklyn Patterson," Kendra said. "Her mom said to come here."

"Yes, Ms. Patterson did call to let us know you were coming." The secretary pulled out a piece of paper. "May I see a form of ID, please?"

They dug out their driver's licenses and showed them.

"Very good," the woman said. "Please have a seat. Brooklyn is still in with the principal."

Kendra looked at Lance as they nestled into the hard plastic chairs. "I still can't believe Brookie got in a fight."

"The report was that she started it," Lance said. "That's why she's suspended."

"Give me a break. Why would they suspend third graders anyway?"

Lance gave her a look. "So they don't grow up to be fighting in high school."

The principal's door opened and Brooklyn trudged out, peeping up at them and then dropping her head back down. Her thick curls were in a loose ponytail with lots of flyaway hairs, and her cute shorts had streaks of dirt on them.

Behind her, the principal extended her hand. "I'm Mrs. Downes," she said.

"I remember you." Kendra smiled, shaking her hand. "You taught second grade when I was here."

"Tell me your name," Mrs. Downes said.

"Kendra Woods."

"Why, yes," the principal said, smiling as well. "I remember you and, later, your brother." It seemed to register. "And I understand your connection to Brooklyn as well."

Kendra nodded. "She's my sister. Her mother asked if we could come get her, since she's at a conference in Illinois today."

"I've already discussed Brooklyn's behavior with her mom." Mrs. Downes gave the little girl a pointed glance. "So I'll leave it to her to tell you two about it if she wants." She looked at Brooklyn again. "I'll see you on Friday, Brooklyn. Think about what we discussed."

Brooklyn stared at her sneakers. "Yes, ma'am."

Kendra signed her out on a clipboard, and they left the building for the five-minute walk to the Woodses' home.

Brooklyn got a little skip in her step. "What're you doing walking up here, Kendra?"

Kendra tweaked Brooklyn's nose. "Coming to get you. I couldn't believe you were fighting, so I had to come see for myself."

Brooklyn kept walking.

"Well?" Kendra said.

"Well, what?"

"Are you gonna tell us what happened?" Kendra asked.

"Do I have to?"

"I'd certainly like you to," Kendra said. "I told Lance I don't care what they said. You couldn't have started it."

Brooklyn turned, eyes narrowed. "I kicked that Sarah Bowman in the leg, and I'd do it again."

"Brooklyn! What did she do?"

"She said my mom is a whore and I'm a bastard."

Kendra gasped, turning to Lance. "And they suspended *Brookie?*" she whispered.

"Probably zero tolerance for physical assault," Lance said.

"What's a whore, anyway?" Brooklyn asked.

"Um . . ." Kendra looked at Lance again. "Sweetie, it's a bad word that kids shouldn't use."

"I already knew what a bastard was."

"What do you think it means, Brooklyn?"

"It means your daddy doesn't love you. That's what Sarah said."

"That's not what it means," Kendra said, "and there's no way Sarah would know that anyway, is there?" She didn't wait for a reply. "Brooklyn, kids just say mean things sometimes, and sadly, they usually get it from their parents. As hard as it is, you have to learn to ignore them."

Brooklyn turned up their street. "All I know is, if she says it again, I'm kicking her again."

Kendra gave Lance a look. She couldn't half blame her.

Brooklyn turned up the walkway. "When does my mom get back?"

"Later this evening," Kendra said.

"During Bible study?"

Kendra shrugged. "I don't know. Why?"

"I'll ask everybody to pray I don't get in trouble."

Brooklyn wasn't kidding. After the meal, when everyone had gathered in the living room, she took to the floor with Lance's permission.

"Could everyone please pray I don't get on punishment—"

"Brooklyn," Lance said, "you have to take your finger out of your mouth and speak up if you want people to hear you."

Brooklyn put her arm down and looked around at the faces. There were fourteen people in the room.

"Okay." She shook out her hands and took a breath. And cleared her throat. "Could you please pray I don't get on punishment . . . for fighting at school . . ." She took another breath. "Because Sarah Bowman called my mom a whore and me a bastard and I kicked her and then she kicked me and we were rolling on the ground and I got suspended."

Kendra's eyes widened along with Lance's. Those little details had been omitted earlier. The others in the room had wide eyes at the name-calling.

Brooklyn looked at Lance. "And that's it . . . I think."

Lance glanced around the room. "Would you all mind if we prayed for Brooklyn before we start the study?"

The adults quickly affirmed his suggestion, and they circled up and joined hands.

"Lord, we pray Ellen has mercy on Brooklyn," Trey said, "taking into account the words that started it, words that hurt Brooklyn's feelings. I pray You would shield Ellen and Brooklyn from words like that. And I pray You would be their peace and their joy."

"Lord, we lift up Ellen to You," Cyd said, "praying You give her wisdom as to how to respond to her daughter in this situation, and how to respond to those who treat them in hurtful ways. I pray,

Lord"—she took her time—"that You would use trying situations like this to draw Ellen and Brooklyn to Yourself. May they know how strong Your love is for them."

"I don't usually pray out loud, but . . ." Molly was standing next to Kendra. "Jesus, the name that girl called Ellen probably fit me more, but You saved me anyway. Can You save Ellen too? Oh, and praying no punishment for Brookie."

Brooklyn grinned.

When they were done, Brooklyn sat on the sofa with Kendra for the lesson and fell asleep partway through. She was still curled up there when Ellen arrived, passing others in the entryway as they departed. Ellen looked slightly confused by the hugs she got from a couple of them.

"Thank you for picking Brooklyn up and taking care of her." Ellen looked worn, her eyes drained. "I didn't know I'd be getting back this late."

"It was no problem at all," Kendra said. "As you can see, she's tuckered out."

"I still can't believe she got suspended for fighting."

"Well, you know what instigated it, right?"

"Mrs. Downes said the girl was name-calling, and Brooklyn hauled off and kicked her." Ellen ran her hands through her hair. "I've told Brooklyn a thousand times, names can't hurt you . . . just let it roll off."

"To be honest, Ellen," Kendra said, "it would be hard for me to let it roll off if someone called my mom a whore and me a bastard."

"That's . . . that's what the girl said to Brooklyn?"

Kendra nodded.

"Did she mention the girl's name?"

"Sarah something."

"Bowman?"

"That's it." Kendra said, "You know her?"

"Her mother works at the university." Ellen stared vaguely. "So now . . . now this crap is filtering down to the elementary school? Now my daughter has to fight on the playground to defend her mother?"

Kendra didn't know what to say.

Brooklyn stirred and, when she glimpsed her mother, sat up, rubbing her eyes.

Ellen pulled her to a hug. "Honey, let's get ready to go."

"Mom . . ." Brooklyn looked up at her. "Sorry I got suspended."

"We'll talk about it tomorrow, after you get some rest," Ellen said. "And we're especially going to talk about how to handle people in a proper way when they say rude things."

"Okay . . . but am I on punishment? Like, will you tell me I can't come play over here?"

Kendra's heart melted. Was that the punishment Brooklyn most feared?

Ellen rubbed her back. "I would never put you on that kind of punishment, Brooklyn."

"Thanks, Mom," Brooklyn said. "And, Mom?"

"Yes, honey?"

"I hate being a bastard. And I hate my daddy."

CHAPTER FIFTY-ONE

THE AFTERNOON SCENE NEARLY RESEMBLED THE NEW ORLEANS service project Lance had been part of a few years back. People pitching in, repairing, cleaning, painting. Part of his charge from Mr. Woods had been to take care of the house. And when he moved in, he'd seen lots of wear and tear, much of which—Trey now readily admitted—was collateral damage from parties. But Kendra's care had taken precedence. Now, with Mr. Woods set to return on Saturday, Lance wanted to get it spruced up for him. But he was no handyman, so he'd sounded the call for help.

"How's it going, guys?" He passed two friends from Living Word who were patching drywall in the hallway off the entryway. Wall damage there and in the lower level had been the biggest issue.

"It looked like somebody put a fist through the wall, if you can believe that," one of them said.

"Oh, I can believe it," Lance said.

The guy backhanded sweat from his brow. "We'll be done with our part today, but it needs to dry. Then the painters can get to work on it."

"Sounds great." Lance patted them on the back. "I can't tell you how much I appreciate your help." He turned and watched another guy replacing pieces of cracked tile in the entryway. "Yours too, Mike. You guys are awesome."

Mike kept at his work. "No problem, buddy."

Lance peeked into the living room and gave a thumbs-up to Trey, who was steam cleaning the carpet.

In the kitchen, Darla worked to replace a few knobs and pulls that had been broken or ripped off entirely.

"I just told Kendra: God smiled on you all," Darla announced. "They still make this style of pewter, and it was in stock."

Kendra looked up from the kitchen table. "And I told Darla: God's smiling on us by her being here to fix it."

"No trouble for me at all," Darla said. "It's good for me to get away from the house and all of Bernie's grousing." She looked back at her. "I could've been over here all along helping with cleaning and such. I'm sorry I didn't think of it."

"Aw, thanks," Kendra said. "Lance has actually been holding it down in the cleaning department. He may or may not be a little anal about it."

"Who, me? Because I posted a cleaning schedule of which rooms need to be cleaned, when, and by whom?" He grinned. "With Trey, Molly, and me here, there's no reason this house shouldn't be spic-and-span on a daily basis."

"That's right," Darla said. "Put the youngsters to work." Her phone chirped, and she looked at it. "See, this is the problem with smartphones. Bernie can grouse over the airwaves." She sighed. "Be right back. I'll go see what he needs."

"Be nice," Kendra said, smiling. She sighed seconds later, looking at Lance. "I'm sad Molly's leaving this week."

"You told her she didn't have to." Lance got back to work on one of his own projects of the week—taking everything out of the pantry, throwing away expired goods, and wiping down the shelves.

"I know, but she thinks it'll be awkward." Kendra sipped some of the smoothie Lance had made for her. "And Brooklyn won't be around while he's here either, according to Ellen."

"Well, what if he's back for good?" Lance asked.

"I don't know," Kendra said. "But I understand Ellen's position. She wants Dad to be the one to initiate a relationship. If Brooklyn's over here, Ellen wants her to feel accepted and welcomed by him."

Lance glanced at the dates on two boxes of cereal and tossed them out. "I have no idea what things will be like when your father comes, but the dynamics are about to change significantly."

Kendra fell silent for a while. Then she said, "I almost wish my dad would stay where he is. I like the dynamics as they are."

CHAPTER FIFTY-TWO

KENDRA HAD DONE A MENTAL SEESAW BETWEEN THE BED AND the sofa. The effects of chemo number five had kicked in with pain and fatigue and the head-to-toe discomfort that demanded all-day horizontal. Her bed was most comfortable, and given the day, preferable. She could delay the inevitable with good reason.

But she felt antsy in bed, as if she shouldn't be there. So reluctantly, in late afternoon, she made her way to the sofa to await her father's arrival.

"Shouldn't he be here by now?" she asked.

Lance sat with her on the sofa. "I should've gone to get him."

"He said he was fine taking a taxi."

"I know, but still . . ."

Trey came downstairs, joining them. "Is it just me, or is it immensely quiet without Brooklyn and Molly?"

"Brooklyn is a force all by herself," Kendra said. "It's amazing how much life she's added to the house in a short time."

"I think she should be here right now," Trey said. "Dad shouldn't be able to act like she doesn't exist."

"I'm with Ellen on this," Kendra said. "What if she's here and doesn't feel embraced? That would be devastating."

"Dad wouldn't diss her if she's right in his face."

"Who knows what his frame of mind—"

A key in the door made the room fall silent.

The door opened, and for a quick moment Kendra remembered the butterflies of youth, when her daddy got home from work and she'd run to the door. Now she waited, and seconds later he appeared.

He looked older, though he was only fifty-eight. Less hair on top, and more gray in what he had. At six three and over two hundred pounds, he'd always been an imposing figure, with a personality that made him gentle. But right now he just looked tired, and Kendra didn't know if it was the long trip or the long months that had passed between them. He set down two big pieces of luggage.

Trey walked over to him, and without a word they embraced. Marlon lingered there. "It's good to see you, son."

"It's good to see you too, Dad," Trey said.

"Sir, welcome home," Lance said, shaking his hand. "I'm glad you made it safely."

"Lance, it's a pleasure to see you," Marlon said. "You've blessed this home tremendously."

"The blessing has been mine," Lance said. "I can't thank you enough for your kindness in allowing me to stay here."

Lance stepped aside, and Marlon set his gaze on his daughter. He came slowly toward her, his eyes taking in the whole of her.

Kendra moved to sit up.

"No," Marlon said. "Stay where you are." He came to his knees beside the couch and brought Kendra gently to himself—and wept. "I've been asking God over and over—why? When I heard you were sick . . ."

Kendra didn't know all that had been bottled up until now, as she wept with him. She'd missed her dad. Really missed him.

"How'd you know I was sick?" she whispered on his neck.

"Pastor Lyles thought I should know." He looked at her. "It grieved me that we had grown so distant that you hadn't told me. It grieved me that I'd made such a mess of my life and of relationships that mean the world to me." He was filled with emotion still. "I had to come home."

Trey moved the piano bench so their dad could sit beside Kendra.

"Thank you, son," Marlon said.

Trey took the floor beside her. Kendra heard the door close to the lower level and realized Lance had left them alone.

"I don't know where we start." Forearms on his thighs, Marlon looked with pained eyes from one of his children to the other. "I asked God the entire flight—Where do we start? Where do we begin to bridge this gap? There's so much ground to cover."

"Some of it has been bridged already," Trey said.

"How so, son?"

"We've gotten to know Brooklyn very well . . . and as a result, we interact with Ellen on a regular basis."

Marlon sat back, stunned. "How?" he asked. "How did that happen?"

"Trey was moved to find our sister and meet her," Kendra said, "and when we met her, a relationship was inevitable. She's infectious." Kendra paused. "And, Dad, I talked to Ellen about what happened between you."

Marlon hesitated. "She told you everything?"

"She told me her side of things."

"I think . . . I might've stumbled on another piece of the puzzle this week," Trey said.

Kendra frowned. "You didn't tell me that. What are you talking about?"

"I didn't know what to make of it," Trey said, "and I knew Dad was coming. So I thought we'd find out together."

"What do you mean, Trey?" Marlon said.

Trey was slow to begin. "I can count the number of times I've been in your room since Mom died," he said. "Only if I need something . . . in and out. But I steam cleaned the carpet in there this week, and under the bed . . ."

"What is it?" Kendra asked.

"I found a letter Mom wrote. Probably shouldn't have read it, but . . . finding anything of Mom's . . ." He sighed. "It was dated shortly before she died, written to another man."

Kendra felt a jolt inside. "What?"

"I'll just read it," Trey said. "It's short." He pulled it out of his pocket and opened it.

> *Lloyd,*
>
> *I appreciate your concern, but I can't see you. When we went our separate ways, I had to commit in my heart that I would never see you again. My illness doesn't change that. Part of me will always love you too. But that love was born out of a sinful relationship. I have to be true to God, even now.*
>
> *His,*
> *Cynthia*

Trey folded it. "I guess she never sent it."

"She didn't have to," Marlon said. "Lloyd called, and I was with her when she said essentially the same over the phone."

"What are you saying?" Kendra grasped for the truth, but this truth was too foreign. "Mom had an affair too? What, as payback for yours? This is crazy."

Marlon exhaled. "I really wish you hadn't found that, Trey," he said, "but maybe this bridge is from the Lord." He stared down a moment. "The truth is . . . your mother's affair was before mine. I discovered an e-mail in which they spoke about a trip they'd taken together. When I approached her, she didn't deny it. She said she loved him."

Kendra felt her world slipping a little more out of orbit. If Trey hadn't found the letter, she never would have believed it.

"As I was dealing with the pain of that," Marlon said, "I'd talk to Ellen. Classic mistake, but for more than a year, Ellen and I were just friends as I walked through this." He paused. "When your mom said she wanted to be with him—that she wanted a divorce—I lost it. And I turned to Ellen in the wake of that."

"But you and Mom obviously stayed together," Trey said. "What happened?"

"You know that Mason—Pastor Lyles—and I are friends. He had been praying for us and began counseling us. It was extremely rocky at first. We laid everything on the table, everything we'd done . . . And surprisingly, when I thought we were too far gone, somehow God took the tiny spark that was left and rekindled it."

"But wait a minute . . ." Kendra put on her attorney cap. "You said you laid everything on the table. This was years before Mom got sick, right?"

"That's right," Marlon said.

"But she didn't know about your affair until she got sick, when Ellen came over and talked to her."

"Mom knew about Ellen years before that," Marlon said. "What she didn't know was that Ellen had gotten pregnant. I didn't know, either, at the time of our counseling sessions." He looked at them both. "When I found out, we'd just gotten to a point where it looked like our marriage could work again. I was so afraid that it would be the last straw, that your mom would walk away, go straight to Lloyd, if she knew about this baby." He sighed. "I'm ashamed to admit that, out of fear, I wanted Ellen to abort that baby. I would've never thought I could sink that low . . . I kept it secret for the same reason."

Kendra and Trey sat in silence, processing, both no doubt grieving the pain their parents experienced . . . the pain their own kids never knew about.

"Dad," Trey said finally, "why didn't you tell us about Mom's affair? Clearly, you knew we were angry with you and blamed you for everything."

"I didn't want that to be your memory of your mother," Marlon said. "I was fine letting it go to the grave with her."

"But what about Brooklyn, Dad?" Kendra said. "Why did you cut off communication with her?"

He took time to respond. "When things are done in the dark, there's always a cloud. I lived with the fear that your mom would find out. I'd sneak to visit, sneak to call . . . and yet, this was my daughter. So I began looking for the right time to tell your mother—then she got sick." He sighed. "It was no longer just a matter of protecting our marriage. It was also protecting her health, wanting her remaining days—our remaining days—to be joyful, stress-free. And as you know, cancer is time-intensive. I needed to be with her. All of this meant I pulled away from Brooklyn."

"What about after Mom died?" Trey said.

"By then I was so upset with Ellen for telling your mom that I'd stopped communicating with her." Marlon seemed bothered by it even now. "She took our last few months together, and she knew Cynthia was sick."

"Dad . . ." Kendra had more emotions than she could manage

right now. "As upset as I've been with Ellen for doing that, she shared something with me that altered my view."

Marlon looked surprised. "What was that?"

"She was coming to talk to *you*, and only because Brooklyn had been crying for ten nights straight, asking why her daddy didn't love her anymore."

Marlon stared at Kendra, then at the ground.

Kendra closed her eyes. Of all she'd heard today, the thing that probably grieved her most was that little Brooklyn had gotten hit in the crossfire.

CHAPTER FIFTY-THREE

LANCE HAD SET A TABLE FOR FOUR IN THE DINING ROOM AND prepared a special meal. After the heavy conversation earlier, which Kendra had told him about, dinner talk seemed purposefully light, mostly about Marlon's time at the University of Ghana and venturing around the country itself. But even those stories carried the undertone that he'd gone to escape the heartache and the scandal.

Marlon was eyeing his daughter. "Ken, I have to tell you: it's a blessing to see you in such good spirits. I didn't expect that."

"Oh, I've been a yo-yo, trust me." Kendra ate lemon sherbet while the others had chocolate cake. "You should've been here two weeks ago."

"She's not lying either," Trey said.

Kendra made a face at him, then touched Lance's shoulder. "The blessing has been this man's effect on my life."

Marlon held them both in his gaze. "As a father, it pains me beyond belief to see my daughter suffering this way, and yet my heart soars knowing she has you, Lance." He drank his ice water. "That was one of the sweetest surprises ever."

Kendra's brown eyes narrowed a little at Lance. "I still can't believe my dad knew you were proposing before I did."

"That's kind of how it's supposed to work," Lance said.

"But he was all the way in Africa, and let's be real . . . Dad and I weren't exactly speaking."

"That had nothing to do with me," Lance said. "Mr. Woods has been nothing but kind to me, and out of sheer respect, I wouldn't ask to marry you apart from his blessing."

"And it took all of two seconds to think about it. And please, call me Marlon."

Lance smiled. "I appreciate that."

"So, Dad, are you here for good, or are you going back to Ghana?" Trey asked. "I thought your sabbatical was until the end of this semester."

"It is, officially," Marlon said, "but there was no way I could stay overseas once I got the news about Kendra. I'm here for good, but still praying about what I'll do."

"You're still on the faculty at Wash U, aren't you, Daddy?" Kendra said.

"Yes, but I'm not sure if I'll return to campus this semester, do research at home, or what."

"Mr. Woods . . ." Lance paused. "It'll take me awhile to get used to not calling you that . . . Now that you're back, I don't want to assume that I can continue to stay—"

Marlon held up a hand, shaking his head. "Nonsense, young man. You're about to be family, which is all the more reason to stay . . . unless you and Kendra want to move out and give your money away to a landlord."

"I'm thankful," Lance said. "It'll be easier on Kendra if she doesn't have to uproot and move somewhere else."

"Hmm," Kendra said, "then I guess the only question is whether I'm moving to the lower level or Lance is moving upstairs with me."

She leaned over and winced. "At the moment though, I think I do need to uproot and move somewhere else to lie down."

Trey stood with his cake. "Let's all move to the living room."

When they'd settled there, Marlon looked long at his daughter. "Ken, you said you have one more chemo session. What happens after that?"

"Testing," Kendra said. "MRIs, cat scans . . . They have to see how effective the chemo has been and whether I can be cleared for surgery."

"This is surgery for a mastectomy?"

"Right. And even though cancer was found in one breast, I'm having a double mastectomy, just in case."

"Okay, so you recover from the surgery . . . Then what?"

"Then I start radiation," Kendra said, "then more chemo."

"And . . . because it's already spread . . ." Marlon couldn't finish his thought.

Kendra nodded. "You already know from walking this out with Mom. Even with all of that, they're not trying to cure me. They don't have a cure. That would take a miracle. They're just trying to prolong my life."

"I'm almost afraid to ask," Marlon said. "How long . . . Is there a time frame . . ."

"What's the life expectancy?" Kendra asked.

"Yes, that's what I'm wondering," Marlon said, "taken totally with a grain of salt. I know God is ultimately in control."

"Amen," Lance said.

"The thing about inflammatory breast cancer," Kendra began, "is that it's aggressive. It grows quickly, and it's likely to come back after treatment."

Lance found it interesting how Kendra could spew the facts from her head with ease at times, but it could turn on a dime.

"The official stats say that 60 to 70 percent of women with the disease don't live five years beyond the diagnosis." Kendra stared away for a moment. "But I've been following this one particular blog, and the woman died this week after . . . after being diagnosed just last year."

"Each case is different," Marlon said.

"I know, but . . ." Kendra took a moment. "She was Stage IV like me, and it was in her neck at diagnosis, like mine."

Lance felt the tears just beneath the surface. He did whenever he thought of losing Kendra, but that it could be as soon as next year was almost unbearable. He had to stay strong for her, had to inject optimism and hope—and it was real. He *was* hopeful. How could they not have hope in Christ? But he loved this woman with every fiber of his being.

Lord, I pray You give Kendra long life, that You would give the two of us long life together on this earth. I'm praying for the miracle.

CHAPTER FIFTY-FOUR

KENDRA HAD PUSHED FOR THE MEETING. HER DAD HAD BEEN back only a day—not a long time—but too much time had already passed. A year and a half, to be exact. There was a little girl who needed to see her daddy, who needed to know her daddy.

Besides, this was Kendra's wedding week. And *this* wedding week she was determined to enjoy as best she could. Which meant she wanted all her loved ones around. She'd figured after church would be a good time to bring it up. When Marlon returned with Lance and Trey, she said simply, "Brooklyn needs you. I'd love to invite her over today."

Marlon had hesitated, and Kendra was certain his thoughts encompassed Ellen, whether he was ready to see her. But his response came quickly, and it was short. "Yes," was all he said.

Ellen had been another story. When Kendra called, she wanted to know how things would go and what Marlon would say. Kendra tried to reassure her that he really did want to see Brooklyn. At least she thought he did, though he hadn't outright said it. Next, Ellen asked whether an apology would be forthcoming, saying she couldn't imagine a meeting without one.

Kendra suggested that both she and Marlon put aside their own issues and let Brooklyn be with her dad, and Ellen finally agreed.

Trey had Brooklyn's favorite games at the ready. Kendra wasn't sure if it was meant to help their dad or if her brother was preparing to step in himself, if need be. Kendra only had energy enough to hang on the sofa, but she intended to stay awake for that same reason. Brooklyn would have a good time regardless, if they had anything to do with it.

The doorbell rang a little past four o'clock. Kendra expected Brooklyn would ride her bike down as she always did when it was light out, but when Trey opened the door, Kendra heard both Brooklyn's and Ellen's voices.

When Brooklyn came into view, Kendra did a double take. She'd never seen the little girl in a dress. It was a chic-looking, green-and-blue, color-blocked fabric, with matching socks and navy ballet flats with glitter. Her hair was neatly coiffed, with a blue ribbon tied around her ponytail.

"Brookie, I missed you!" Kendra extended her arms. It had only been two days, but it seemed like weeks.

Brooklyn's eyes darted around before she came running to Kendra for a hug.

"You look so pretty," Kendra said. "Is that a new dress?"

Brooklyn beamed. "Got it today."

Ellen walked over, giving Kendra a look. "She insisted we run to the mall."

Something about that hurt Kendra's heart. Did Brooklyn feel she had to look a certain way to be loved?

Heavy footsteps sounded on the stairway, and everyone seemed to pause. Ellen cleared her throat, bringing Brooklyn near.

Marlon walked into the living room, and Ellen stared him down.

He approached anyway, and Brooklyn moved behind her mother, looking away.

"Ellen," Marlon said, "there's a lot we need to discuss. I'm sure we agree now is not the place or the time, but hopefully very soon. Is that okay?"

Ellen eyed him. "I've been looking forward to a discussion, so yes."

Marlon took a floor seat next to Kendra. "Brooklyn, may I talk to you?"

Brooklyn shifted slightly, peeking out from behind her mother.

"Brooklyn," Marlon said, "I haven't been a good dad. I haven't called you like I should. I haven't seen you in way too long—and look at you, you're so much taller . . . Brooklyn, I'm sorry . . ."

Kendra looked down, surprised by her dad's tears, which started her own.

"I've asked God to forgive me," Marlon continued, "and one day, I hope you find it in your heart to forgive me too." He let the tears slide. "You're my daughter, and I love you. I hope you'll allow me to be in your life, to get to know you." He glanced at Kendra. "When Kendra was your age, she used to beg to get ice cream from Maggie Moo's or pizza from Imo's. I want to learn the things you like and enjoy them with you."

Brooklyn pulled on Ellen, and she bent down and listened as her daughter whispered.

Ellen looked over at Marlon. "Brooklyn says she likes Maggie Moo's too."

"Yeah!" Trey said, smiling.

"I don't know if you've had Sunday dinner yet," Marlon said, "but how would you like to go right now, with Trey and me?"

"Umm . . ." Brooklyn twisted around without moving from her spot. "I think I'd like it okay." She looked at Ellen. "Can I, Mommy?"

Ellen's face had the makings of a *no*. "You haven't eaten yet," she said, staring into her daughter's pleading eyes, "but go ahead."

"Thank you, Mommy!" Brooklyn hugged her waist. "And I can just eat here." She took her hand and led her to the door. "Okay, Mommy, I'll be fine now."

"Oh my goodness, Brooklyn, you're ushering me out?"

"No. Just saying you can go home."

Trey laughed. "I guess she's back in the saddle, Ellen. We'll make sure she gets home safely."

"Thanks, Trey." Ellen looked at Marlon.

"Call you tomorrow?" Marlon said.

"That'll be fine," Ellen said.

She walked out, and a moment later Brooklyn ran to the door.

"Wait! Mom? Can you bring me back a change of clothes? I can't play right in this dress."

Chapter Fifty-Five

October

KENDRA WAS BANISHED FROM HER OWN HOUSE.

She'd been bedridden more than usual and unable to wedding-plan the way she wanted. Simplicity was all she was after, but even that took energy and focus she couldn't muster. In frustration she'd finally said, "I need a fairy godmother who can wave a magic wand and make a wedding appear."

Without missing a beat, Lance had replied, "Your wish is my command. A wedding you shall have."

Kendra laughed. "If only you could plan a wedding."

"Oh?" Lance said. "You don't think I could do it?"

"I think you could plan a ceremony," Kendra said, "as in, call the justice of the peace and ask what hours they're open."

"Okay." He nodded, smiling revenge. "I'm planning the wedding."

"You're not planning the wedding."

"I'm planning the wedding."

She didn't believe him until he picked up the phone and implemented the first part of his plan—her exile. He asked Cyd if Kendra could stay at her home the Friday before the wedding, so whatever plans were made could be a surprise. And now that Friday was here, Cyd's chariot had whisked her away in the early evening.

Kendra glanced at Cyd as she drove the three blocks to her house. "Any idea what Lance is up to?"

Cyd smiled at her. "Not totally."

"Can you give an inkling of what you do know?"

"Not a bit."

Kendra glanced around as Cyd pulled into her driveway. "Are all these cars at *your* house?"

Cyd cut the engine. "You're always looking for evidence, aren't you?"

"And you're always responding without responding."

Cedric came out the front door. "I'm charged with making sure you get safely inside."

"Lance is ridiculous," Kendra said. "Please tell that man I can walk."

"Nevertheless," Cedric said, "I'm doing my duty."

He opened her door and helped her out as Cyd grabbed her bags from the trunk. Leading her inside, they stepped across the threshold—

"Surprise!"

A small army of women greeted her in the entryway. Kendra saw Molly, Jess, Darla . . . and lots of other faces she didn't recognize, all of them smiling.

Kendra smiled back at them. "What is this?"

"We'll explain that very shortly," Cyd said from behind.

Cedric whispered to his wife, "If you all are okay, I'll head on over to the Woodses' home."

Kendra turned. "Why? What's happening at my house?"

"Oh, never you mind," Cedric said.

Cyd took over, looping Kendra's arm in hers. "We have a special place for you in the family room," she said, leading her there.

The women parted so they could pass and followed behind.

"Where's Chase?" Kendra asked.

"He and the dog are giving my dad more gray hairs right about now," Cyd said. "Mom is in that crowd of women behind us."

Kendra stopped when she saw the room—festive white balloons filled the ceiling, trays of food and assorted beverages were on a table in the corner, and the focal point of the room was a cushiony recliner outfitted with a plush white blanket, a white pillow, and white fuzzy slippers at the base.

"This is so beautiful," Kendra said.

"Let me escort you," Cyd said.

She helped Kendra get settled into the recliner and exchanged her shoes for the slippers.

"What can I get you to eat and drink?" Cyd asked and told her the choices.

Kendra smiled. "I'll take the peanut butter crackers"—she knew they were specially ordered for her—"and water will be great. Thanks."

The other women got appetizer plates and drinks and filled the sofa, love seat, and floor space. Molly plopped down on the floor by Kendra and grinned up at her.

When everyone was seated, Cyd stood in the middle of the room. "I'm so excited about this evening," she said. "And I'm moved by your presence because many of you don't even know Kendra personally. But you know her family, and when I shared her story with you, you wanted to be here."

Cyd walked closer to Kendra. "Ken, I wanted to give you a bridal shower, but I knew you'd said no gifts."

Kendra nodded. She'd done a registry with Derek and had to return gifts to people who'd sent them early. This time around, material gifts weren't a priority. Celebrating love with friends and family was their gift of choice.

"Most of the women here are from Living Word, and I've known many of them for years. And instead of showering you with gifts," Cyd said, smiling, "we're going to shower you with wisdom!"

Cheers went up around the room, and Kendra got goose bumps. These women didn't know her, but wanted to take part in this?

When they quieted, Cyd continued. "As you all know, Kendra is battling a rare and aggressive form of breast cancer called inflammatory breast disease. It has already spread and is considered incurable. Thus, Kendra is very aware that tomorrow is not promised and that every day is a gift from above to be treasured."

Kendra felt the eyes around the room on her. But she felt the love behind them as well.

"But here's the thing," Cyd said. "Shouldn't we *all* live with that awareness? Tomorrow is not promised for any of us, though we tend to live like it is. I know for myself—I don't treat every day as a gift. I don't ask how I can make the most of it, to the glory of God. But in watching Kendra, I'm learning, and I'm thankful for that. And that's what inspired the idea for this shower."

Cyd picked up a Bible from the coffee table. "Molly, will you read our two shower verses?"

Molly jumped up and turned to a bookmarked page. "From James chapter 4: 'Yet you do not know what your life will be like tomorrow. You are just a vapor that appears for a little while and then vanishes away.' And"—she turned back a few pages—"in 1 Timothy 6 we are told to fix our hope on God, 'who richly supplies us with all things to enjoy.'"

"Thanks, Molly," Cyd said. "So, knowing our life is a vapor and we should enjoy the days God gives us, each woman was challenged to come up with a wisdom gift." She smiled, looking at Kendra. "They're going to share their wisdom as to how you can enjoy every day God gives you—in life and, in particular, in your marriage to Lance."

"Ooh, I'm looking forward to hearing these," Kendra said.

"They've written their wisdom nuggets on keepsake note cards for you to take with you as well." She looked around the room. "Who's going first?"

A hand went up. "I'll go." The woman stepped forward. "Kendra, my name is Dana. I grew up with Cyd at Living Word, and I think I remember you. Were you in a Christmas play the teens put on one year—one of the worship dancers?"

"Oh wow, I forgot I did that," Kendra said. "And I can't believe you remember it!"

"Yes, it was awesome," Dana said. "Okay, this is very simple wisdom from a woman who's been married eighteen years and dealt with a very public ordeal of my husband cheating on me, yet experienced God's faithfulness." She opened her note card. "God is faithful every single day. In the sun and in the rain. In the chirping of birds outside your window. In the embrace of your soon-to-be husband's arms. Look for His faithfulness daily. Be blessed by it."

Dana put the note card in a basket on the table. "I knew I couldn't do it without crying," she said, grabbing a tissue as she sat down.

Kendra slid a finger under her eyelid. "If this is any indication how the evening will go, I need two boxes of tissues over here." She looked at Dana. "Thank you."

Another woman got up and came forward. "I won't even try not to cry," she said, "because I'm so moved by all of this." She smiled sweetly at Kendra. "My name is Kelly, and I'm Cyd's sister-in-law—"

"Oh, Cedric's sister?" Kendra said. "I've heard so much about you and your husband's music ministry."

Kelly nodded. "Then you might know that in our concerts we talk about how we aborted our baby back when we were teens." She paused, exhaled. "And it's given me a unique perspective on life. So . . ." She looked at her note card. "Every day of life is a day purposed by God, a day purposed for you. Ask what He wants to do in you. Whose life does He want to impact through you? And whatever the day brings, know that God loves you fiercely, cares for you completely, and watches over you zealously."

Kendra was playing back the words already. She tended to dwell on the days she wouldn't have. But living for today, knowing it counts, has purpose . . . "Kelly, that was on time. Thank you."

"I'd like to go next," a woman said.

Kendra wondered how she'd missed her. It was Pastor Lyles's wife.

"Kendra, I'm Thelma Lyles, and I'm so blessed to be here."

"I'm blessed to have you here," Kendra said. She'd never really known Mrs. Lyles, but the pastor's wife had always been kind. She'd seen her last at her mother's funeral.

"I don't know if you knew this, Kendra, but I had breast cancer in my forties," Mrs. Lyles said. "It was Stage II, and I had a mastectomy and radiation. My wisdom stems from that perspective." She put on her glasses and opened her card. "God will love you through your husband. He will care for you through your husband. He will even spoil you through your husband. When Lance anticipates your need, even when he overestimates your need, receive it as specially packaged by God. *Lance* is your gift, specially packaged by God. Enjoy your gift, girl."

Mrs. Lyles's words seemed so simple. Kendra knew God had blessed her with Lance. But she'd never thought of it as God's loving her, caring for her, even spoiling her through Lance.

Kendra held her tissue. "I can't wait to show Lance this one, Mrs. Lyles. Are you sure he didn't write it?"

Mrs. Lyles chuckled as she dropped the note in the basket and went back to her seat.

Two hours later, Kendra had been saturated with such wisdom that it felt like her soul was sloshing in the goodness of God—as if He'd arranged the night, the words, the love, just for her. Which He had. But it was hard to wrap her mind around it.

As much as Kendra's spirit soared, though, by the time the women had gone, she was beyond fatigued. Cyd showed her to her room and made sure she had everything she needed.

"Don't you hesitate to call out if you need anything else," Cyd said. "And if your mouth hurts too much to call out, pick up your phone. I'll come."

"I'm so overwhelmed by what you did tonight," Kendra said. "I'll never forget this."

"As Mrs. Lyles said, this was God loving you through every woman who was here," Cyd said. "You probably have no idea how much it blesses all of us to witness the love you and Lance share. It's beautiful, Ken." She grinned, shoulders hunched. "And you're getting married! Tomorrow!"

Kendra smiled, her eyes closing on their own, her thoughts stretching toward the man she missed greatly, only a couple blocks away. Lance Alexander.

CHAPTER FIFTY-SIX

THE LAST THING LANCE EXPECTED TO BE WAS NERVOUS. HE knew he'd be worried about everything coming together. He'd bitten off way more than he could chew.

But wedding plans wouldn't make him nervous. It was marriage that was making him nervous. Being a husband—a good husband—that was making him nervous. He'd never seen it modeled in the home. And he'd never known anyone who married "in sickness" like this. How would he know what to do? It was one thing to come up to Kendra's room and ask what she needed. Now he'd be responsible for her, before God. That was huge.

Lance stared out the kitchen window at the workers who'd gotten started early in the backyard. He'd been careful to clear every phase of planning with Mr. Woods. But that was another thing—he wasn't sure how he felt about being here. He always figured he'd have his own house when he married. A small one, sure. But it would be his. Theirs. Would it be weird to live with his father-in-law? Was it okay to stay here for free, work less, and care for Kendra?

That's what he wanted to do, care for his wife. Like a job, but not a job. He wanted to give himself to it, learn what he needed to learn, help however he needed to help. Which also made him nervous. What if he failed?

Marlon came downstairs and into the kitchen. "Today's the day," he said, smiling.

Lance turned to him. "Yes, sir, it is."

"How are you feeling?" Marlon asked.

"Truthfully?" Lance said. "Nervous."

"That surprises me," Marlon said. "I don't think I've seen anyone more prepared for marriage."

Lance looked at him. "I don't understand why you'd say that. I don't make tons of money. I don't even have my own home."

"Son, there are countless men with a big bankroll and a large home who aren't prepared to be husbands," Marlon said. "You love the Lord. You have the heart of a servant. You're prepared for marriage the way Jesus intended."

Lance thought about that as Marlon joined him at the window.

"Do you think everything will be done in time?" the older man asked. "I'm beginning to wonder."

Lance chuckled lightly. "I started wondering days ago. They were able to do minor things while Kendra was here, but most of it had to wait until she was gone." He did a slow shrug. "I don't know. The good thing is the wedding's not until five o'clock."

Marlon got orange juice from the refrigerator. "And between now and five o'clock, we've got how many SWAT teams descending on the place?"

"I know," Lance said. "I'm sorry it's gotten out of hand."

"No, no, it's great." Marlon gestured toward him. "Orange juice?"

"Sure," Lance said. "Thanks."

"There's something very special happening here today." He poured Lance a glass and passed it to him. "I'm grateful I'm able to see it."

Lance wondered if Kendra's first planned wedding went through his head, the one he wasn't invited to.

"Join me for a minute at the table, Lance," Marlon said. "I'd like to talk to you about something."

Lance followed and sat across from him.

"There's so much going on today to prepare for the wedding," Marlon said. "I'm not sure if you've planned for after the wedding—specifically, moving your things into one room."

Lance let his head fall into his hand. "I knew I was forgetting something." He looked at Marlon. "You're right. I need to move Kendra's things downstairs. One more thing for the to-do list today."

"Actually, I'm offering another alternative," Marlon said. "I want you to take my room."

"I can't do that," Lance said. "That's your room, the one you and your wife shared for decades. There's no way we could move in there."

"I've given it a lot of thought," Marlon said, "and it makes sense. It gives you two added privacy as a married couple."

"Sir, we have plenty of privacy downstairs. That'll be just fine."

"Also," Marlon said, "the master bedroom is the only room with its own bathroom. Kendra needs that more than anyone."

Lance nodded. "It would be beneficial for Kendra, but I don't think it's a big enough deal to move you out of your space. There's a full bathroom downstairs."

"Okay," Marlon said. "I was going to wait to tell you and Kendra together, but since that wasn't enough to convince you . . ." His expression was kind. "I'm moving."

"I didn't realize that," Lance said. "Are you headed overseas again?"

"No, nothing like that," Marlon said. "I want to be near my children, all three of them. I've decided to buy a duplex in the neighborhood. I'm working with my Realtor on it. But in the interim,

I'll move into the lower level, and you and Kendra will take the master." He eyed him. "And that's my final say on the matter."

Lance sat back in the chair, thinking. "It's too much. Everything about this day is too much. I don't even know what to make of it."

"The truth is, Lance . . ." Marlon took his time. "There will be difficult days ahead. I know this firsthand. So when God gives a day like today, just live in it. It's a marker you can look back on to remind you that God is faithful and that He's with you every step of the way."

Lance let the words settle. "And today is a mighty big marker." He downed his juice and stood, his mind on his bride. "I'm praying this will be the most special day Kendra has ever known."

CHAPTER FIFTY-SEVEN

KENDRA HAD AWAKENED FEELING AS SHE'D PRAYED TO FEEL—pain-free enough to get out of bed and insert herself into the day. She'd learned to function with aches, spasms, stiffness, fatigue, and the like. As long as it stayed short of debilitating, she was determined to make the most of this day.

She'd been able to eat, too, a just-right breakfast of oatmeal and bananas, with the just-right company of Cyd and Molly. It was actually kind of nice not knowing what was going on at the house, because it meant she didn't have to stress. Her part was easy—get dressed at Cyd's and arrive in time for the wedding . . . and she had hours before she needed to do even that.

Cyd's doorbell rang, and she popped up. They'd been in the family room talking honeymoons, imagining where she and Lance could go if a window opened up between the end of chemo and surgery. She didn't think it likely, but on a wedding day it was fun to dream.

"Hi, we're looking for Kendra Woods," a woman's voice said.

The house was so quiet that they could hear from the family room. Kendra turned to Molly, mouthing, "What's that about?"

"Sure, she's in here," Cyd said.

Two women and a gentleman came into the family room with Cyd, carrying garment bags, duffel bags, and tote bags.

"You're Kendra Woods?" one of the women asked.

"Yes," Kendra said. "How can I help you?"

"I'm Roxie," she said, then, pointing left, "and this is Stella and Rudy." She looked back at Kendra. "We're here to help you get ready for your wedding."

Kendra frowned a little. "Excuse me?"

"Well," she said, looking at the others, "we understand you were going to keep things simple, wear the ivory-colored dress you got from the mall . . . but we wanted to give you the dress you've always deep-down wanted, but maybe weren't bold enough to wear."

Kendra glanced at Cyd and Molly. Was she on some reality show, being recorded right now?

"I am so confused," she said. "How on earth would you know what dress I've always wanted to wear? *I* don't even know what dress I've always wanted to wear."

The three of them glanced at one another again.

"How about we let you see it?" Roxie shrugged. "Who knows? You may not like it at all."

They put down all of their bags, draping a couple of garment bags on the sofa. Stella lifted the biggest garment bag while Roxie pulled down the zipper. Kendra, Molly, and Cyd had their eyes glued to the bag, wondering what would come out.

"*Wow.*" Kendra let down the recliner and got up.

"No, no," Roxie said. "Stay there. We'll bring it to you."

Kendra sat back, staring. "I've never seen anything like that. It's absolutely gorgeous."

"The gown is satin with a chiffon overlay," Roxie said. "A-line silhouette, bodice slightly beaded and ruched, sheer long sleeves to hide the bruising on your arms . . ."

Kendra touched it lightly as she spoke. "And it's such a deep, rich purple . . ."

"It's sooo gorgeous," Molly said.

"It's so romantic looking," Cyd said. "You just want to stare at it."

Kendra looked at Roxie. "But how did you know?"

"Your photo blog."

Kendra tilted her head, more curious. "I don't understand."

"You posted a picture you'd taken at the botanical gardens," Roxie said, "of a beautiful cluster of purple-and raspberry-colored flowers. You wrote that it was your favorite color combo and you'd always dreamed—"

"Of making them my wedding colors—with a purple wedding dress. I would've never had the courage though."

Roxie smiled. "Is anything stopping you now?"

"It better not be," Molly said.

Kendra's brows bunched. "But hold it. Let's go back ten steps. Why were you even on my blog? Why are you here with the dress and whatever else? Who *are* you?"

Roxie laid the dress across the love seat. "I have a good friend, Eva, who's a wedding planner, one of the best in the area, and she attends Living Word Church. She said Lance asked her what he needed to do to plan a simple wedding that was two weeks away." Roxie laughed. "Eva thought he was joking. Then she learned the circumstances, and that woman was suddenly on a mission."

Kendra turned to Cyd. "Did you know about all this?"

"Once the ball started rolling," Cyd said.

"Eva called everybody she knew who was remotely associated

with the industry to see who could help. I was one of the first people she called because she wanted to know if I could make a dress."

"You made this?" Kendra asked.

Roxie nodded. "I really hope you like it."

"I love it," Kendra said. "But how'd you know my measurements?"

"Believe it or not," Roxie said, "Lance put us in touch with your former maid of honor, who put us in touch with the bridal salon you went to in DC."

Kendra blank-stared. "Y'all were serious."

Roxie gestured to her associates. "Stella is here to do your makeup and headpiece, and Rudy's got his camera, ready to capture this entire process."

Kendra took a second look at him. "You're not Rudy Lehigh, are you?" At his nod, she grew wide-eyed. "I follow your blog! I've learned so much from you."

He had a rugged smile. "Eva saw that you hat-tipped me in one of your captions . . . When she told me about you, I had to be here."

Kendra pondered all of it. "I can't believe someone cared enough to want to do this, and that you all cared enough to respond. I could never thank you in any way that would seem adequate."

"I think I speak for all of us," Roxie said. "Being able to witness you saying 'I do' will be all the thanks we need."

❧

The limousine rounded the bend toward Kendra's home at exactly four forty-five, with an excited Kendra, Molly, Cyd, and Brooklyn inside. Cars lined both sides of the street as far as Kendra could see.

"Didn't we say we were having a small, intimate wedding?" Kendra asked, staring out the window. "Umm . . . is that a news truck?"

"Where?" Molly moved to Kendra's side and followed her gaze. "NBC local is here?"

"I see a lot of Living Word people getting out of cars and heading to your house," Cyd said.

"They're probably friends of Lance," Kendra said.

"Or they're crashing because they heard the story. Hey, that reminds me"—Molly laughed—"I was set to crash your first wedding."

"And now look where we are," Kendra said. "You're my only attendant, looking absolutely fabulous in raspberry, I might add."

"I am so dying my hair this color." Molly fluffed her hair, which looked tame without spikes or a faux hawk. "But I'm glad it's jet black right now." She smiled. "Anything else might've clashed."

"Roxie did an awesome job with these dresses," Cyd said. "Brooklyn's is about the most adorable flower-girl dress I've seen."

Brooklyn ran her hands over her full skirt. "And it's my favorite color—purple!"

"You're rocking that headpiece too," Molly said. "It's like a scarf and veil in one."

"What touched me the most," Kendra said, "is that they were so creative about accommodating my needs."

The limo slowed to a stop in front of Kendra's home.

Kendra gasped, looking out the window again. "Look at the walkway."

Both sides were lined with shepherd hooks holding glass jars filled with bouquets of purple- and raspberry-colored flowers.

The limo door opened, and a woman leaned inside.

"Kendra, I'm finally meeting you," she said. Petite with a cute, short haircut and stylish pantsuit, she had a walkie-talkie in hand. "I'm Eva, and I've been doing a little work with your wedding."

Kendra shook her hand. "More than a little," she said. "Thank you so much. You're a wonder woman. I'm amazed by what you've done."

"Let me tell you," Eva said, "there was no way Lance could've told me your story, and I *not* do this. It was like the Lord shook my heart and said, 'Eva, give this couple a dream wedding.'" She leaned in, her eyes big. "And then *He* did all the work. Oh my, the doors He opened to get this done." Eva pulled a tissue from her pocket. "No smudging your makeup, young lady," she said, dabbing the outer corners of Kendra's eyes.

"I'm just . . . overwhelmed," Kendra said.

"You can't be overwhelmed yet," Eva said. "The party's just beginning."

Molly was laughing. "I like her."

Eva introduced herself to the others and then spoke to someone in her walkie-talkie.

"This is what will happen," Eva said. "Your dad's coming to get you, to escort you inside . . ."

Kendra smiled at that. She'd asked her dad a few days ago if he would escort her down the aisle, and he'd answered with tears in his eyes.

Eva continued, "The bridal party will walk through the house and out the back door, where you'll see a pathway that will be your aisle. Molly will go first, then we'll tell Brooklyn when to go. And then, Kendra, you'll walk the aisle with your dad to the trellis." She winked. "And guess who's waiting for you there?"

Someone squawked from Eva's walkie-talkie.

"Where's Jody?" Eva spoke back. "Hello? The ceremony's about to begin. Yes, they're here in the limo, just pulled up."

The front door opened, and two women rushed out to the limo with beautiful bouquets of dark purple, lavender, and raspberry, one for Kendra and a smaller version for Molly.

Kendra lifted it to her nose. "Oh, I need my camera. This is too gorgeous."

"Don't worry." Eva smiled. "Rudy will get a thousand shots of it."

"And here's the flower-girl basket." One of the women handed a basket with purple, lavender, and raspberry petals to Brooklyn. "Sprinkle these as you walk down the aisle."

Brooklyn grinned. "Then can I pick them back up and keep them?"

"You are too cute," Eva said. She turned to Kendra. "How are you feeling? I want to make sure I keep checking with you. Weddings can be grueling, and we want this to be as comfortable as it can be for you."

Kendra exhaled. "I'm really good."

As they waited, Kendra took a moment with her thoughts, gazing at the bouquet. The day had already been incredible—and thank God she'd had time for a nap—but she hadn't seen Lance. She hadn't even talked to him. Being away from him for twenty-four hours made her realize how crazy in love she was with this man. She couldn't wait to lay her eyes on him.

Chapter Fifty-Eight

LANCE STOOD UNDER THE CUSTOM-MADE TRELLIS IN A BLACK tuxedo, looking past the rows of white chairs filled with guests, awaiting his bride. He'd never anticipated a moment like this in his life. He never knew marriage could loom so large in his heart and mind, that the thought of a woman becoming his wife could so fill him. But not just any woman. *This* woman. As beautifully as everything had come together, his mind wasn't on the new landscaping or the canopy of lights. It was on Kendra.

Pastor Lyles watched him from a couple feet over. "How are you doing, son?"

"You already know," Lance said. "Anxious."

The pastor smiled. "I thank God for you."

Lance quirked a brow at him.

"The first time I saw you, you were hard, cold, and lost. Now I look at you . . ." Pastor Lyles nodded, as if holding back emotion. "I thank God for you," he said again.

"Don't get me started up here, Pastor," Lance said. "I'm having a hard enough time as it is."

"Here they come," Trey said, standing next to him. "There's Molly."

Music had been streaming through a speaker system set up for the wedding—with easy approval from surrounding neighbors. But as Molly came up the aisle, the song changed to "I Can Only Imagine"—and for Lance, emotion swirled all the more. Thinking of seeing Jesus face-to-face and what that would be like, and that Kendra might see Him sooner than he *wanted* to imagine . . . he almost lost it. Still, the song's beauty and imagery, today of all days, was captivating.

Molly walked slowly up the pathway and took her place at the front, and Brooklyn started down at the top of the second verse, to a chorus of "Awww." She was beaming and adorable as ever, dotting the pathway with pretty petals. Ellen stood on the aisle near the back, raising a tissue to her face.

Brooklyn sprinkled the last of her petals and stood in front of Molly. The guests stood and turned to the back. Lance's gaze was already there, waiting.

As the chorus built and the singer belted, "Surrounded by Your glory, what will my heart feel . . . ," Kendra appeared. He'd had no idea what she'd be wearing, but royal purple couldn't have been more stunningly suited. She looked like a queen. As she made her way toward him, her gaze was fixed on his. Lance let the tears roll.

Kendra's pace with her dad was slow, but it seemed a purposeful slow, not a painful slow. Cyd had assured him she was feeling okay today, but he was relieved to see for himself.

Kendra and her dad came near as the song closed—"I can only imagine, when all I would do, is forever . . . forever worship You . . ."

Something clicked in Lance's heart, and he pondered it even as Pastor Lyles began his opening remarks. No matter what happened this side of eternity, he and Kendra would both worship the Lord forever. And there would be no sickness.

"Who gives this woman to be married to this man?" Pastor Lyles was saying.

"I do," Marlon said, "with the firm belief that Cynthia would love and support this union just as much as I."

Marlon sat down, and Lance moved closer, facing his bride. Kendra passed her bouquet to Molly and slipped her hands inside Lance's.

"Lance and Kendra," Pastor Lyles continued, "you stand before us very aware that marriage is not to be entered into lightly, but reverently. It is a covenant before God, a union to which heaven itself bears witness. As children of God, redeemed through Jesus Christ, your marriage is a reflection of Him—of unconditional love, of selflessness. Of sacrifice. But I know you know this"—he looked into their eyes, as if speaking to them only—"because your very union is an illustration to all of us of love and sacrifice."

Lance saw a flicker of something in Kendra's eyes, like she was laboring to focus. They'd met with Pastor Lyles at the house this past month as he counseled them, and in the last session, they'd gone over the service and decided to keep it short—no songs, no readings—given Kendra's health. Now Lance wondered if she'd even make it through this.

Pastor Lyles looked out at the guests. "Lance and Kendra have written their own vows, which they will now share with—"

Everyone gasped as Kendra suddenly slumped—but Lance caught her in his arms. He picked her up and carried her to the front row, where Cyd and Cedric had quickly risen to make room.

Lance laid her on his lap, cradled in his arms, comforted that she was looking at him.

"What are you feeling, sweetheart?" He searched her eyes. "What's hurting?"

"I don't know what happened," she murmured. "My legs just . . . lost power." She shifted her head slightly and saw the guests standing, staring. "I'm so embarrassed."

"If embarrassment is your main concern, we might be good." He sighed. "You have no idea how much you scared me."

Darla ran forward with bottled water and peanut butter crackers. "Here," she said. "It's helped in the past."

Lance took them. "Thanks, Darla." He unscrewed the cap and lifted Kendra's head, helping her drink.

She took a couple gulps. "My lip gloss'll be messed up."

Lance shook his head at her, amused. "Can we just get you strong enough to say your vows and become my wife, and you can worry about lip gloss later?"

He took a cracker from the pack, broke a piece off, and gave it to her. Kendra chewed it slowly, then drank more water.

"How are you feeling?"

Kendra finished the cracker. "I feel okay, but the test will be when I try to stand."

"We can do our vows right here, just like this."

"I want to try though," Kendra said. "I want to stand."

Lance helped her to a sitting position, then helped her to her feet. Slowly she walked, hand in his, to the foot of the trellis, as the guests cheered.

Pastor Lyles whispered to Kendra, "We can do this sitting, no problem."

Kendra leaned on Lance. "I'll make it."

"Without further ado," the pastor announced, "we'll move to the vows." He turned to Lance and gave a nod.

Lance looked into Kendra's eyes. "There is no me without you. You're a gift from God that I will treasure all of our days." He paused, swallowing emotion, wanting to get through it. "I can't love you with my love because it's not enough. I promise to love you with the love God gives me for you . . . and He tells me it's endless. I promise to seek Him for your every need, to trust Him with every one of our days, and to believe that His goodness and loving-kindness will follow us all the days of our lives."

Lance paused again. Maybe it was the excitement of a few minutes ago, but his mind had suddenly gone blank. He couldn't remember the last part of his vows.

He winged it. "For better, for worse, for richer, for poorer, in sickness, and in health?" His tone said that was a given. "Girl, I would lay down my life for you. I will cherish you, protect you, pray for you, and be to you everything that God gives me the grace and strength to be." He flicked a tear away. "I love you, Kendra."

Kendra's hands were shaking in his as she tried to hold it together. "You were my knight in shining armor when I felt abandoned and alone. You were salt and light when my world had spoiled and gone dark. You were an answer to a prayer I hadn't even prayed." Her voice broke, and she squeezed his hands. "You are God's goodness to me. You led me to truly know Jesus, and you've shown me what it truly means to be loved."

Lance glanced at Pastor Lyles, surprised as the pastor dabbed his eyes with a handkerchief.

"I don't know if I'll be able to be the wife you need, and that scares me . . ." Tears rolled down Kendra's eyes. "But I promise to ask God to help me. I promise to spend every day loving you more than I ever thought possible. And I promise to spend every day in wonder that I even have another day to live with you." Her gaze lingered with his. "I love you so much."

Pastor Lyles needed a moment himself before he continued. He proceeded with the exchange of the rings, then put his hands on their shoulders, smiling.

"By the authority vested in me as a minister of the gospel of Jesus Christ, I declare that Lance and Kendra are now husband and wife . . ."

Lance didn't hear the rest. His mind stopped at husband and wife. She was his *wife*.

". . . You may kiss your bride."

He felt his heart knocking in his chest as he drew Kendra near. They'd never kissed. Not by agreement—they'd never talked about it. He just wanted everything to be right, and in his heart, it seemed right to wait.

Their arms enfolded each other, and for a moment they simply gazed into each other's eyes. Then his lips brushed hers, and softly he kissed her.

The backyard erupted with applause and cheers as everyone stood. A cameraman stood within a few feet, filming the action. The photographer had been near the entire time.

Pastor Lyles did a final charge and benediction, and Lance took Kendra's arm in his as they started to walk back down the path. But partway, he decided he wasn't taking a chance. He picked her up and carried her, to even louder cheers.

"I was about to say this is silly, and I can walk," Kendra said, "but I like being in my husband's strong arms."

"That's a good thing," Lance said, "because I don't want a day to pass when I don't hold you in my arms."

She snuggled in, holding him as he held her. "I'll never forget the day I became Mrs. Alexander. This is the best day of my life."

CHAPTER FIFTY-NINE

KENDRA ROLLED OVER AS LANCE WALKED INTO THE BEDROOM.
"I was wondering where you went." She smiled. "Honeymoon week?"

"Yep, honeymoon week continues." Lance set the tray on the
bed. "Early breakfast in bed."

"You're spoiling me," Kendra said, propping herself to see what
he had brought.

"I can do that honeymoon week," Lance said. "Next week, it's
every man for himself." He fed her a piece of banana he'd cut up.
"Have you gotten used to being in your parents' room?"

"It's still weird, but I'm really thankful," Kendra said. "It's room-
ier, and having a bathroom in here makes a big difference."

He nodded toward the wall. "How do you like the flat-screen?"

"That's the best part," Kendra said, smiling at last night's honeymoon week gift. "Now we can snuggle in bed and watch movies."

Lance kissed her cheek. "Snuggling is the best part."

Kendra hesitated. "Lance?"

He looked at her.

"We haven't talked about the elephant in the room."

He frowned. "What elephant is that?"

"We're supposed to be consecrating our marriage, becoming one flesh." It was hard to look at him. "It's not much of a honeymoon if your wife isn't up for sex."

"Isn't 'up for sex'?" Lance moved closer to her. "Sweetheart, that's not what this is. Everything is challenging for you right now. You're undergoing aggressive chemotherapy for aggressive breast cancer."

"That's the other thing." Kendra didn't know why this was all coming out now. There were moments when real melancholy came over her. "I feel like you must be so repulsed by my body, by this . . . cancer in my breast. I don't want to look in the mirror myself. So you've got this new wife with a deformed body who can't make love to you. And on top of that, who keeps you awake with all her tossing and turning." She stared at the bed. "That's what I meant about not being able to be the wife you need."

"Oh, sweetheart . . ." He put the tray on the nightstand and brought her into his arms. "My love for you is so beyond anything physical. Do you know what it does for me, just being able to go to sleep and wake up by your side? Do you know how much I love being able to talk to you when you can't sleep?"

"But, Lance, you're a man, and—"

"I'm a man, so all I think about is sex?"

"No, I'm not saying that, but . . ." Kendra looked at him now. "I want you to be honest with me. I want to know what you're feeling."

Lance was quiet a moment. "Okay, that's good. I want that too." He lightly stroked her back. "You're my wife, I love you, and you're drop-dead gorgeous. So of course I want to make love to you. But I'm not thinking about it, if that makes sense."

She looked at him, waiting for more.

"I could put it this way," Lance said. "I've prayed for God to give me grace for our marriage, to be the husband you need. And He knows when the time will be right for us to come together in that way. Until then, there's grace to wait, to not dwell on it, to enjoy you in all the ways I can enjoy you now—and that's plenty."

"I guess I should pray more for that grace too," Kendra said.

"What do you mean?"

"It's not one-sided." Kendra laid her cheek against his arm. "You're my husband, I love you, and you're incredibly handsome. I can't even kiss you like I want to because of my mouth sores. Being physically challenged is rougher in a whole new way now." She sighed. "But I want to see what happens after the last chemo today."

"That's also why I brought you breakfast in bed," Lance said. "To celebrate the end of chemo."

"We don't know if it's the end."

"And we don't know that it's not," Lance said.

"My mind is already on all the upcoming testing, to see if they can schedule surgery next month." Kendra looked up at him. "What if the new chemo cocktail had no effect?"

"You know I'm not going there."

"I know," Kendra said. "No speculation."

Her phone rang, and she reached for it on the nightstand. She did a double take at the caller ID and showed it to Lance.

Lance frowned. "Is he serious? Want me to answer it?"

"I'll answer," Kendra said. She clicked the phone on. "This is Kendra Alexander."

"I heard—or should I say, *saw*," Derek said. "That's what prompted the call."

"You saw what?" Kendra asked.

"Cable news picked up the touching story of the woman with

a terminal illness who was given a dream wedding, after her former fiancé broke up with her—a week before their planned wedding—because of her illness. You didn't have to put me out there like that."

"No one gave your name."

"Everyone who knows us, knows," he said. "Up until now, most assumed it was by mutual agreement because you were sick."

"Excuse me . . . Did you really just call, after all this time, to gripe because people know why our wedding was canceled?"

"I'm just saying, you didn't have to reveal that," Derek said. "Obviously, you got over it, and quickly, since you're already married."

Lance tugged on her. "Can I let the old Lance get with this dude? Just two minutes?"

Kendra stifled a laugh. "Derek," she said, "I shared that on my blog, and I want you to know why. When you broke up with me, I thought it was the end of the world. But I discovered that God had a different plan for me. He saved me, and He showed me His love through Lance." She didn't know why she was telling Derek all this, but maybe there was a reason. "I wanted people to know that no matter what life throws at you, there's hope in Jesus.

"Basically, you became my testimony. And if you still don't understand, that's okay." She sat up straighter. "But let me say this— this will be the last time we talk. Take my number out of your phone, and I'm blocking yours."

Lance tugged again. "Tell him I said hi."

Kendra swatted him.

"So you're saying I might never talk to you again?" Derek asked.

"That's exactly what I'm saying. Bye, Derek."

"He didn't even ask how I'm doing." She hung up, marveling at that, then looked at Lance. "Thanks to Derek, I feel good about my marriage again."

Lance gave her a look.

"You know what I mean. I was a little depressed about what we don't have because of the illness." She let the new thought settle. "But wow, what if we had those things, but not the things we *do* have, the things that make up the soul of our marriage?"

"I thought that's what I was trying to tell you," Lance said.

"Maybe. But I had to get it for myself." Kendra eyed her tray. "My oatmeal is cold."

"Whose fault is that?"

Kendra turned on her best puppy-dog eyes.

Lance grabbed the bowl. "Be right back."

She called after him, "Did you know I love you more today than I did on our wedding day?"

"Yeah, yeah," he called back.

Kendra took another piece of banana from the tray. Right now, she couldn't take the thought of being in a chemo chair in two hours and suffering the effects over the next two weeks. But she was learning to savor moments. And she would savor *this* moment, the time she had this morning with her soul mate.

CHAPTER SIXTY

IT WAS ALMOST A MANTRA WITH LANCE—NO SPECULATING. No anguish over horrible things that exist only in the mind. But he was guilty of it himself this week, plagued by thoughts that Kendra's CT scans and MRI would reveal terrible news . . . that her cancer had not only not improved, but gotten worse.

The bad part was it looked like he wouldn't be able to make it to the appointment with Dr. Contee to hear the news himself. Due to a scheduling conflict, the doctor had to move it up an hour, to ten o'clock. It worked for Kendra, but Lance had had a photo shoot for nine scheduled weeks before. Kendra assured him it was fine. She'd get the results alone. But this was important to him. He wanted to be there.

And he'd be on his way if the Rickshaw family hadn't decided at the last minute to include their dog in the shoot. Every year, they were one of the first to book their Christmas photo shoot, and every year they asked if they could include the family dog.

"I don't do pets," Lance always said, readily offering info for a great photographer who did. For whatever reason, they'd stuck with him. But this year, they'd shown up anyway—with the dog. This really wasn't the day to try his patience.

"Bunny," Mrs. Rickshaw sang, coaxing with a toy, "be a good girl and cooperate."

Bunny had decided she'd much prefer to exercise her legs in the open space and run to and fro. Lance had gotten plenty of candid shots of the family playing with the dog, but Mrs. Rickshaw was bent on having everyone, including the Wheaten terrier, pose portrait style.

"Jacob, you try," Mrs. Rickshaw said.

The four-year-old patted his legs. "Bunny, come. Come on, girl. Come on, girl."

It was a game now. The more they called, the more Bunny darted this way and that.

"I don't know what's going on with her," Mrs. Rickshaw said. "She never does this."

Lance checked his watch. Nine forty-five. They'd probably be done by now if they'd left Bunny home.

"Honey," Mr. Rickshaw said, "we may have to put Bunny in the car and take the portrait without her."

Lance turned a hopeful glance toward Mrs. Rickshaw.

"She won't play like this forever," Mrs. Rickshaw said. "She'll calm down shortly."

"Can't you put her on a leash?" Lance asked.

"But that'll take away the feel that she's part of the family," Mrs. Rickshaw said. "I don't want her to look like an animal."

Lance sighed to himself. "How about we put her on a leash and position her in the photo in such a way that it doesn't look like she's on a leash. In fact, if any portion of the leash shows up, I can erase it when I edit the photos."

Mrs. Rickshaw's eyes lit up. "I didn't think of that. That's perfect."

They got Bunny on the leash and took several family shots in different poses. And Lance jumped in the car and headed to Dr. Contee's office. Kendra was still there when he texted, and he was only ten minutes away. If he could hear a quick synopsis from the doctor, he'd take it.

But by the time he found parking and took the elevator to her office, Kendra was walking out of the office suite.

Lance groaned. "I can't believe my morning got hijacked by a terrier named Bunny, and I missed the meeting." He searched her face for clues. "Well . . . what did Dr. Contee say?"

"The surgeon was there too." Kendra moved to the side of the hall. "That's one of the reasons why the appointment time changed, so he could be there. And they'd spoken with the radiologist as well."

He couldn't read her.

"The cancer is still in several spots in my breast," Kendra said. "There's some enhancement in the breast, lymph node enlargement. But there's no indication that the cancer is bigger or worse, and it's away from the chest wall. So it's operable."

"That's what we wanted to hear, right?"

Kendra nodded. "And they also said"—she looked confused, like it didn't make sense—"that they don't see evidence of cancer in my neck."

Lance pulled her closer. "Say that again."

"They used that term 'NED'—no evidence of disease—regarding the cancer in my neck, because of the chemo."

Lance wanted to pick her up and twirl her around. "Sweetheart, that's an answer to prayer! No evidence of cancer in your neck, plus your breast is operable, so *that* cancer will be removed." He paused. "Why aren't you more excited?"

"I've read so much about this disease," Kendra said. "We don't know what's around the corner."

"Can we take a moment to praise God for what's at *this* corner?" Lance said. "You don't know how relieved I am."

"Mr. Alexander, you weren't imagining the worst, were you?"

"Um, not the worst, just a sort of nightmarish . . . Okay, yeah." He took her hand and led her to the elevator. "We need a mini-celebration. I say we do something to celebrate every bit of good news we get as thanks to God, even if it's just stopping for a bakery treat."

Kendra smiled at him as they awaited the elevator. "I think we can do better than a bakery stop."

Lance waited, hopeful.

"They scheduled surgery for mid-November," Kendra said. "I was thinking in about two weeks, when I'm feeling better from the last chemo, maybe we could take that trip I talked about."

They hopped on the elevator.

"You think you'd be up for a long road trip?" he asked. "I don't know . . ."

"I can pack my pillow and sleep in the car," Kendra said. "What does it matter if I have pain spasms at home or on the road? I want to do this."

The elevator opened, and they walked off.

"It could be our real honeymoon," Kendra said.

Lance stared after her. "Who takes a honeymoon to the federal pen?"

CHAPTER SIXTY-ONE

November

KENDRA AND LANCE DROVE TWELVE HOURS TO TALLAHASSEE, arriving Friday evening. They wanted to be able to rest and be at the prison before eight thirty, the start of visiting hours.

Kendra almost wasn't allowed to come. Visitors needed to be preapproved, and the inmate needed to know the visitor prior to incarceration. But thankfully, the prison granted an exception for the new daughter-in-law of one of the inmates.

Inmate. Kendra thought about it and talked about it during the drive, what it was like to be locked up. It wasn't Lance's favorite subject, but as she probed, he willingly shared. And Kendra found herself getting sadder. This was his mom's life, day in and day out. No freedom. No real choices about where to go, what to do. No thought as to how you might enjoy a nice day, because, how could you, other than sitting in the prison courtyard? The beauty of flowers blooming in spring or leaves changing in fall . . . How did one miss that for *years*?

She was especially moved once they arrived at the facility itself. The wire, the guards. Filling out paperwork. Clearing the metal detector. All the hoops that had to be cleared just for an inmate to have contact with someone from the outside world. And now, watching the faces of eager kids waiting to visit with their moms . . .

Kendra didn't know what she was feeling. But there was something about life and its twists and turns, the way things didn't turn out as planned. Lance had told her some of the stories of the women here. Many weren't hardened criminals. One bad decision, often the choice of a boyfriend, had started the downhill slide. And Kendra knew—as an attorney—if you got snagged in the federal system, you could get decades behind bars for a drug-related offense. More time than murderers and rapists. Time away from these little kids.

She felt a weird kinship with their stories. An interrupted existence. An unexpected journey. Being suddenly very aware that your life is not in your control.

Lance put an arm around her as they waited. "You okay, babe? You've been quiet."

Kendra nodded. "Just . . . this little girl right here, probably Brooklyn's age. She can't sit still. She's full of so much anticipation. I wonder when was the last time she saw her mom . . . and how long before she'll see her again?" She looked at Lance. "Life. You know?"

"Breaks my heart whenever I come," Lance said.

The door opened and the visitors stood, looking for their loved ones. The little girl ran forward, saying, "Mommy! Mommy!" Her mother broke into a wide grin and held her tight.

"Here comes my mom." Lance smiled, moving forward.

Anticipation built in Kendra's heart as she searched faces. She'd seen pictures of Lance's mother and knew she'd recognize her—and there she was, in khaki pants and shirt, her hair pulled into a ponytail. Kendra saw the resemblance immediately between mother and son, more so than in the photos, although his mom was petite. And she saw the love between them, too, as they embraced.

When they let go, his mom came directly to Kendra and hugged her too.

Lance laughed a little. "Mom, this is Kendra. Kendra, this is my mom, Pamela."

"I got all the intro I needed through the letters and pictures Kendra sent," Pamela said. She smiled at Kendra. "I couldn't wait to see you. Oh, you don't know how excited I was to hear about the wedding. You were a gorgeous bride."

"Thank you, Pamela," Kendra said. "I really wanted to share the day with you."

They walked into the courtyard and sat together at a table.

Lance leaned in. "So how are you, Mom? Catch me up."

Pamela beamed. "They got me in here preaching now."

Lance looked impressed. "All right now." He grinned. "Tell me about it."

"Well, the women call it preaching," Pamela said. "I'm just sharing one evening a week from my own Bible study." She winked at him. "Those notes you send from your messages come in handy. I tell them when something I'm saying is from you. They know I'm proud of my son."

"Tell them I'm proud of my mom." Lance put an arm around her and squeezed her. "I really am. This is awesome."

"Pamela, I'd love to hear what your last message was about," Kendra said.

Pamela started right in. "Girl, I was coming from Matthew 6, where Jesus is telling them, 'What are you anxious for? God is feeding the birds and dressing the lilies *Himself*, and you think He can't take care of *you?*'" Her entire self got animated. "I wanted the ladies to know that even here behind bars, God cares about us, and He's taking care of us." She chuckled. "Shoot, if it didn't encourage nobody else, it sure encouraged me."

"Wow," Kendra said, pondering it, "that encourages me too."

Pamela looked at her. "How are you feeling? I know about your illness, but I'm wondering how you're feeling inside, in your soul."

"That's a good question," Kendra said. "I don't get that one very often." She thought about it. "I get depressed sometimes, especially if I'm focusing on the illness. So I try to make myself focus on God's goodness, which always includes Lance." She glanced at him. "You raised a phenomenal son."

The light faded a little from Pamela's eyes. "The way he turned out had nothing to do with me. It was in spite of me." A hint of emotion entered her voice as she looked at her son. "I thank God every day for this boy, and for saving him—and then using him to save me."

Her words struck Kendra. "That's really something, Lance. God used you to save your mom and your wife."

"It *is* something," Lance said, "because He used Pastor Lyles to save me, when I was locked up."

"Pamela," Kendra said, "I'd like to ask you the same question. How are you feeling, in your soul, knowing you'll be here for a long time, especially when a twenty-year sentence is so unfair?" She added, "I honestly think I would go crazy."

"I 'bout did go crazy," Pamela said. "I couldn't believe my ex-boyfriend hardly got any time, and he was the dealer. But he gave up another dealer, and that's what the prosecutors wanted. I felt like my life was over, like there was no point to anything."

Kendra nodded, imagining herself in her shoes.

"But you know what?" Pamela gave her a look. "God checked my whole perspective. I blamed my ex-boyfriend, but I knew what he was doing, and let him do it from my house, because I was a user. And if I hadn't gotten locked up, I might still be a user." She'd thought about this—that was clear. "And it was here that God got my attention and brought me to my knees for the first time in my life. So I found freedom in Christ after losing my freedom in the world."

Pamela had barely let that settle when she added, "We've got something in common, daughter-in-law."

Kendra had yet to wrap her mind around the other words. "What's that?"

"I can focus on the length of my sentence and stay depressed, like you with your illness. Or I can focus on God's goodness and know that I'll have an eternity to enjoy with Him."

Kendra sat back, rocked by her words. "I wish I could say we have that in common," she said. "I don't do that enough—focus on eternity. Even when I'm focusing on God's goodness, it's about what's here and now, like Lance."

"Honey, by all means, enjoy your here and now," Pamela said. "Enjoy freedom, both kinds." She chuckled at that. "But keep your eyes on the hope to come. Ooh, when I think about it. It'll be glorious!"

Kendra got goose bumps. "When I told Lance I wanted to come here, it was to meet his mom, but I was also thinking it would be good to come and encourage you." She shook her head. "You've encouraged me, and we haven't even been here an hour."

"Don't think I'm not encouraged," Pamela said. "It does my heart some kinda good to see that my son chose you as his wife. That right there . . ." She pointed between her and Lance. "That's real love. It still exists. That encourages me."

Kendra and Lance stayed in the courtyard several hours with Pamela, and before they knew it, a guard was announcing, "Five more minutes!"

"It's three o'clock already?" Kendra asked.

Around the visiting area, the excitement of the morning was

turning into sadness, especially as kids began to cry, saying good-bye to their moms.

Kendra felt sad herself as they stood. "I'm so glad I had this time with you," she said. "Now I know my phenomenal husband has a phenomenal mom. I loved seeing the two of you together."

"And I loved seeing the two of *you* together," Lance said. "My two favorite girls in the world."

Kendra hugged her. "I don't know when I'll . . . see . . ." Tears choked her words, if she'd had words. She didn't quite know what to say.

"Seeing you right now today blessed me like crazy," Pamela said. "I have a daughter." She hit Lance. "You take care of my daughter, you hear me?"

Lance's eyes had welled with tears, and Kendra knew it was because he wouldn't see his mom for a while. "I'll take care of Kendra," he said, "and as always, trusting God to take care of you."

"Can't nobody do it better," Pamela said. She held tight to her son. "Love you, my baby boy."

Kendra and Lance watched her disappear behind the thick, locked door.

Chapter Sixty-Two

Lance couldn't wait to see the look on Kendra's face. They were headed back to St. Louis as far as she knew, and she'd fallen fast asleep soon after they left Tallahassee. But less than three hours later, he'd exited off the highway toward another destination. He wondered how long it would take Kendra to wake up and figure it out.

Using the map feature on his phone, he'd navigated his way. He parked and cut the engine.

Kendra stirred and stretched. "Stopping for gas or are we eating?" she asked, eyes still shut.

"We'll probably do both . . . during our stay here."

Kendra peeked open an eye. "Where are we?"

"On our honeymoon."

She sat up and looked around. "Where?"

"Pensacola Beach."

"Oh my goodness, seriously? How did you do this?"

Lance looked at her. "Are you acting like it's a miracle that I've planned something? You saw our wedding, didn't you?"

"Which you didn't plan."

"I asked a question that put the plan in motion," Lance said. "Same thing."

"Uh-huh," Kendra said. "So what question did you ask that put *this* in motion?"

Lance laughed. "I asked about vacation spots in this area, since we'd be down here. Somebody knew somebody who owned this condo and made a call." Lance looked up at the building. "It's supposed to be the penthouse."

"Are you serious?" Kendra asked. "How long will we be here?"

"Three nights," Lance said. "It's not long, but I didn't want to take a chance. I knew you needed to get back soon for lab work and other tests before surgery."

Kendra looked at him. "Three days and nights with my husband, at the beach, on a honeymoon . . . sounds like forever to me."

Lance had already been full from the visit with his mom, but this—special time with Kendra—was taking him over the top. They'd done a little shopping—"for the things I would've packed, had I known"—had a romantic dinner by the water, and slow-walked the beach. It almost felt normal.

And while "normal" for Kendra came with physical challenges, it was as if God had given them a vacation even from that. At least from the worst of it. On the balcony reclined on a double chaise with his wife, soaking in an amazing view, there was no place he'd rather be.

"So when do you see yourself becoming lead pastor of a church?" Kendra asked.

Lance eyed her. "Where did that come from?"

"Popped into my mind," Kendra said. "You always say you don't 'see' it, so I'm wondering when you think that'll be."

"How would I know?" Lance asked. "I'd have to see it first. Then I'll know."

"Is it that you're still uncomfortable because of what happened in high school?"

"Actually, no," Lance said. "Once the Bible studies got going, that fell away. But that's the thing. I love what we're doing Wednesday nights. It's fruitful. People are being impacted." He sighed. "I've prayed a lot about the church-plant idea, and I really don't hear God saying to take that big step."

"But if you felt that's what God was saying, you'd go that route?"

"Absolutely."

"Okay." Kendra paused. "I just don't want you to hold back on anything God's telling you to do because of me."

"Well, that's funny," Lance said, "because you *are* what God's telling me to do."

She leaned into his shoulder. "What were His exact instructions?"

"Very simple. To love you." He snuggled closer. "How am I doing?"

"Hmm . . . I don't know," Kendra said. "I think I need more evidence." She tilted her head up and kissed him lightly, then tossed her eyes, thinking. "I'm still not fully persuaded . . ."

She turned more toward him and kissed him again, and slowly it grew deeper . . . deeper than they'd ever experienced.

"I love you so much," Kendra said, kissing him still.

Lance could feel her heart beating against his. "I love you too."

Kendra pulled away, got up from the chaise, and took his hand. He stood with her, and she kissed him again.

"Let's go into the bedroom," she said, "where we can be more comfortable."

Lance hesitated, not wanting to assume.

She held him. "I'm sure, Lance."

"But what if . . . I don't want to . . ."

She was kissing him again. And this time he allowed himself to get lost in it.

꙰

"Oh my gosh!" Kendra's voice sounded as though she could barely contain her excitement. "Look! Look! I got the shot!"

Lance came over and checked the back of her camera. "Look at that!" he said, smiling. "Perfect."

"Really?" A balmy breeze swept across her face. "You're not just saying that?"

"The picture speaks for itself," Lance said. "You caught a flock of seagulls taking flight, with different wingspans, different heights off the ground. You're becoming a pro with shutter speed."

"Aww," Kendra said, pointing to a corner of the picture. "I just noticed these two about to take off, looking at the others like, 'Hey, wait for us!'"

"Very cool, Mrs. Alexander."

She sat on a blanket, working on a close-up of a seashell. "Every vacation we take needs to be by the water."

"Because?"

"The photography vibe," Kendra said. "Being out here at sunrise and sunset, catching the colors reflecting off the water . . . amazing." She glanced up at him. "What?"

Lance sat beside her. "That's the first time I've heard you talk about anything future with respect to the two of us."

Kendra rested the camera on the blanket. "And I didn't think before I said it."

"It's nice to think about though."

She picked up some sand, let it run through her fingers.

Lance intertwined his fingers with hers. "Sometimes, especially these past two days, I can't help but hope. I find myself thinking, what if? You know? *What . . . if?*"

"I was thinking something else these past two days," Kendra said, "that it's like a dream, being with you. And I wouldn't have it—I wouldn't have you—if I had a normal life with normal thoughts about a normal future. And I knew without a doubt . . ." She looked at him. "I'd take you and this over normal."

Lance felt like his heart would burst. *Lord, if You take this woman from me, I don't know what I'll do.* What he hoped—what he wanted—was for them to beat the odds . . . for this honeymoon to be a foretaste of a long life together.

CHAPTER SIXTY-THREE

THE MORNING OF SURGERY SEEMED TO COME QUICKLY. KENDRA arrived at the hospital before dawn. She wanted to get this done, to have the surgeon remove all the milk ducts, lobules, fat, blood vessels, lymph channels—and cancer—from her chest, as well as the lymph nodes from under her armpit. Her left breast had been the cancerous one, but they were going to remove the right breast as well, as a precaution. Although everything about this entire process was painful, and her mind couldn't yet fathom a flat chest, she couldn't wait to be rid of the heavy weight—both physical and mental—that she lived with daily. She couldn't wait to believe that today, just maybe, she'd be cancer-free, or well on her way.

Lance had come to the pre-op area and, with word that surgery would begin shortly, had just finished praying with her.

He leaned over her, holding her hand. "In June, you had chemo ahead of you," he said, "plus surgery and radiation. You knocked the chemo out, and after today, the surgery will be behind you. You know we'll celebrate that."

Kendra nodded, a slight apprehension coming over her about going under the knife. "Will you be here when I wake up?"

Lance kissed her. "Where else would I be?"

A nurse approached. "Mr. Alexander, I'll have to ask you to move to the waiting room."

Kendra squeezed his hand. "I love you."

He traced her eyebrows, which were starting to fill back in. "I love you too, babe."

Kendra watched him go, then closed her eyes. She'd started memorizing Psalm 18, one of her favorites, and that's what she needed on her heart as they wheeled her to surgery. She let it scroll through her mind—*"I love You, O LORD, my strength. The LORD is my rock and my fortress and my deliverer, my God, my rock, in whom I take refuge; my shield and the horn of my salvation, my stronghold . . ."*

She woke up vomiting. Vomiting so severely that she was barely able to catch her breath. And the pain was so excruciating she thought the anesthesia must have worn off in the midst of surgery. But when she got her bearings she realized she was in recovery, and from what she could grasp, she'd been there several hours.

She glimpsed Lance in a chair a few feet away, but medical personnel surrounded her. Something about her blood pressure dropping. She writhed in pain, and her arms moved in the space above her chest, empty space. *They're gone.* The surgery was over, and she was alive—in pain, but alive. And the deformed breast was gone.

Groggy still, Kendra couldn't make sense of what was going on. And she didn't know if she wanted to. Her eyes closed as her upper torso shifted, weightless. Gone.

With Lance's help, Kendra slipped her arms one at a time, very slowly, into one of his old button-down shirts. She couldn't lift her arms to pull a shirt over her head, and her own button-downs weren't roomy enough. She needed space to accommodate the drains inserted by the surgeon, which moved fluid from her chest to bulbs attached at the end of the tubing. Lance had been emptying the drains every few hours, helping her shower, and picking up and reaching for things she needed. She had no idea what she'd be doing without him.

It was five days since the surgery, three since she'd been home. She'd been looking forward to being rid of her cancerous breast—and she was indeed relieved—but somehow the pain that would result from surgery had escaped her. At times, it was excruciating still, and she was almost counting down minutes until the next pain pill.

A knock sounded at the bedroom door.

"Who is it?" Lance buttoned her up.

"Hey," Trey said, "I'm headed to campus, but Ellen just stopped by to see you two."

"Come in, Trey." Kendra waited for the door to open. "Did she say what she wanted?"

"She brought a casserole or something, but she also asked if you were available." Trey hunched up his backpack, which was sliding. "Should I tell her it's not a good time?"

Kendra had been about to climb back into bed, but Ellen had never just stopped by out of the blue.

"Tell her I'll be down," Kendra said.

"All right." Trey turned to leave, then turned back. "You need anything? I can stop by the store on the way home."

"Thanks, but I don't think so."

Kendra checked herself in the mirror. A little 'fro was trying to grow in, now that she'd stopped chemo.

"You want your phone?" Lance asked.

"Yes, thanks." People had been calling to ask about her surgery, and it helped to have it with her.

They made their way downstairs and saw Ellen in the entryway.

"I'm so sorry to bother you," Ellen said. "I really could've come back another time."

"It's okay." Kendra was fatigued, her breathing labored. "Trey said you brought some food. I really appreciate that."

"No trouble at all," Ellen said. "I think he tucked it away in the refrigerator." She looked a little uncomfortable. "Should we sit in the living room?"

"Sure," Kendra said.

Lance helped her get settled on the sofa, which was now a feat since she had to position herself in such a way that she wouldn't bump the tubing or the drain under her shirt.

Ellen sat across from them in a chair. "I talked myself out of coming several times, because it feels odd," she said. "But ever since your wedding, I don't know . . ."

Kendra and Lance glanced at each other.

"It's okay," Lance said. "Say whatever's on your mind."

"First, Kendra, I didn't know until the news report that your former fiancé had broken up with you over your illness, which had to be just awful." She looked at Lance. "And I never knew you had a small bit of history here in Clayton, Lance."

Lance sighed. "Yeah, I wasn't thrilled when the local paper thought it was 'interesting' to dig that up as part of the wedding piece."

"But knowing these bits of background," Ellen said, "and

witnessing your wedding myself . . . It's made me think . . ." She groaned. "This sounds so wishy-washy. I knew it would."

"It's not wishy-washy at all." Lance shrugged. "And even if it is, who says anything's wrong with wishy-washy?"

A sharp pain shot through Kendra, and she clutched Lance's hand to bear up under it, so Ellen would feel free to continue.

Ellen smoothed her hands down her thighs. "I guess what I'm trying to say is it gives me hope . . ." Her jaw tightened. She was clearly stifling emotion. "I feel like, if you two could find something so beautiful after what you've been through—and in the midst of what you're still going through—then just maybe . . ."

Lance leaned forward. "Ellen," he said softly, "you feel like you need hope?"

"I do." Her face contorted, but there was nothing she could do. The tears came. "I didn't want this to happen," she said, wiping them quickly. "I feel so foolish." She got up. "I don't know what I'm doing here anyway. I'm the last person you would want to hear from about anything—"

"Ellen." Kendra felt a piece of tubing poking her and shifted a little. "I'm glad you're here," she said. "And if you've got time, Lance and I would love to tell you how we found hope."

✤

Two hours later Ellen rose to leave, after they'd prayed together.

"I didn't expect this when I came," she said, "that you would take this kind of time with me." She exhaled. "I just shared things I'd never imagined sharing . . . and in the unlikeliest of places."

"God does that," Lance said. "Coming to live here was the

unlikeliest of places for me. For that matter, marrying Kendra, the popular Clayton cheerleader, was 'the unlikeliest' for me."

"Hey!" Kendra said.

"Being real, babe."

"Thank you." Ellen shouldered her bag. "And thank you for the Bible. I'm still not sure about everything. I'm not ready to take any big steps. But I'll ponder the things you said."

Kendra's phone rang, and she looked at it, then looked at Lance. "It's Dr. Contee."

"You go ahead," Ellen said. "I'll let myself out. Thanks again."

Kendra answered. "Hi, Dr. Contee."

"Hi, Kendra, how are you feeling? Are the pain meds working?"

"It's been pretty bad, but better than yesterday," Kendra said, "so I'm hoping for even better tomorrow."

"Well, I know you've got an appointment tomorrow, when we'll check your drains and see how you're recovering," Dr. Contee said. "But I thought you'd want to hear some news from the preliminary pathology report."

Kendra whispered it to Lance. "Preliminary pathology report."

He moved closer.

"It's what we were looking for," Dr. Contee said. "Clean margins with your left breast."

Kendra closed her eyes. *Thank You, Lord.*

"What?" Lance said.

"Clean margins," Kendra whispered.

They both knew what it meant, that the surgeon had been able to cut out the tumor completely, with a rim of healthy tissue all around.

"The report also found cancer in your right breast," Dr. Contee said.

Kendra's eyes widened.

"But it was a small amount, and that, too, was removed with a clean margin."

"Thank God we did a double mastectomy," Kendra said.

"Exactly," Dr. Contee said.

"So what does this all mean?" Kendra asked.

"We'll talk about it more tomorrow," Dr. Contee said, "but as of now—the cancer is gone."

CHAPTER SIXTY-FOUR

December

KENDRA FELT BETTER THAN SHE'D FELT IN A LONG TIME. NOT pain-free by any means. But the words *cancer-free* had been enough to set a new course. Yet it was more than that. Without the diseased breasts and the chemo effects, the pain was lessening. Her energy was returning. Her hair was growing. She could even taste more of her food. She almost felt . . . normal.

But radiation would start tomorrow. And based on what she'd heard, it could knock her back a few steps. Some felt very little in the first few weeks. Others had nausea and sickness. But eventually, it seemed, almost everyone suffered intense radiation burns. She'd have eight weeks of it, five days a week, and at the end she hoped to have a real celebration.

But this morning she'd decided to take advantage of a feel-good day by going to Living Word. Lance had left early this morning, as usual. For months, Kendra hadn't had the energy. Just the thought of sitting in a pew for any length of time was tiring. And the couple of Sundays she probably could have gone, she'd chosen to rest.

But this morning she had a real desire to go, not necessarily to the main church, but here, to the building in which she'd spent so much time as a teen—to listen to her husband. On the edge of her seat, Kendra marveled that this was her first time hearing him like this. The dynamic in the living room was far different from the dynamic on a stage, in a room full of teens. Here, the man was electric.

Kendra hit her brother's arm. "Did you know Lance could preach like this?"

Trey gave her a look. "Where've you been?"

"At home in bed, usually."

"Okay, good excuse," Trey said. "But yeah, this is why Molly, Timmy, and I come to both services every Sunday, even though we're supposedly too old for this one."

Molly chimed in. "I told Lance, on Wednesday nights, he's all laid back"—she slumped in her chair—"but up there, he goes into a different zone."

"Uh, hello, people." Timmy spoke from two seats down. "There's an enlightening message going forth, in which we can all partake, if you'd only have ears to hear and mouths to close."

Molly narrowed her eyes at him.

Kendra laughed quietly, whispering, "Timmy's right. My fault."

"Imagine Joshua running in a pack," Lance was saying, winding up. "What if he said, 'No, I don't want to be different, don't want to look different, talk different, definitely don't want to *do* different . . .'"

Lance paced before them. "What if Joshua said, 'You know, God, I'd really rather not be strong and courageous, because no one else is strong and courageous, so how would that look? I mean, there's Caleb, but people think he's wack.'"

The teens chuckled, looking at one another.

He stopped, looking at them. "But notice God didn't ask a whole clique of people to be strong and courageous," Lance said. "He only needed one—and that strong, courageous *one* would lead and inspire the rest."

He jumped down from the stage and walked into the audience. "What I want to know is, which one of you will it be? Who's willing to be different, to be greatly used by God? Who's got the courage to say, 'The rest of y'all can get involved in all that foolishness if you want, but as for me . . .'"

Timmy stood, then Trey and Molly. Kendra thought they were playing along, but their expressions said otherwise. They were willing. And true to what Lance had just said, they inspired others to stand.

When the service ended minutes later, Lance was back there in a flash.

"What are you doing here?" he asked her. "I thought I was seeing things."

"I wanted to see what you do every Sunday." Kendra eyed him with admiration. "Can I tell you what I saw?"

"What did you see?"

"I saw a man who has said, 'Yes, God, I'm willing to be strong and courageous for You.'"

He stared at her a moment. "So you think you can just come into my workplace and make me emotional in front of these teens." He wiped a nonexistent tear. "No, ma'am, it's not gonna happen."

"It just occurred to me," Kendra said. "I hadn't seen this side of you, but they've probably never seen the sensitive side of Lance Alexander. Hidden camera footage would probably be golden."

"They'd never believe it," Lance said. "My reputation is fixed. All man. Macho. Never a tear."

Molly was with them, listening. "Kendra, you forgot . . . the wedding video has gone viral. You know, where the groom breaks down at the altar as his bride appears."

"A man broke down at the altar?" Lance said. "Seriously? Ugh. Ruins it for everyone."

Timmy cleared his throat. "What it does, in actuality, is inspire the Romeo within to dare to be entranced by, deeply smitten with, a love that comes but once in a lifetime." He lifted Molly's hand as if to kiss it.

Molly yanked it back. "You can drink the Kool-Aid by yourself, dude."

They all laughed. "I keep telling you two," Trey said, "one day . . ."

Lance took Kendra's hand as they walked to the main building.

"Hey, you guys," Kendra said, "tree-trimming party tonight. Don't forget."

"B.Y.O.E.?" Timmy asked.

Kendra tried to puzzle it out. "Bring your own . . . ?"

Timmy smiled. "My favorite holiday drink. Eggnog."

Kendra eyed him. "As long as it's not spiked with that Romeo Kool-Aid, we're good."

❧

"Look what Daddy and I made!"

Brooklyn came running into the living room with Marlon following and a small box of ornaments they'd been working on.

"Great timing." Kendra hung a silver ball waist high, still unable to reach very far. "We saved the last spots on the tree for the most special ornaments. Ooh, what's that there?"

Brooklyn had pulled one out. "We traced a cookie-cutter Christmas tree on felt, cut it out, and punched holes in it. Then we glued sparkly beads over the holes." Her eyes were bright. "We made Christmas trees for the Christmas tree!"

"It's beautiful!" Kendra said. She looked at her dad. "Since when did you become artsy-craftsy?"

"Brooklyn's teaching me," Marlon said, smiling at her. "She's very creative."

Kendra looked into the box. "You've got all sorts of pretty things in there. Let's get these beauties on the tree."

"Daddy, can you help me put this Christmas tree one up high?"

"You ready?" Marlon said.

Brooklyn giggled. "Yes!"

He picked her up and hoisted her high.

"Whoa! I didn't know you were gonna do that!" Brooklyn placed it carefully on a branch.

Marlon continued helping Brooklyn hang their ornaments. "Did I tell you all I have a closing date on the duplex?" he asked. "Second week in January."

"Where is the duplex, Mr. Woods?" Timmy asked.

Marlon chuckled. "At the other end of this street."

Timmy had been working on the lights, but he paused. "Will you be renting apartments? If so, I'm interested."

"Absolutely," Marlon said. "We'll talk."

When all the ornaments had been hung, Kendra turned to Trey and Timmy. "Are the lights ready?"

"They're hung, but we didn't test them yet," Trey said.

Everyone stood back as Trey turned the lights out in the room, then flipped a switch for the Christmas tree lights. A gasp of awe went around the room.

"This is really beautiful," Marlon said. "Special." He looked at Lance. "You picked the perfect tree."

"With a lot of help," Lance said. "It was my first time getting a real one."

"With everything that happened last year," Trey said, "we didn't even have a tree for Christmas."

"And I didn't come home for Christmas," Kendra said.

"And I was stoned last Christmas," Timmy said.

Molly stared at the tree. "What a difference a year makes."

Kendra hugged Lance's waist, lingering. Anxiety about tomorrow was creeping in, what radiation would be like, how her body would react. But she forced her mind to stay here. In this moment. And in her heart, she bottled and stored it.

Chapter Sixty-Five

Lance sneaked downstairs early to wrap his gift for Kendra and put it under the tree. He'd been filled with excitement all week, simply because it was Christmas . . . and his first Christmas with the love of his life. He'd already gotten *his* gift—Kendra was cancer-free and doing well on radiation. Granted, it had only been a little over a week, but he was thankful nonetheless that it hadn't overwhelmed her. She'd had some nausea and fatigue, but in their world that was very manageable. After this morning's appointment, he was looking forward to soaking in the holiday—cooking and baking, watching Christmas movies, and doing lots of snuggling by the fireplace.

He went back upstairs to see what Kendra wanted for breakfast, but when he walked into the room he found her sitting up in bed, tears streaming down her face.

He ran to her. "What's wrong?"

"I can't . . . move my neck." She stared straight ahead. "It hurts really bad when I try to move an inch."

Lance stared, feeling helpless. "It just came out of the blue?"

"The last few days it's been hurting. Like muscle soreness. But when I woke up this morning, it stopped me cold." She tried to shift a little and cried out in pain.

"Let's take some pain medication," Lance said.

"I did," she said. "A half hour ago."

"Okay," Lance said. "We're going to the hospital."

Lance got Kendra out of bed and helped her dress, praying as she cried out at the slightest movement. Other than the immediate aftermath of surgery, he'd never seen her in this much pain. In the car he called Dr. Contee, who sounded concerned, confirming that Kendra needed to get to the hospital.

Lance parked in the circular drive at emergency and carried her in. Before the woman at the desk could even ask him a question, he blurted out, "My wife's a cancer patient, on radiation, can't move her neck, in severe pain . . . please, can someone help her?"

The woman got some additional information. "Be right back, sir."

"Lance, I'm scared," Kendra moaned. "It really hurts." She kept her head stock-still in his arms.

"I know, baby," he whispered. "I know."

Her tears, the look of fear, made him desperate to help her himself. Where did the woman go? Someone somewhere in this place could help Kendra. Where were they?

A gurney rolled through the double doors moments later, and Kendra was taken from his arms and positioned on it.

"Can I come with her?" Lance asked. "I'm her husband."

"We'll let you know when you can come back, sir," they said.

Lance moved his car to the garage and then paced the waiting area, asking more than once for an update and for permission to join his wife.

Finally, almost an hour later, a nurse escorted him back to one of the rooms. Kendra was hooked to an IV, her head angled to the side, which she hadn't been able to do before. Her eyes looked anxious still.

"Is that pain medicine?" Lance asked, pulling up a chair next to her bed.

Kendra nodded. "It's helping a lot."

"What'd they say?"

"They gave me a CT scan. Now I have to wait for the results."

"What do they think caused the pain?"

"They didn't say," Kendra said, "but I could tell they were worried." Tears came again. "It's not good, Lance. I know it's not good."

"Shh . . ." Lance took her hand, heart rate on double time. "One step at a time. Thank God they gave you something effective for the pain."

"Why did this have to happen on Christmas Eve?" Kendra stared at their hands. "I was excited about having a Christmas where we didn't have to think about doctors and hospitals and illness. I really wanted that."

"Me too, baby," Lance said. "And we may yet have that. Hopefully they'll send us home, saying, 'We don't know what happened, but the scan is clear.'"

After several hours, Lance and Kendra walked into the house. Marlon and Trey were in the kitchen cooking, where Lance had planned to be today.

Marlon looked curiously at them. "You two must've done some last-minute shopping after radiation. We tried to call, but I guess your phones were off."

Lance had wanted to call them from the ER, but Kendra wanted to wait until they knew something. Then she didn't want to talk at all, not even to him.

"I just . . . need to go up," Kendra said, heading for the stairs.

"We'll be back," Lance told them.

He saw their confused faces, but he had to be with Kendra. Lance followed her into the bedroom, where she stood staring at a miniature tree he'd gotten for the dresser. They'd decorated it with miniature ornaments they'd chosen together. Kendra turned on the lights and watched them blink.

Lance sat on the bed several minutes, head in his hand, not knowing what to say. If he had to be honest, he was mad at God. It was Christmas Eve. *Christmas Eve.* If He wouldn't give them the miracle—if she wouldn't be completely healed—couldn't He at least give them *this*? He'd prayed so fervently for a Christmas they could enjoy, a Christmas where normal was within reach, like their trip to Pensacola Beach. He wanted Kendra laughing, snapping pictures, enjoying family.

God, why? Why couldn't You give us that?

Lance looked at Kendra, almost catatonic by the tree. This was one of those difficult days Marlon talked about on their wedding day, when they needed to remember that God is faithful. It was a day Lance needed grace for himself as well as Kendra. *Lord, we need You. We desperately need You.*

The Christmas gift came to mind, and Lance rose suddenly and went downstairs to get it. When he returned, he handed it to her.

Still in front of the tree, Kendra looked at him. "What's this?"

"Your Christmas present," he said. "Go ahead and open it."

She tore off the colorful Christmas paper and opened the oblong box inside.

"Lance . . ." Tears spilled as if a dam had broken, a new one. Her fingers shook as she lifted a bracelet, reading each charm. "My refuge, my fortress, my God . . ." Her entire body shook now as she entered his arms, sobbing. "It's so hard to see God that way when I'm dying. All I want is to live with you forever . . ."

Lance wanted to be strong for her, but his tears fell hard too. He needed God to be his refuge and fortress.

"You're not dying," Lance said. "It's a setback, but——"

"Lance, the cancer is spreading, that fast. Two months without chemo, and it's in my neck again." She blew out a breath. "I knew it was aggressive. I've read where it happened to countless women, just like this. But I *hoped*."

Lance clung to her as if he dared anyone to pry him loose. "I hoped too, Ken." He swiped his face. "I said on our wedding day that I would trust God with all of our days, but I won't lie. I'm struggling right now. I wanted the miracle. I wanted you to stay cancer-free."

He held her, trying to make sense of it all, finally leading her to the bed, where they sat on the edge.

"I guess, Ken," he said, "if God is a refuge, this is when we find out how much of a refuge. This is when we find out the strength of the fortress." Emotion stuttered his speech. "You know what?" He gently tipped her chin. "*Today*, we have one another. *Today*, you're here in my arms. *Today*, I can look into your beautiful brown eyes and say, 'I love you with everything that's in me.'"

Kendra's watery eyes were fixed on his.

"If I don't live fully in today"—Lance paused, trying to keep it together—"I'll go out of my mind."

Kendra clutched him and held him, then slowly pulled back, holding up her bracelet. "Can you put this on for me?"

Lance wrapped it around her wrist and fastened the clasp.

She read each of the charms again, then looked at him. "Tomorrow is still Christmas."

He sighed, nodding. "And as God gives us breath, we'll live fully on that day of all days, celebrating Christ . . . our hope."

CHAPTER SIXTY-SIX

July

A GORGEOUS RUSSET SUNSET ENVELOPED THE OSAGE BEACH SKY. From a chaise under the gazebo, Kendra aimed her camera at it and the shimmer of the lake beneath, and got the shot. The camera felt like lead now, too heavy to lug around. But at times like this—in nature, by the water, under an open sky—she kept it near.

Kendra scrolled through the pictures on the back of the camera, enjoying them all over. She'd managed to shoot a lot this week, mostly family shots. They'd driven two hours to the Lake of the Ozarks on Tuesday—she, Lance, Marlon, Trey, and Brooklyn. No one said it, but it was a last hurrah. Time for them all to gather, laugh, relax. Time with Kendra.

The cancer had spread further, lately to her bones. She'd had to stop radiation months ago and return to weekly chemo. But her body wasn't responding adequately to the drugs. They weren't prolonging her life to the extent they'd hoped.

"Ohhh! You killed that one!"

Kendra looked over, smiling at the fun. They'd rented a home on the lake with a gazebo, fire pit, deck near the seawall, and lots of grass to run and play. Trey, Lance, and Brooklyn had played Frisbee earlier. But Molly and Timmy had shown up, and now they'd moved to the volleyball net. They hadn't thought about it when they chose this vacation spot, but what a treat when they realized they wouldn't be far from Molly's home, where she'd gone after graduation.

Lance and Trey had their game faces on, waiting for Timmy's serve. "He's gonna serve it long," Trey said. "Get back."

The ball sailed over the net, and Lance set it to Trey, who spiked it—but Molly got under it and hit it back over, to their surprise.

Timmy cupped his mouth. "And score another point for Molly and Timmy."

Brooklyn looked at Lance and Trey, shaking her head. "They're pretty much killing you guys."

Marlon rejoined Kendra with two twelve-ounce plastic cups. "I made us some delicious smoothies," he said.

"You're just . . . trying to get something in me." Kendra's speech was slower at times, when it was hard to catch a breath.

"You caught me," he said.

Obliging him, Kendra took a short sip. She had little appetite. Mostly she wanted to sleep.

"Dad," she said.

Marlon looked at her.

"You've done so much for Lance and me. We haven't had to worry about a mortgage and so much else . . . Thank you sounds so lame, but I am . . . so thankful."

"You and Lance have thanked me enough," Marlon said, "and I don't need thanks anyway. You're my daughter. Don't you know there's nothing I wouldn't do for you?"

"But after the way I treated you," Kendra said. "I didn't even invite you to my wedding to Derek." It grieved her when she thought of it. "It was so wrong."

"We're not spending a single second revisiting that," Marlon said. "And I know you sure don't want to think about ol' what's-his-name."

Kendra laughed inside.

Marlon stared at the water. "I didn't realize how little I'd seen you over the last decade. Time flies so fast."

Kendra looked at him, wishing she could go back and spend more time with her mom and dad.

"But the times we've spent these last months . . ." Marlon looked over at her. "These have been the sweetest of our lives."

She felt it deeply. "You really think so?"

"I know so," Marlon said. "We had *time*. And by the grace of God, we made the most of that time." He groaned a little. "Forgive me, sweetheart. I hate that I just said that in past tense. I could kick myself."

"It's okay, Daddy," Kendra said. "I only heard the heart behind it." She reached for his hand. "I'm so glad you came back to the States when you did . . . so glad God gave us this time, even this week. It's been incredible."

Brooklyn came over to the gazebo. "Can you believe they're playing *another* volleyball game?" she asked. "Lance and Trey think they'll win one if they keep playing *one* more."

Kendra winked. "Molly's too good for them."

Brooklyn lay beside her on the chaise. "I wish you could play with us."

"Me too, sweetheart." Kendra smiled at her. "But it's fun to watch."

"But . . . I know you're sick and . . . sometimes, I get really scared."

Kendra looked at her. "Why do you get scared, Brookie?"

"Because you might die. And I'd be really sad." Brooklyn fisted a tear away.

Kendra closed her eyes. *Lord, help me. I don't want to break down in front of her.*

"Brooklyn," Marlon said, "you know how we talked about Jesus and how we can live with Him forever?"

Brooklyn nodded, looking down.

"When Jesus lives in our hearts," Marlon said, "we don't have to be scared of dying. Do you know why?"

"Because we go to be with Him?" Brooklyn asked.

"That's right," Marlon said.

Brooklyn turned to Kendra. "Does Jesus live in your heart?"

Kendra looked at her, eyes smiling. "He sure does, sweetie."

"Are you scared to die?" Brooklyn asked.

Kendra thought about it. "I'd be sad, because of you and Dad and Lance and Trey . . . but I won't be scared." She was thankful she could say it and mean it. "I could never be scared, not when I'll get to see Jesus."

She was thankful to have that hope. That's the hope she'd been dwelling on.

⁂

Excitement was building for fireworks over the lake. They'd heard the show was spectacular, and they had a front-row seat. The guys had even gone inside to rustle up snacks for the occasion.

Kendra had taken a short nap and was now back out on the deck, under a blanket to ward off the chill. The back door opened. She glanced up and smiled.

"Hey, you," Molly said.

"Come sit next to me," Kendra said.

"Uh-oh." Molly eased herself into the chair. "Timmy told me you had a few words for him earlier. I feared my time was coming."

Kendra wanted to laugh, but her laughing muscles hurt. She

smiled a lot, mostly with her eyes. "You look great, by the way," she said.

Molly tousled her hair. "So, yeah, I thought I'd give my natural color a go. Mousy brown is so *blah*." She added quickly, "But hey, I do like it better than blond."

"You look beautiful, Molly." Kendra eyed her. "I bet Timmy thinks so too."

"I knew that was coming."

Kendra smiled. "Tell me about it."

"Well . . ." Molly stared out at the water. "Right before graduation, I don't know what happened . . . It was like, we talked more, about real things. And he started calling. And when he suggested coming down today so we could hang out with y'all on the Fourth, I actually got . . . excited." She looked at Kendra. "Extremely weird, huh?"

"Molly, it's okay," Kendra said. "You want to protect yourself. But do it. Give yourself permission to love him."

"*That* I didn't see coming." She pulled her knees up to her chest. "Why would you say that? What makes you think I love him?"

"I know you. I've watched you two." Kendra paused. "Timmy loves you too. And if I've learned anything, real love is special, and you can't waste time being afraid of it."

The back door opened and clapped shut again. Trey sat down by them with his Doritos bag. He crunched a chip, then looked at them. "Is it just me, or is this a really solemn vibe?"

"Your sister says I love Timmy."

"And this is news?" Trey popped another chip into his mouth.

Molly took a chip from his bag and threw it at him.

"Ah, the man himself," Trey said, glancing up as Timmy walked out onto the deck.

"Molly," Timmy said, "I don't want to be too forward, but I wondered if . . . given the beautiful night and the fireworks to come, you might want to go for a walk . . ." He cleared his throat. "With me."

Kendra and Trey looked at Molly, and she narrowed her eyes back at them.

Turning to Timmy, she said, "That might actually be nice."

"They make me smile," Kendra said as Molly and Timmy walked away. "And you make me smile."

Trey kicked back in the seat. "Where did the last part come from?"

Once again, Kendra fought to rein in her emotions. It was one of those days. She had them lately, when she needed to express what was on her heart.

Kendra looked at her brother, already losing the battle. "You are such a special person, Marlon Woods III. The hand of God is upon you in such a real way."

He put the chip back in the bag. "I'm not sure what you're talking about."

She took her time. "The way you're praying to embrace singleness. I know it's not easy. Even though you never saw yourself getting married, you have to get lonely. And yet, I'm seeing you grow so close to God as you work all of this out in your heart. You inspire me."

Trey blew out a breath. "You just blindsided me." He looked at his sister. "I wasn't expecting that. It means a lot."

"I've never told you this," Kendra said, "but watching you has helped me on my own journey."

He frowned. "How?"

"You live with an awareness that this life is not meant to be our best life. What's that passage you like to quote?"

"From 2 Corinthians?" He nodded. "I had to memorize it to

encourage myself. It says, 'Therefore we do not lose heart, but though our outer man is decaying, yet our inner man is being renewed day by day. For momentary, light affliction is producing for us an eternal weight of glory far beyond all comparison—'"

Kendra finished it for him. "'—while we look not at the things which are seen, but at the things which are not seen; for the things which are seen are temporal, but the things which are not seen are eternal.'"

"You memorized it too?" Trey asked.

"Memorizing Scripture gives me strength . . . and keeps me sane." She focused on him. "But, Trey, that's how you live. You fix your hope on what's to come, on the eternal. And your example helped me do the same."

"*You* . . ." Trey pointed at his sister, his eyes glazed. "You've helped me understand what it is to truly live with suffering. When I lapse into self-pity, I look at you and the way you've endured. I know God's grace is sufficient because I've seen it in you."

Kendra dissolved into tears. "Come here, boy."

He knelt beside her chaise, and they embraced.

"You're the best sister in the world. I love you, Ken."

"I love you too, Trey."

Moments later, Lance, Marlon, and Brooklyn came out with a tray filled with goodies, including freshly popped popcorn.

The first fireworks shot into the night, whistling, bursting with beauty.

"Whoa!" Brooklyn ran to the edge of the deck, looking skyward. "Did you see that?"

Lance nestled next to Kendra. "How you feeling, babe?"

She didn't have to ponder. "It's been one of the best days ever."

Chapter Sixty-Seven

October

Lance lay awake on his side, watching Kendra sleep. Most nights she was the one awake, in pain and often in tears, trying to find respite. But right now she seemed peaceful. He traced her eyebrows growing in once again. They'd made the decision to stop chemo seven weeks ago. It was too painful, with no measurable offset. Kendra craved a better quality of life, for however much longer God would give her.

And thankfully, He'd given them a one-year anniversary—and the sweetest time together. To celebrate, they played their wedding song, "I Can Only Imagine," and danced in their bedroom. Holding her, swaying with her, feeling her arms around him . . . He memorized every bit of it, taking none of their moments for granted.

Like now. He wanted to remember what it was like to lie beside her, to watch her chest rise and fall as she slept and the way her bottom lip sometimes moved.

Kendra exhaled slightly, and her eyes opened. She looked around, seeming confused.

"I'm here, baby," Lance said. "You okay?"

Kendra looked at him, then glanced around again. "I guess . . . I was dreaming."

"What was it about?" he asked.

"It felt like . . . I was in heaven." Her breathing was labored. "I was walking . . . normal . . . and twirling, like . . . dancing. Happy."

"That's what's coming," he said. "No pain. No sickness. Just . . . joy."

"It seemed like . . . it's coming . . . now. Like . . . it's time."

Her words landed deep in his gut. He'd known this moment would come, but he wasn't ready. He'd never be ready. *Lord, not now. And yet I don't want her to keep suffering.*

Lance caressed her face. "God gave you to me as a treasure, to have, to hold, to love, and I'm so grateful." His heart had never ached like this. "You couldn't be more precious to me. You couldn't be a better wife and friend. I couldn't be more madly in love with you."

Kendra gazed into his eyes. "I don't know why God . . . loved me so much . . . that He'd give me His Son, and then . . . give me you." She worked to get a breath. "Lance, God gave us this time . . . and even though it's my time to go . . ."

Stop saying that. Lance let the tears flow.

". . . it's not yours." Kendra touched his face. "Baby, keep letting God . . . use you . . . to love. His well in you . . . is deep." She coughed away a nasty rattling sound. "I'm saying it whether . . . you like it or not . . . You are . . . *amazing*. I hope I loved you . . . half as much . . . as you loved me."

Kendra coughed again, her chest lifting slightly from the bed. And when she exhaled, her head fell softly to the side.

Lance brought her to himself. "Kendra?" *Oh, God . . .* "Kendra?"

The grief contracted from deep within, rippling through his gut. Lance rocked with her in his arms, sobbing, needing the sound of her voice once more, the light in her eyes. How could she be gone? Just like that? How could their life together be over?

Lance stayed there, Kendra in his arms, sadness washing over him in a flood of memories. But with the memories, he was hearing a soundtrack. With one arm, he reached for his phone on the nightstand and played the song—"I Can Only Imagine."

Now it was the words to the song washing over him, and the realization that he was the only one left imagining. Kendra no longer needed to. She knew what it was like to see Jesus, to be surrounded by His glory.

Fresh tears flowed—tears of grief still, but also tears of joy. He held her body, her diseased body, but Kendra was with the Lord. He laid her gently down and moved out of bed, getting down on his knees.

Lord, she was Your treasure before she was mine. You love her more than I ever could. Thank You for allowing me to love her for a short while. He exhaled hard, trying to get out from under the tears. *Thank You for giving me such a gift in my lifetime.*

Chapter Sixty-Eight

May
Seven months later

Lance stood in the designated prayer room before the start of service, in casual jeans and a button-down shirt, somewhat anxious.

"We said from the beginning we'd look to the Lord to lead us in everything," he said. "We won't be caught up in numbers or anything else. If He only sends a few people week to week, then those are the few who are meant to be here. Amen?"

"Amen," sounded around the circle.

A core group had committed five months before to be part of the launch of a church plant in Clayton. But God had assembled them almost two years before—Trey, Cyd and Cedric, Molly, Timmy, Darla, and others from Wednesday nights, along with Marlon. They'd been praying fervently every step of the way, including prayers about the name. They'd agreed without hesitation that this was the one— Living Hope Church.

They'd prayed about a location, too, debating whether to launch from the Woodses' home or a school or someplace else. But a local church heard about the effort and knew the story of Lance and

Kendra. Their congregation had dwindled, and they were no longer holding regular services. They were willing to let them use the building for free, with the option to purchase over time. The launch team had been blown away time and again by gestures like that . . . clear answers to prayer.

Molly raised her hand. "What if God sends a lot of people? It could happen, given the article in this morning's paper."

"What article?" Lance hadn't seen the Sunday paper.

Cyd dug into her purse. "I cut it out this morning to show you, then forgot when I got here." She handed it to him.

Lance skimmed it, a short blurb from the local section with the headline, "'Amazing Love' Update—Pastor Plants a Church." It struck him that two years ago, he'd been concerned that people would be talking about his past at Clayton High or his criminal record if he started a church. There was no mention of either of these things.

"I don't know how many people will see it," Lance said, "but that's a nice article. Funny how they refer to the 'Amazing Love' story."

"I keep telling you it impacted more people than you think," Cyd said.

"But it's weird thinking about it like that," Lance said. "I was just loving my wife. It shouldn't be a big deal, you know?"

"Oh, but it is. Trust me," Darla mumbled.

Lance looked at Molly. "So, Moll, let's hear your answer. If God sends a lot of people, what will we do?"

Molly rolled her eyes up, thinking. "I don't know for sure, but I'm thinking prayer'll be the first thing."

Lance smiled. "You got it. I have to thank all of you again," he said, "for your hard work. It's a big job starting a church plant, and you've put in so much time. And you're still willing to serve." His eyes traveled the circle. "But this is more than a church plant. You're family. You've been there more ways than I can count, especially after Kendra . . ."

He couldn't go there, not right now. He exhaled.

"Group hug!"

Lance wasn't sure who said it, but they all squeezed in for a big, rocking hug.

"I love you guys," Lance said, holding on still.

"I'm curious," Timmy said. "Has anyone given thought to the cosmic greatness of God's handiwork with this group?"

Molly eyed him with amusement. "I dwell often on such cosmic realities, now that I'm married to a cosmic thinker."

"People, I submit to you that *that* is amazing love," Timmy said, hugging her. "That this woman puts up with me."

Lance chuckled. "You'll get no argument there."

"I can't believe it's here, y'all," Trey said. "Living Hope Church is actually launching today."

A cheer went up among the circle.

"All right, everybody, it's time," Lance said. "Let's pray and head out."

Lance greeted people in the lobby area as they arrived. A lot of Living Word members were coming to support the first service, but Lance had never seen most of these people. He shook hands, casually asking how they'd heard about it. Word of mouth and the newspaper article had been the main sources.

Lance turned, surprised to see Ellen and Brooklyn walk in. "Hey, I didn't know you were coming."

"Brooklyn didn't want to miss it," Ellen said.

"Look," Brooklyn said, sticking out her arm. "I wore my very special bracelet."

It hit an emotional nerve, seeing the Psalm 18 bracelet, which Kendra had given her. Lance hugged her, unable to speak.

Ellen looked at him. "You know I'm still grappling with God and church and all of that," she said. "I've still got lots of questions. But as I think about it, I could've sent Brooklyn with her dad. Maybe . . . maybe I wanted to be here."

Lance hugged her. "And it means a lot to have you here."

Ready to begin, Lance walked into an almost-full sanctuary as worship music played. His heart was full. Kendra had wanted to see this day. She'd encouraged him toward this day. But he couldn't see it until she was gone. It wasn't meant to be until she was gone. God knew her time—*their* time—would be short. And He'd given Lance grace to devote himself to his wife in a very special way.

As he thought about it, looking out among the people, Kendra was indeed with him, watching him. And he knew what she would say—live fully in this day.

Lance took a steadying breath. God would give him grace for this too.

READING GROUP GUIDE

1. As she prepared to marry Derek, Kendra knew he wasn't a man of faith and that even she wasn't who she needed to be. Yet she was comfortable pushing these realizations aside. In your own life, have you acknowledged that, spiritually, you're not where you'd like to be—and left it at that? Or did you begin to take steps toward positive change?

2. Did you find Derek's decision to leave Kendra understandable? Do you think you could love someone enough to marry him if you knew he'd been diagnosed with a terminal illness?

3. If you've never grappled with same-sex attraction, you likely know someone who has—though he or she may not have shared it. Would you be a safe person with whom someone could share this struggle? Would you listen with compassion and show love?

4. Lance told Trey, "When something is in our lives that brings affliction or suffering or any struggle we can't control, we're more aware of our need for God." Have you experienced affliction, suffering, or a struggle that made you more aware of your need for God? Did you see His love and care in deeper ways? Explain.

5. The Wednesday night Bible study was called The Shadow. Have you ever lived in shadows of doubt, fear, or shame? Have you experienced what it's like to dwell in a different shadow, one of refuge and blessing—the shadow of the Almighty?

6. At Kendra's "wisdom shower," they noted that tomorrow is not promised for any of us. In what ways could you intentionally treat each day as a gift? How can you glorify God daily?

7. Kendra told Derek that when he broke up with her, she thought it was the end of the world. But he became her testimony. Have you ever experienced the pain of a closed door, only to see it later as God's goodness? Did that closed door become your testimony? Explain.

8. Kendra found great comfort in Psalm 18 as she began to know God's attributes personally. Do you know the Lord as your strength, your rock, your fortress, your deliverer, your refuge, and your salvation? How has He made Himself known with respect to any one of these?

9. In the midst of a very difficult season, have you experienced unimagined blessings—*hidden blessings*—from God?

ACKNOWLEDGMENTS

I AM INDEBTED TO MANY WOMEN WHO HAD THE COURAGE TO blog throughout their battles with inflammatory breast cancer. Their insights as to what it was like to live with this disease—physically, mentally, emotionally, and spiritually—often brought me to tears.

I am indebted as well to those who have had the courage to voice past and/or present struggles with homosexuality, in particular the ministries of Christopher Yuan, Jackie Hill, and Julie Rodgers. I credit Christopher Yuan for the statement (spoken through Lance) that the opposite of homosexuality isn't heterosexuality but holiness, from his book *Out of a Far Country*. To the three of you, thank you for helping the body of Christ to grow in compassion.

Finally—always—I am indebted to the Lord for giving me grace . . . to write, to love, to hope, and to endure.

OTHER NOVELS BY KIM CASH TATE

"Tate expertly crafts an intriguing narrative that explores unrequited love, true faith, and the complicated politics of change in the Christian church . . . [an] affecting tale about forgiveness and following God's call."

—*Publishers Weekly* (on *Hope Springs*)

ABOUT THE AUTHOR

KIM CASH TATE IS THE AUTHOR OF *THE COLOR OF HOPE*, *HOPE Springs*, *Cherished*, *Faithful*, *Heavenly Places*, and the memoir *More Christian Than African American*. A former practicing attorney, she is also a Bible teacher and women's ministry leader at The Gate Church in St. Louis. She and her husband have two children.

Visit her website at www.kimcashtate.com

Twitter: @KimCashTate

Facebook: kimcashtate